"Author James P. Stobaugh is quite an elegant writer verging on the poetic. *Growing up White* is very much a novel of mood and meaning and yes, quite explicit in religious intent. Clearly Stobaugh knows his material as in his day-to-day life he is a pastor as well as quite a gifted writer. One cannot help but admire writers who have a clear love of language and Stobaugh clearly has that. His words, images and just general flow of his bayou-like pacing are common enough in excellent poetry; a rarity in prose."

—Herbert O'Hearn, *San Francisco Book Review*

"*Growing up White* gifted me with soft memories that expatriate southerners have—rendezvous with suntanned southern boys at soda fountains, and family gatherings in pecan groves. I am also reminded of some memories I would like to forget-- stringy barbecued squirrel, for one, and racist comments for another. Yet, I share with Jake, the joy of the journey. And there are days when I close my eyes and yearn again for one more Delta dawn Stobaugh so eloquently describes in this tour de force."

—Lisa Mormon, Political Analyst, London, UK

"The true value of *Growing Up White* is that it is written from the point of view of a White person who has had a sort of painful 'awakening' to the evils of White power and privilege and is struggling to let go of his 'father's world.' Fortunately, Jake learns that there is something better than the old ways. However, he also comes to realize that his desire to let go of the old world causes him to become a victim of the prejudices and discrimination that Blacks face. *Growing Up White* would be a good supplement for a sociology course that deals with race and ethnic relations."

—Mary A McGehee, PhD, Arkansas Dept of Health

"Part historical, part theological, part philosophical, part autobiographical but a fully remarkable tale told with interesting reflection and insight."

—D. C. Washington, Lt. Col., U. S. Army (retired)

"Just as the Mississippi Delta renews its life annually, so do we develop and enrich human relationships under God's guidance in James Stobaugh's lyric story *Growing Up White*. On his 59th birthday, Jake Stevens realizes that with God's help he has indeed remade his own world from childhood experiences of inexplicable racism to acceptance and deep love for all souls. This is a story of one man's journey from the tortures of Southern inhumanity to being born again and renewed in the spirit of love through his four beautiful children, 'all shades of white and black . . . ripe with promise and hope.' Stobaugh has a natural gift for language that brings the reader from precise observations of the pesky female cardinal in the morning, and the all-too-vivid remembrances of past gruesome events to the lilt of love from his beloved Yankee wife, Anna. A marvelous, soft, inspired story of growth, fulfillment and reflection by a gifted writer."

—John Barell, Author, Professor Emeritus, Montclair University

"The narrative touched me deeply . . . it deals with repulsive issues that most of us have attempted to whitewash. However, much like a rainbow after a cleansing rainstorm, there is a message of hope and of healing that is honest and beautiful. It really is a powerful story."

—Julie Braswell, Home Educator

"Stobaugh's literary metaphors add so much to the central theme that is both compelling and endearing."

—Alouette Greenidge, Student, Wheaton College

# Growing Up White

## James P. Stobaugh

New York

Harvard Square Editions

2014

# GROWING UP WHITE

Copyright © 2014 James P. Stobaugh

Cover design © Daphnide McDermet

Special appreciation to David Garber, Ph. D., for editorial support.

Scripture marked NIV is from the Holy Bible, New International Version®. NIV®. Copyright © 1973, 1978, 1984, 2011 by Biblica, Inc.™ Used by permission of Zondervan. All rights reserved worldwide. www.zondervan.com

Scripture marked NRSV is from the New Revised Standard Version of the Bible, copyright © 1989, by the Division of Christian Education of the National Council of the Churches of Christ in the United States of America.
Used by permission. All rights reserved.

ISBN 978-0-9895960-0-8

Published in the United States by Harvard Square Editions
www.harvardsquareeditions.org

None of the material contained herein may be reproduced or stored without permission of the author under International and Pan-American Copyright Conventions.

This book is a work of fiction, yet true to life as experienced in the USA, South and North. Names, characters, and situations are the author'sinvention. Any resemblance to actual people, living or dead, is purely coincidental.

*For Mammy Lee*

"O foster-mother in whose arms there lay
The race whose sons are masters of the land!"

—James W. Johnson, "The Black Mammy"

# 1

THE SPRING SUNRISE SILHOUETTED scraggly, sugar maples guarding my ten-acre Pennsylvania Laurel Highlands farm.

A soft May spring breeze teased juvenile leaf buds struggling to make up for lost time at the end of a winter that began before Veterans Day and extended beyond Memorial Day. The beginning of the Laurel Highlands winter saluted living warriors and the end honored the dead ones. Until late May, frosty cold impeded solstial warmth. May in the Laurel Highlands was just a slightly warmer version of March and 80 degrees warmed the Highlands only once or twice a year. It was as if summer never arrived. Or, if it arrived, it stayed so briefly that no one noticed.

Or so it seemed to this expatriate southerner.

Sunrises came and went effortlessly and with no fanfare. They came and went too quickly for my liking. I no longer contemplated their going and their coming. My world was rich with other things, but not allegory. Corporeal existence in the real time world dulled my perspicuity in ways that I had not anticipated.

It was my birthday and I was 59.

My grey farmhouse was on the edge of a rolling hill whose bottom abuted my musty basement and whose top stroked God's azure grandeur. My bedroom was somewhere between musty and azure.

In my bed was my lover, my wife for 34 years. Her slumbered magnificence, undiluted by pasty make-up and morning sobriety, nonetheless brightened dim morning light. Even in vulnerable repose this woman was supple and sinuous! I was tempted to ravish the fair maiden but denied myself in tribute to faithful sleep.

I tiptoed down the creaky stairs to the kitchen.

The kitchen was the command post of my ailing, ancient Mennonite-built farm. The farm and the kitchen were the very essence of practicality. No granite counter top or shiny modern faucet adorned this kitchen. There were no enticements to worldliness or pride; no, this kitchen drew aspiring cooks to plain cooking and faithful diners to Godly living.

One fortunate gift from my former Anabaptist owner was frequent and mammoth kitchen windows. Built when coal heat was cheap and abundant, the kitchen was sincere about blessing its visitors with plentiful sunlight. Light cascaded into the inviting kitchen where the former and present tenants spent most days contemplating the Holy Scriptures and the beauty of God's creation.

I walked in sock feet toward the stainless steel sink.

I filled the teakettle and put it on the stove. I first moved the start knob to the right—wrong way—as I have done since we got the darn thing—and then back to the left—the right way. It exploded into a cascade of burning blue propane gas searing the hairs on my right hand.

"Good morning world!"

Surrounded by leviathan whales, ship crews will throw out a tub in order to divert the attention of their behemoth sentinels. The whales amuse themselves by tossing the tub into the air, as children do with a soccer ball. While their attention is diverted, the formerly endangered ships sail away. Hence, "Throwing a tub to the whales!"

On my 59th birthday, I, Jake Stevens was surrounded by a myriad of whales, and I was throwing my tub to the Goliaths.

Outside the kitchen window an irascible female cardinal was tapping on my window.

Two years before a cardinal couple was building a nest outside our side kitchen window in a privet hedge. Too low, in my estimation, to escape our ferocious barn cats. These birds would become red bird-take-out if I did not intervene.

I did. I tore down the nest before the stupid cardinals could birth cat food.

Unfortunately, the proprietors, especially the female, did not appreciate my thoughtful act.

In fact, every morning, for two years, she waited until I came down the stairs and tapped in angry clatter at my entrance.

Tap! Tap! Tap!

"I thought cardinals only lived about 18 months," I growled.

I was an incongruity. A study in contradictions. A southerner, who married a northerner. An alumnus of several elite universities, who lived below the poverty line. Overweight due to my morbid lifestyle, I nonetheless was effusively healthy. My family physician, which looked and lived a lot like me, was obviously disappointed: he himself suffered under sundry maladies and wondered why I didn't. Yet last week, with some satisfaction, he warned me that my vitamin D3 levels were low. Glad to throw a tub to my doctor's whale.

I was a part-time Presbyterian minister, who wrote nonfiction books that only nerdy precocious prodigies read. It was one of the smallest niche markets in the history of humankind, which my paltry pocketbook and choleric publisher could attest.

By this time, though, the kettle was whistling. And the lovely maiden, Anna, came down the stairs.

Anna descended with a certainty in Providence that gave her gait a strong assurance—there was no creak on the stairs when she descended. Anna approached the new day with more than a modicum of caution though. She was unwilling to commit to unbridled optimism until she identified and measured the obstacles before her and the resources that she could marshal to meet them. Anna was disinclined to embrace luck, or chance, for my careful wife did not believe in such things. Her God controlled her future and He would show her the path to follow this new day. She trusted her God, but her husband, Jake Stevens, was an entirely different matter. God only knew what he would do, especially on his birthday.

"Happy birthday, Jacob," she smiled as she entered the kitchen.

"Good morning, sweetie," I responded.

I placed one Earl Gray, three PG Tip tea bags in the teapot and wrapped it in a tea cozy. As Anna, whose parents were from Raasy, Skye, Scotland, were fond of saying, "The tea is stewing."

And so it was.

Anna joined me at the stove.

She measured out half a cup of steel cut oatmeal and put it into a pot.

I kissed her. "Morning."

The effervescent mist of the stewing tea mingled with Anna's silver hair reflecting the morning sun. Anna's hair started turning grey when she was 38 and had progressed into a processional of hoary splendor.

"Let's sit down," I invited.

Our solid oak oval kitchen table was cluttered with strewings. Anna was an inveterate note taker. She went through realms of sticky notes every year. They decorated napkin holders and saltshakers and even her Bible. Sticky notes organized, alerted, and scolded us with epistemological pretension that offered very little metaphysical comfort but helped us organize our kaleidoscopically complicated lives.

Out our window gluttonous gold finches consumed overpriced striped sunflower seeds. For thirty-four years we had held hands, prayed together, lived together. For twenty of those years we had greeted the morning sheen at this kitchen table.

We quietly enjoyed the commencement of this new day.

Timid whitetail deer moved from thicket to spring. Stripped chippies dodged spiteful blue jays and scurried along stone fences. Conscientious crows hopped among pokeberry bushes tossing hard black berries into ravenous beaks. Swopping orange crowned chipping sparrows to plume their nests snatched whispy hair from our dozing barn cats.

I recklessly held my tea cup with two fingers and blew my steaming tea until it cooled; Anna held her cup in two hands. She was unwilling to invest effort into something that God and circumstances would bring about naturally.

The brown, orange beaked ADHD female cardinal moved to the bird feeder, which, we also provided gratis to my aviary friends. The visitor was not welcome, but how does one racially profile cardinals?

"Jacob, what are you doing? Are you daydreaming?"

While everyone else called me "Jake," Anna used my formal, name "Jacob." "Jake" reminded her of tobacco-chewing Nascar fans. "Jacob" was an investment of faith. She wanted to be married to an erudite, arcane "Jacob" not a parochial hick named "Jake," which in truth, was what I was. Anna did not believe what she saw, nor was she moved by what she felt. She was only moved by what she believed. Faith annihilated mutability, destroyed vastness, and brought history at once into possession.

"No, of course not, I am hypnotized by your radiant beauty."

And what I could see was beautiful. She was wearing her favorite LL Bean green-checkered flannel nightgown that revealed nothing and was more resistant to wandering hands than a flak jacket.

"What are you thinking, Jacob?"

Anna returned to the kitchen counter to fill two blueberry-decorated bowls with oatmeal, Greek yogurt, and homemade granola. The delicious mixture was Anna's creation and appreciated by this hungry boy on most days but not on my birthday. I had higher expectations.

"It is hard to be 59." I whined.

"Come on, Jacob. Eat your breakfast. Do you want some more tea?"

"I love oatmeal Anna, but it is my birthday. Why can't I have eggs, grits, country ham, biscuits, and red-eye gravy?"

"When did I ever cook you eggs, grits, country ham, biscuits, and red-eye gravy?"

"Never."

"Do you look like you need eggs, grits, country ham, biscuits, and red-eye gravy?"

"No?" she continued. "Looks to me like you need oatmeal, yogurt, and granola."

At the same time, Anna announced my absolution with a smile.

Anna's smile was epic. It began on the edge of her red cheek and ended in my heart. Nothing pleasured me more than an Anna smile.

Meanwhile, my plaid flannel shirt covered belly had conveniently captured about two grams of porridge that had escaped from my roguish spoon. I deftly scooped the absconder before it despoiled Anna's imported Persian carpet.

Anna was observing all with amused annoyance.

"This belly is useful for something," I said with a questioning smile.

"Indeed."

Yes, Anna could do two things at once. Even three or four. She dazzled everyone at the Harvard Graduate School of Education while I was slumming at the Harvard Divinity School.

"It is hard to be 59," I repeated. "Is it harder being 61?"

I loved teasing my slightly older Anna about marrying a 'younger man.'

"Cougar," I smiled.

"You have acted like an 80 year old since I first met you," Anna came back. "You were the only Harvard man I know who could not wait to attend the 'oldies but goodies' Boston Pop concert."

"It was memorable—especially 'Moon River.' Remember?"

"How can I forget?"

"God that woman is beautiful," I thought.

Scottish Raasy Anna had a ruddy complexion and piercing brown eyes with a feisty disposition to match both. Her tight curly silver hair, somewhat tamed by childbirth, accentuated her earnestness and sincerity. Anna had a sense of humor, but it was uncorrupted by frivolous exaggeration. There was no connotation in her denotation.

Idealism was realism to this woman. I doubt that she had ever told a lie. Surely our galaxy would catapult out of the universe if she did! The problem was that the woman was nearly perfect and expected an approximation thereof from her spouse. Still, Anna, like a vintage red wine, grew mellower with each new vicissitude of life.

Anna accompanied me through my 59th year, a time when I found myself in Alighieri Dante's darksome wood. The darkness of Dante's forest was intimidating: growing old is no fun, but it can be tolerable if one has a friend growing old with oneself. I was glad to have had the companionship for these thirty-four years.

Anna was my Beatrice, Dante's ideal woman, and like Beatrice, Anna no doubt would guide me to Paradiso.

"Sweetie, you are my Beatrice!"

"Who?" She exclaimed.

"What exactly do you want for your birthday?" She asked without waiting for an answer.

"You know." I smiled.

Anna scooped the remainder of her granola into her mouth.

An angry blue jay drove away all his cousins. The wasteful interloper scattered more striped sunflower to the ground than he ate.

Anna was obviously restless. She still worked for a living.

"Honey, this is interesting, but I have work to do. Can we talk later?"

"Absolutely."

"Happy birthday again!" Anna said as she kissed me with centennial enthusiasm.

As Anna wandered upstairs, I wandered back in time.

# 2

"Dad, where are we?"

I was nine years old and with my dad in Devil's Den Swamp hunting whitetail deer, and as usual, we arrived way too early.

"Nice night, dad," I sarcastically quipped. Perhaps it was an insight to my dad's personality that his nine-year-old son was already a cynic.

Nothing about this morning resembled its raison d'être. I stared into the heavens and contemplated the absurdity of our situation.

The Devil's Den was a thousand acre quagmire. It was the last wheeze of antediluvian mayhem in the wild Mississippi River Arkansas Delta before somnolent pilgrims entered the subdued lowland piedmont.

Other little boys, waiting for trophy bucks, were relaxing in comfortable shelters on the edge of Milo maze fields. But no, not me. I was sloshing around in the Devil's Den.

With no hint of dawn, Dad and I languished in a slough of despair.

"We are right where we should be, Jake." Dad smiled. "If we follow the North Star we shall surely be near the deer stand before dawn."

"Okay, Dad," I muttered deferentially.

We were doing no such thing. We were following Venus. Venus, squatting on the right of the first quarter moon, had been in the same place for a millennium. Nowhere near the North Star.

We were following Venus, not the North Star, but I discerned that it was not propitious to challenge Dad's misapprehension of the universe.

My dad was a 28-year-old dad, Martin Stevens. Five feet eight inches tall, he wore heavy canvas camouflage pants and a grey flannel shirt. He wore his favorite green knee high rubber boots with tiny brand name red balls peering over the top of murky swamp water. In truth, he looked more like my older brother than my dad.

"Dad, where are we?"

"I don't know, but we are fine."

I was not so sure. There was quicksand in the Devil's Den. I wondered if Dad remembered that. I knew a lot about quicksand—it regularly gobbled up unwary travelers in Saturday morning Tarzan movies.

Three years ago, while duck hunting, Jedidiah Morris walked into the Devil's Den and never returned. Old-timers claimed he fell into quicksand and disappeared forever. I was certain, this morning that I would step on old, slimy, Jedidiah's head.

We were headed to the "deer stand," which was a euphemism for a rickety wooden structure strapped to an ancient pin oak tree. Earlier that spring, fighting bloodthirsty mosquitoes and angry water moccasins, we built our deer stand on an obscure Indian mound in the middle of the Devil's Den.

Remote and unapproachable by man and deer alike, on this early November, the deer stand awaited our arrival and the debut of the first deer-hunting trip of the season.

I wore camouflage attire, although I had pinned captain bars to my authentic Marine fatigue camouflage shirt. I was a captain in the Corps, but I expected to be promoted any day, like my cousin Major Eddy Jones, a U. S. Marine Phantom II jet pilot, who flew beer between Manila and Saigon. Even at age nine I knew it was a terrible waste to use a genuine American hero like Uncle Eddy and his superior flying machine the Phantom II to transport Budweiser when both hero and machine could be more profitably used to bomb the Hell out of Charley.

At age nine I was experimenting with curse words. Apparently, in extreme stress, I was allowed to use a few mild curse words like "hell" or "damn." I first learned these words at our hunting camp when High Pockets Sargis regularly cursed the St. Louis Cardinals for losing to the Milwaukee Braves.

"Son of a bitch," he exclaimed when the Braves scored a winning run.

I asked my Mamaw what he meant and she said High Pockets was the best example she knew of one.

I regularly heard John Wayne use these words at the Majestic Theater, and since he was just below Jesus in the pantheon, it must be ok.

I went too far though.

I used my new vocabulary to ask Mammy Lee "what the Hell" she thought she was doing.

Mammy Lee washed my mouth out with soap. Dad preferred that I use these words sparingly and Mammy Lee forbad them altogether.

I was a perceptive child who learned quickly the protocol of late 20th century southern Arkansas.

Yes, Dad and I plodded through knee high, brackish swamp water, to our deer stand, in the middle of the night, in the middle of Devil's Den Swamp, to hunt whitetail deer.

Dad was hunting deer. I was after bigger game.

The previous week, in the Philippines, an unrepentant, Imperial Japanese soldier, hiding for 20 years, surrendered to authorities. If one was hiding on Mindanao, why not in the Devil's Den Swamp?

Taciturn even in a crowd, in the embryonic break of day, Dad was a veritable hurricane of stillness. He preferred it so, and I dutifully took his cue, and quietly moved in the direction of Venus and, hopefully, our deer stand.

We both knew no man or beast was awake—nocturnal animals had started their diurnal repose, and diurnal animals finished their nocturnal repose. Only a little boy, and his hyperactive Dad, were awake.

In the Arkansas Delta, the last few moments before dawn were an immense cosmic tease. There was no real, sustaining, light, only the promise of light. To this nine year old, hope was nearly lost.

There were reasons to hope. Grey dawn slowly coated the tops of trees. A cool, comforting breeze stirred these sentries of the dawn. In the tops of pecan trees parsimoniously holding on to the corpses of brown leaves, tentative birds reticently chirped or tweeted, but with no devotion. To me though, it might be dawn in the top of the trees but at the base it was still murky. Where it really mattered, at the epicenter of subsistence, there was still more gloom than luminosity.

"Dad, what time is it?"

He did not hear me.

He was enjoying, no doubt, the enormity of being in Devil's Den Swamp before the dawn erased its clandestineness. When he was in the woods, in a slough, walking in a field—no matter where he was, as long as he was hunting, it was sacramental. He was communicating with his God.

However, what if God wasn't listening? What if, even as we languished in the Devil's Den, the world was already expiring?

I was not persuaded that dawn would actually arrive. The sun had risen every other day, but who knew if that would happen today? Maybe the world ended last night while I slept, and I just didn't know that the world had ended. I might be waiting in vain for the dawn to come.

The end of the world would have to come sometime. I learned about the Apocalypse in the First United Methodist Church 9-12 year old boy's Bible class.

I listened to the voice full of dread and foreboding, as much dread and foreboding as one could manage in a Bible class for 9-12 year old boys. My Sunday school teacher, 42 year old, slightly balding, moderately overweight, Evan Nash, whom I affectionately called Uncle Evan, wearing the same wide lapel sky blue polyester suit with a dark blue and white striped tie, warned me that someday the sun would turn black like sackcloth made of goat hair. The whole moon would turn blood red, and the stars in the sky would drop to earth. I would call to the mountains and the rocks, "Fall on me and hide me from the face of Him, Who sits on the throne and from the wrath of the Lamb! For the great day of wrath has come, and, who can withstand it? (Revelation 6:14-18)."

"The only antidote is the Parousia, the Second Coming," Uncle Evan explained.

"Apocalypse" and "Parousia" were two of my first big words and I felt wise and important as I muttered them under my breath.

In the middle of the Devil's Den Swamp, as the world was about to end, or had already ended, I pleaded, "Come quickly, Lord Jesus!"

The day of the Lord will come like a thief. The heavens will disappear with a roar; the elements will be destroyed by fire, and the earth and everything done in it will be laid bare (2 Peter 3:10). I stood in the Delta dawn and waited for the wrath of God to fall on me, as it might have done to others last night. Conceivably, on the other side of the world, little Chinese boys like me were already burning in Hell, and my time was coming.

I imagined it was like the movie I saw in school about the Atomic Bomb falling on Hiroshima. The wrath of God dropped from the bowels of a B 29 Super Fortress Bomber, exploded, and the air shimmered like sparkling ripples on Bayou Bartholomew. Last night, colossal clouds of dust and debris darkened the skies of Shanghai, and would soon reach the Devil's Den. We were doomed.

Yes, that was why it was taking so long for the darkness at the core of things to recede, and light to appear.

However, looking again to the sky, I realized, no, the world had not ended. Not yet at least. The dawn was evident in the spectral shadows of cypress, oak, pecan, and sweet gum trees.

Still, there was room for doubt. While the dawn apparently had come to the tops of trees, my world was still dark. My world was not at the tops of things, but at the base of things, where there were rattlesnakes, bobcats, and Samurai warriors, who could hurt even a plucky United States Marine captain.

Then suddenly, for a moment, it was quiet. No bird, boy, or man made a sound. The dawn arrived. Inexorably, the light came.

It was not earthquakes, or the sound of birds, but it was silence that filled the Delta morning. The hushed light graced the living and the dead alike, little boys, and all sorts of living things.

First, darkness absorbed the repartee dawn, but the dawn was clearly winning the epic struggle. The wrath of God would not fall today. The Apocalypse was delayed. We might live after all.

I shivered, not because it was cold—November in southern Arkansas was never cold — but I wished I was six because, when I was six, on hunting trips, Dad still held my hand, and even put me in his lap when we stopped to rest. Snuggling into his tan hunting vest, I would scrap my nose against number six twelve gauge Federal shells. It was an olfactory amalgamation of Three-in-One gun oil, rotting squirrel blood, and stale tobacco smoke.

Still, I wished the sun to illumine quickly the forest, the lake, and the cotton field. In the daybreak, pervasive shadows, the verisimilitude of verve itself, was in question. But, the sun knew it had won, and was in no hurry to claim its victory.

Dawn came. Like a Pentecostal church, faithful squirrels and contrite mockingbirds, both with unguarded anticipation, broke out in glossolalia. Rodent, bird, and magnolia blossom awakened their lovers, their children, and me to imminent sunrise possibilities.

Some unrepentant saints were still tentative and doubtful—backsliding eastern turkeys, wayward mourning doves, and reprobate armadillos. They had not yet come to the altar to claim their redemption. Like Aeneas, they had crossed the river separating the mortal realm from the land of the dead but had not yet reached the Tiber River on the other side. They languished in purgatory.

But, most creatures, the morning dove, the crow, the opossum, and the raccoon, with joy and gladness, met Dido, Aeneas' spurned lover. To them, Dido, Aeneas, and agnostics alike, the dawn may be full of regret. But there was Odysseus, who was immensely happy in his watery grave. Reticent deer moved in the safety of dawn to watering holes. Like Odysseus they preferred the darkness to dawn.

Odysseus, Dido, and other lost souls had to give way to the dawn. We all must. The light was already here.

At sunrise, Aeneas and the Sibyl, Aeneas' tour guide and a prophetess, everyone, at all times, come to a fork in the road. One had to decide to take the left path leading to Tartarus, the lowest point of Hades, or to take the right path leading to Elysium, the height of Heaven. One must choose Tartarus or Elysium. The Delta dawn required a decision, and the moment of decision was at hand. One had only one quick moment to decide.

With strong purpose, the Delta dawn conquered all. Invading morning illumination dissipated coruscations of coolness. No, the world did not end last night, or if it did, God, stepped into the chaos, into the dim cotton field, and murky slough, and created the world again. God said, "Let there be light," and there was light. God saw that the light was good, and He separated the light from the darkness. God called the light "day," and the darkness He called "night." And there was evening, and there was morning—the first day. Life began again. Clarity returned. Hope was restored. God breathed life into man. Aeneas and all other mortal creatures turned their ships to sea, their sterns to shore! The Delta dawn arrived.

It was the most real thing in the world. On this new day, from its commencement, every living creature knew that the sun was a force to be reckoned with, and living was serious business. The Delta dawn was grand even before it reached its apogee. It awakened water bugs, which bounced on the surface of hundreds of rivers, lakes, bayous, sloughs, and swamps. It quieted royal bullfrogs, which retreated from moonlight darkness to a meridian nadir. The Delta dawn awakened the whole world. Upon the land and the water new life arrived. Like the old Egyptian poet in his Book of the Dead "Hail, thou Disk, thou lord of rays, who risest on the horizon day by day! Shine thou with thy beams of light upon the face of Osiris Ani, who is victorious; for he singeth hymns of praise unto thee at dawn…"

The hunting trip at the Devil's Den, like so many of our hunting trips, ended in nothing more than cheerful memories. The new day arrived, but our trophy buck did not.

There would be many other dawns.

Often, as a child, I lay in bed and wondered when everyone else in my household would wake up. I had no way to know what time it was, so I estimated time by bathroom urges, and the labored snoring of my brother. My brother snored the way long distance runners breathed—at first, with a labored overture, then with a roaring symphony, and finally with a wheezing finale.

I was a slightly obese, little boy, weight that I lost in my teen years, only to regain with a vengeance in my middle age years. I had incisive blue eyes that I inherited from my dad, and big hips I acquired from my mom. My dad nicknamed me "Satchel" after baseball star Satchel Page, although my mother was horrified at the appellation.

"Martin, Mr. Page is a nigra."

Like my parents craved an early morning cigarette and a cup of coffee, I fervently wished to read a book but had no way to do that. I had no discreet night light or lamp, whose sheen would allow me to obtain my fix. The cognitive depravity was more painful than the evocative dissoluteness.

For Christmas, my dad's brother, Uncle Ray gave me an illustrated Howard Pyle's The Story of the Champions of the Round Table. "Son forget not that you are a king's son and your lineage is as noble as anyone's on earth . . ." It was all true and Sir Lancelot made me noble as I read it. Like the Holy Scriptures, to this nine year old, to read about someone made me that someone. Howard Pyle, and the disciples gifted me, "Silver or gold I do not have, but what I do have I give you. In the name of Jesus Christ of Nazareth, walk (Acts 3:6)."

Brave Sir Lancelot and Sir Percival protected coy ladies from duplicitous wizards and fierce dragons. Duplicitous wizards and fierce dragons were in short supply in southeast Arkansas. Uncorrupted, intrepid, and felicitous, in the face of imminent butchery, fanciful in the early morning light, my knighted champions slashed through the early morning, like the four horsemen of the Apocalypse. "I watched as the Lamb opened the first of the seven seals," St. John wrote, "Then I heard one of the four living creatures say in a voice like thunder, 'Come!' I looked, and there before me was a white horse! Its rider held a bow, and he was given a crown, and he rode out as a conqueror bent on conquest (Revelation 6:1-2)."

Brave Sir Tristram was dying. The lovely Lady Belle was summoned from Ireland to save the valiant knight. "Belle because of her wonderful beauty. . . she alone may hope to bring Sir Tristram back to life and health again, for I believe that if she fail no one else can save him." Sir Tristram loved this young maiden, but his paltry ardor paled in comparison to my blazing passion.

A "rose-tree up from Sir Tristram's grave, and down upon the grave of the Lady Belle; and it is said that this rose-tree was a miracle, for that upon his grave there grew red roses, and upon her grave there grew pure white roses. For her soul was white like to thrice-carded wool, and so his soul was red with all that was of courage or knightly pride." Lying among all those roses, I wanted to spend eternity with my Lady Belle!

The Story of the Champions of the Round Table was the first book I was to own and it was a brawny book, a book any boy would proudly display on his chest of drawers, or take to show-and-tell in school. It as an exotic, foreign book, published in London with strangely spelled words like "favour" and "theatre." It was sensual and seductive in its rich, exotic imagery. It replenished my soul with metaphor and syntax.

I offered my bath robe tie to Mammy Lee, our housekeeper, nanny, and surrogate parent, and offered in a condescending southeast Arkansas English accent, "Ma Lady, you have my favour and can accompany me to the theatre."

I knew London was overseas in England. My Uncle Ray, whom I told my Bible Class was Omar Sharif, recently returning from a dangerous mission against the Ottoman Turks. He was actually a boring, Tulane educated MBA Monsanto oil chemical engineer, who lived in Dickenson, Texas. He had been in Inverness, United Kingdom, coordinating oil drilling in the North Sea. It could have been Nairobi, Kenya, or Mena, Arkansas, for I had been no farther away from home than Watson, Arkansas. Uncle Ray brought me this treasure that blazed brightly in the early sunrise of the Delta dawn.

# 3

THE DAWN ALWAYS BROUGHT mixed feelings to me, especially on my birthday.

I remembered hunting and fishing trips that I would never experience again. I thought of a place on the Deep Lake Road, where Dad and I successfully killed our limit of grey squirrels, and pledged to one another that we would one day return, but we never did. However, what most bothered me, were my memories of Bo Dean Taylor.

Bo Dean Taylor was born in the Arkansas Delta in the early 1930s, on or near the longest bayou in the world: Bayou Bartholomew. God lost all sense of proportion when He created Bayou Bartholomew and Bo Dean Taylor. He was an extraordinary person born in an amazing place in an astonishing time.

To be born near Bayou Bartholomew, was to be born at the epicenter of the universe. No one was quite sure when Bo Dean, affectionately call Bo by his friends, was born, nor did he know where Bayou Bartholomew began. If the Arkansas Delta was Eden, Bayou Bartholomew was the place where God first stood and blew his clarion horn. The bayou, and the man were born in mystery but in hope.

Bayou Bartholomew began as a small, unpretentious bayou, and remained so, throughout its 375 miles. In Southeast Arkansas nomenclature, a "bayou" was bigger than a stream, smaller than a river. Or as my dad so descriptively explained, "If you can just about piss to the middle of it, it is a bayou."

The world, into which Bo Dean Taylor was born, was held in perpetuity between the Bayou, and the Mississippi River, both extravagant and cheerful in longevity and opulence. Folks caught fat red belly brim, prickly crappie, and colossal catfish in its turgid waters. Timid alligators hid among shedding cypress knees.

People swam and fished in it, held barbecues and picnics by it, and were baptized in it. In baptism, God claimed us, and sealed us, to show that we belonged to Him. Likewise, the Bayou held its faithful servants in its arms. In the Bayou, God freed humankind from sin and death, uniting it with Jesus Christ in His death and resurrection. But, God did not neglect corporal needs. Bayou Bartholomew freed all converts from fear of hunger or want. There was no end to its food supply. At the beginning of each new day, on Bayou Bartholomew, God announced His pleasure at the admission of new converts into His family. Newly baptized converts said, 'We give you thanks, Eternal God, for you nourish and sustain all living things by the gift of water. In the beginning of time, your Spirit moved over the watery chaos, calling forth order and life.' Likewise, Bayou Bartholomew residents daily lived in the sustenance and nourishment of Bayou Bartholomew, whose predictable, steady water called forth order and life, out of chaos.

In the Mesopotamian Creation myth, the main god, old Marduk, rolling his thunder and storms in front him, shot an arrow down evil Tiamat's throat. It split her heart, and she was slain. Marduk took his club and split Tiamat's water-laden body in half like a clam shell. Half he put in the sky and made the stars. Across the heavens Marduk added the moon and sent both in perpetual movement across the heavens. From the other half of Tiamat's body, Marduk made the land and all that lived on it. From Tiamat's eyes, he made the Tigris and Euphrates, and surely the Mississippi River and Bayou Bartholomew. Upon this land grew grains and herbs, pastures and fields, forests and orchards.

Bo Taylor was born in the midst, then, of profligate plenty.

Bo lived with his wife Minnie Lou and his nine-year-old son Little Tommy on Red Fork Road, sixteen miles from Bayou Bartholomew. Red Fork Road abruptly turned off Highway 1 at Watson and paralleled Highway 1 to MacArthur. Whereas urban southern communities were strictly segregated, rural southern communities were not. Buddy Cook, Raleigh Parker, and Bo Taylor lived next to each other on the Red Fork Road.

Bo, Minnie Lou, and Little Tommy lived in an unpainted shack on 38 acres, a gift to Bo's father, by the Farm Bureau Administration. He really owned 40 acres, but Mr. Raleigh Parker claimed two acres of Bo's land. On the Red Fork Road, in Choctaw County, Arkansas, Bo knew better than to claim from a white man what was rightly his.

A cypress cluttered, overgrown slough, covered two acres of Bo's property. With Bo's permission, Dad and I hunted perky wood ducks in his slough, a gracious gesture that we repaid by giving Bo half of our kill.

Some Sunday mornings, we were wicked, and fished in nearby Kate Adam's Lake. Before Dad went to Pedlam First, and Minnie Lou went to Red Fork Holy Ghost, Dad gave Minnie Lou a silver dollar and, for further penance, one-half of our catch of black bass and all the brim, to clean our fish so that we could quickly return home before Sunday School. Minnie Lou had a gift: Minnie Lou, her hands moving like wild birds, could clean, dress, and fillet black bass faster than any living person.

To supplement his income, Bo worked at Buddy Cook's farm and Enos Gould's Spirit of Red Fork Lion gas station.

Bo loved the morning. In the warm mist of Delta mornings, Bo dared to believe that God loved him as much as anyone else, and that God was good indeed. Even to black folks.

Each morning, Bo optimistically checked his trotlines on Macon Bayou. Cotton twine, with fish head adorned hooks, draped cypress knees. The trotline wriggled every time a catfish snagged its breakfast. The captured catfish, and the morning, then, belonged to Bo, and it pleasured him greatly.

Bo also chopped cotton at Buddy Cook's farm. "Chopping cotton" was a euphemism for removing grass from cotton rows. Dancing a minuet in the dawn, with a six-foot sharpened hoe held almost straight up, moving perpendicular to the ground, working as earnestly as an assembly line worker, Bo eloquently emasculated Johnson grass. Carefully removing weed roots and plants from Mr. Cook's cotton rows, Bo vigilantly preserved prosperous cotton plants. A good cotton chopper was much appreciated by all in the Arkansas Delta.

Buddy Cook, Raleigh Parker, and Bo Taylor lived on the edge of the Levee, a forty-foot abutment that protected all Terre Haute, from St. Louis to New Orleans. In a land where there were no mountains, not even small hills, a levee was an impressive thing, especially to me, a nine year old. The land between the levees, one on the Arkansas side, and one on the Mississippi side, was full of panthers, bear, and wild bucks. Nothing permanent could be built between the levees. No matter what the structure, it would not survive the perennial floods of the Mississippi and Arkansas Rivers. There was a feeling of impermanence between the levees, with nothing truly enduring but the lingering smell of damp decay. In April and May, as melting snow churned the River from Minnesota to Louisiana, water bubbled up under the levee, and flooded low areas of all three farmers' land.

These three farms were the last permanent attempt at taming the land before the wilderness between the levees. Like Roman sentries on Hadrian's Wall, Buddy, Raleigh, and Bo held back the Scots, Picks, and Britons from overwhelming the good citizens of Choctaw County. Like mysterious Druids, they patrolled the levee looking for signs of weakness and disrepair.

If Buddy, Raleigh, and Bo were sentinels on the wall, Enos Gould's Red Fork Lion Gas station, called The Spirit of Red Fork, was a trading post on the edge of Indian Country.

Enos Gould built the Red Fork gas station on Highway 1 at the end of the summer of 1927. During the 1927 Flood, Highway1 became a canal, an interior waterway as open for boat travel as it once was for car travel. While paddling in a long boat down Highway 1 to and from Elouisa Cuthbertson's country store to buy Saltine Crackers, sharp cheddar cheese, and Vienna sausages, he found the perfect spot for his new entrepreneurial venture. As Mr. Gould drew close to the levee, he noticed that Highway 1 took a propitious turn to the east, toward St. Charles, Arkansas. He knew that once Highway 1 dried out, Lake Charles moonshiners would need gasoline and succor before they braved the final run to Pedlam.

"This is where I will build my store," he thought.

It was located in Red Fork, Arkansas, and he had the idea to build the store while Charles Lindbergh was landing his airplane in France. A frenzied mob of 100,000 spectators greeted shy Charles Lindbergh, and over the radio beamed all over the world, Lindbergh said his forgettable "Well, I made it."

At the very moment, Buddy had his vision.

Enos Gould named his new store, which was one of the early Lion Oil and Gas Company franchises, headquartered in El Dorado, Arkansas, 90 miles away, "The Spirit of Red Fork Lion Gas Station." He only regretted this name once, when Lindbergh collaborated with the Nazis in the 1932, but it was too late to change the name or his $18 sign, a handsome sum in 1927. So, he retained the name and the sign.

Almost every Saturday, Dad and I would be going to or coming from somewhere across the levee. The Spirit of Red Fork was a natural place to purchase gas, to buy a frosty RC Cola, and to use the bathroom.

The bathroom was a unisex bathroom with a sign "whites only." A smaller sign with "coloreds" painted on it, pointed to the left. Enos had thoughtfully provided a roll of toilet paper for black patrons squatting in the bushes.

Mr. Gould's gas station stayed open 24 hours per day. Even as a child, it seemed foolish to me to keep a gas station open all night in the middle of a population base of 350 people. Also, by the 1950s, Highway 1 had been thoroughly supplanted by shiny, white paint lined, Highway 144, twelve miles to the West. Mr. Gould simply gave into inertia, like a ball on the end of a string, and, for over 30 years, he had never closed the gas station. Like a respirator-sustained life, the gas station sustained him, and, as long as it stayed open, he lived. In any event, tobacco-chewing fishermen, with grizzly white beards, replaced bleary-eyed moonshiners. Mr. Gould had set up a small, metal table, thoughtfully covered with tacky plastic wrap, to protect table and fishermen from splashed coffee. Around 8 PM every night, he put a sign on the front door, "Pump your own gas. Use the bathroom but lift the lid. Help yourself to coffee. Put your money on the counter."

We often stopped at the Red Fork Lion gas station to visit with Mr. Gould, and with Bo Taylor, who worked there on the weekend.

Every Sunday, Bo, Minnie Lou, and Little Tommy attended the Red Fork Spirit Filled Holy Ghost Church.

The Red Fork Spirit Filled Holy Ghost Church was an uninsulated, but clean and well maintained, one room, pinewood shack built on cinder blocks annulated with mold. To the right of the building was a huge, silver propane tank, which provided warmth to faithful saints, who needed more than the Holy Spirit to warm a January morning. On rainy Sabbaths, the pitter-patter of water on the tin roof soothed the most discouraged saint. Behind the church building was an outhouse tastefully decorated with a Celtic cross peep hole. Inside the outhouse, to tempt unsaved patrons, Holy Ghost Church Deacons lay Gospel tracts next to the toilet paper roll.

The Gospel tract warning, "Meet Jesus now or spend eternity in Hell," no doubt constipated wayward sinners, involved in more mundane, earthy pursuits.

The church building was full of golden colored glass windows, which harvested the munificent mid-morning Delta sun. Ardent saints clapped their hands with extravagant bliss. Clapping hands launched sunshine graced, dazzling dust toward heaven and toward whirling spirit filled, swaying dancers, moving hip and thigh, in faithful response to the unction of the Holy Spirit, to the beat of the out of tune piano.

"Wooooo, Lord! Thank you Jesus!" the Holy Ghost saints chanted.

Three –hundred-pound, sweating, Brother Obadiah T. Williams, pastor of Holy Ghost Church, waved his hands in unison with his congregation's response. In his right hand was a white handkerchief that he occasionally wiped spittle from his ample mouth.

"Jesus, Jesus, Jesus. We need you Jesus!"

"Yes, sir! Yes, sir! Yes, sir!"

"And we know, that in all things," Brother Williams paused for effect. "God works for the good of those, who love him, who have been called according to His purpose."

"Preach it Reverend!"

"What, then, shall we say in response to these things? If God is for us, who can be against us? Do you hear me—what shall we say in response to these things?"

"We are saved! Saved! Saved! Saved!"

"What then shall we say?"

"We are redeemed by the blood of the Lamb!"

Waving their hands, to and fro, back and forth, then in frenetic joy, the Holy Ghost saints pleaded, "Wash us Jesus! Wash us! Wash us!"

They all were saturated in the blood of the Lamb and they rocked in remonstrative triumph.

"So if we are saved and we are redeemed, who shall separate us from the love of Christ?" Brother Williams remitted.

"Shall trouble or hardship or persecution or famine or nakedness or danger or sword? Shall lynching and beatings and injustices and such, shall they separate us from the love of Christ Jesus!"

"No, oh no! No! No! No!" the feverish congregation affirmed. "Nothing! Nothing! Nothing shall separate us from the love of Jesus!"

"No, indeed brothers and sisters! No, in all these things we are more than conquerors through Him, who loved us. Neither death nor life, neither angels nor demons, neither the present nor the future, nor any powers, neither height nor depth, nor anything else in all creation, will be able to separate us from the love of God that is in Christ Jesus our most precious, our most wonderful, our most powerful Lord!"

"Ohhhhh yes, Lord! Yes! Yes, Lord!" the saints groaned.

And then an explosion of corporate triumph erupted. Glossolalia, waving hands, and cries of ecstasy punctuated this cosmic moment, when God and humankind united in euphoric conquest. People, falling prostrate to the rough, unsanded pine wood floor, were slain in the spirit; attentive deacons spread white cloths on prostrate exposed female knees.

"Give into it, sister, give into it," caring deacons whispered. "Let the Spirit heal your troubles."

And He did. The revived saints would lie in rapture for several more minutes contemplating the goodness of the Lord.

"We are more than conquerors, more than conquerors! We have nothing to fear! We have Jesus! We have Jesus!"

Brother Obadiah then broke in with a chorus of "I'll fly away Oh glory, I'll fly away."

God was good. The world was good. Tomorrow was full of hope again.

Church was a defining moment in the lives of Bo, Minnie Lou, and Little Tommy. For an hour or two each week, they were, who God intended them to be. In the eyes of man, God, and demon, they were redeemed by the Blood of the Lamb. They were equal to all.

There was no Sunday school, no children's church, and no youth group. Red Fork Spirit Filled Holy Ghost Church saints stood in defiant solidarity against the injustice that infected their land and persecuted their souls. For an hour or two each week, in Red Fork, Arkansas, black men, women, and children, poor, weak, haughty, humble, altogether, stood in the Holy of Holies, and they were more than conquerors in Christ Jesus!

Mr. Gould would sometimes put up his sign and go to his home church, Pedlam First United Methodist Church, eight miles away. Most Sundays, though, Mr. Gould would turn his radio to KVSA, 1490 on the AM dial, turn the volume to full throttle, and would listen to Judge Jim Murphy regularly vilify in the name of Jesus godless Yankees and Anti-Christ Communists.

Dad, with optimistic, bright blue eyes, drove our black 1952 Chevrolet truck, next to the gas pumps, so that Bo could fill the gas tank with red dyed, regular leaded gasoline.

Bo wore a dark blue industrial shirt with a bright golden Lion insignia on the back, tucked into matching slacks. He always wore Korean War, army issued black leather boots, gifted Bo on his birthday by Minnie Lou. No one knew when Bo's birthday was, but Minnie Lou and Bo decided it would be on Labor Day because Bo always got that day off from work.

Dad and Bo, away from the supervision of my mom—who strictly forbade all egalitarian intercourse between the races—squatted on the cracked concrete surrounding the gas station and shared an unfiltered Camel cigarette. Dad and then Bo, approximately the same age and size, alternately took drags, talked about the weather, where the fish were biting, and when the first frost would occur.

"Bo, have you seen any mallards yet?"

"No Mr. Martin, but I sees some wood ducks in my slough. I believe they is done nesting and should be ready for the skillet in a few weeks."

"Did Bud grow any corn this year? Do you see any doves over there?"

"Yes sir, I do. Mr. Bud must have left some corn bait in that field 'cause I sees hundreds of them."

"Thank you Bo," Dad smiled. Dad now had the key to Fort Knox and he planned to kill his limit of doves before the first frost.

These intimate tête-à-têtes, however, in no way distracted Bo from another of his amazing talents: cleaning windshields. Spraying water from a rusty oil spray can in which Bo, with keenness and foresight, replaced 30-weight oil with pure alkaline well water, he carefully washed our cracked front window and dried it with an Arkansas Gazette. Using the society section because it had the most black ink pictures, Bo reclaimed our windshield from interloping, squashed June and stinkbugs. Rigor mortis bug guts, some of which for weeks had obstructed the sheen of our automotive universe, could not withstand the concentration that Bo devotedly committed to this task.

Slowly, but inevitably, Bo and his Arkansas Gazette, triumphed!

To celebrate the subservience of everything creepy-crawly to Bo's acuity, my dad bought Bo a brown bottle Orange Crush and Hershey candy Bar. To emphasize his victory, Bo full of justified hubris would say, "Mr. Jake, put on your daddy's blades."

I put on my dad's blades and heard the whine of dry rubber on redeemed glass. We listened to our squeaking wiper blades with joy, promise, and hope, with no worry of a future rendezvous with rapacious bugs, who were willing to sacrifice their lives, and guts, and eternity, for one brief moment of dazzling, vehicular, chimerical fame. Dad and I knew that no matter how full of dust and bug gut our window might be, cleanliness and decency would prevail. For a few moments, without saying it, without really thinking it, we experienced transcendent fraternity, equality, and felicity. Decency, kindness, and virtuousness would prevail.

We profusely thanked Bo for his gift. We thanked Bo for the end of a memorable day in the woods or on a lake. Every outing was rewarded with kind Bo, with his oilcan and Arkansas Gazette, greeting us at the Spirit of Red Fork Lion gas station. I loved Bo the same way I loved an early southeast Arkansas spring morning. They were both strong and enduring.

Smiling, Bo lifted his Orange Crush in salute as Dad drove away!

It was to be the last time we saw Bo alive.

# 4

EVAN NASH TOO, was born next to Bayou Bartholomew.

Celebrated by scion and pauper alive, Evan grew up on an antebellum plantation, Willow Lane. Massive in design and expectation, it was a fitting testimony to the Nash legacy. Willow Lane appeared to belong to a king or a duke or the Caliph of Egypt, but not to a prosperous Delta planter. A brick walk escorted visitors into a massive hallway that was larger than most sharecropper cabins. There were eight bedrooms, each remodeled with its own bath during the 1920s. When a toilet was flushed, bubbles emerged from the depth of Bayou Bartholomew. Young Nash tied bacon to cotton twine and caught scores of crawdads enjoying the noisome deposits. Hooks were optional.

Evan's paternal great-grandfather, Abner Nash, was born in nearby Napoleon, Arkansas, in 1845. Napoleon was the largest town in Choctaw County. During the Civil War, young Abner served under Captain Henry E. Green, Company E "Napoleon Grays" Choctaw 6th Militia Regiment, founded on February 28, 1861. The Napoleon Grays were absorbed into Brigadier General Pat Cleburne's 15th Arkansas in March 1862. Private Nash distinguished himself on the first day at the Battle of Shiloh by leading the Grays into the Hornet's Nest and, when Captain Green was killed, was promoted on the spot to the captain of the Napoleon Grays. Promoted to colonel after the battle of Franklin, Abner Nash commanded the 15th Arkansas and was mustered out near Bentonville, North Carolina in May of 1865.

Evan Nash was one of the wealthiest residents of Choctaw County. He had real money, not money gained through crafty business investments or spouting oil wells. This was money farmed from the land, money that lasted, as the land lasted. It was everlastingly virile. Evan was part of the land; he was part of the chosen people and he embraced his calling with humility and resoluteness.

I stared at a 1962 Pedlam First United Methodist Church directory and I saw a smiling middle aged Uncle Evan, the Grand Wizard of the Arkansas Ku Klux Klan. He was a medium sized, handsome man whose engaging smile and Christian testimony convicted the most backsliding sinner, and inspired the most pious saint. His three lovely children were apoplectic in their normalcy. His attractive wife was a poster mom for the PTA. Mrs. Nash was Arkansas State Worthy Advisor until she married Evan, when she was promoted to the head of the Eastern Star.

Evan Nash was an officer in the Lions Club. He was a 33 Degree Mason, Knight Commander of the Court of Honor. He could quote by heart the entire Book of Ephesians and the Magnum Opus. In the annual Christmas Parade, following Sag Sherman dressed up as Santa Claus, Uncle Evan, in his Bozo the Clown outfit, rode his unicycle down Main Street throwing Hershey Kisses to grateful Pedlam residents. Along the parade route, Bozo the Clown occasionally stopped and gave five-inch round, rainbow lollipops to appreciative children.

Uncle Evan did not neglect his ecclesiological duties. Besides teaching my Bible class, he chaired the Lay Administrative Board of Pedlam Church.

My Bible class met in a small room at the end of the third floor hall and, appropriately, right above the Pastor's Study. We had the pastor in our bowels and glory at our crania.

My cosmology was enriched with God, angels, prophets, and venerated saints. I rode to Heaven in Elijah's chariot of fire. "Open your Bible," was the beginning of a sacred ritual I enjoyed every Sunday morning. Uncle Evan arrived one-half an hour early to evoke prayerfully the anointing of the Holy Spirit on our gathering.

Shadrach, Meshach and Abednego replied to King Nebuchadnezzar, "King Nebuchadnezzar, we do not need to defend ourselves before you in this matter. If we are thrown into the blazing furnace, the God we serve is able to deliver us from it, and He will deliver us from your Majesty's hand."

"Would you trust God if you were thrown into a fiery furnace?" Uncle Evan asked.

"Yes! With all my heart!" I replied.

For three years, he taught me about King David, his many wives, rebellious Absalom, and pliant Solomon. Uncle Evan was careful to include redaction criticism and practical application to his Bible lessons. "God especially loves nigras," Uncle Evan taught. "It is our job to love them as Jesus loved them."

My adoration of the man was akin to worship. I believed all that Uncle Evan taught me and I wanted to be like God, King Solomon, and Uncle Evan, in that order.

Nor did he neglect the physical body. Every Sunday morning Uncle Evan brought coconut snow ball cupcakes. Sometimes Mrs. Nash came too, bringing a pitcher of frosty lemonade, with pieces of real lemon peel floating lusciously in the mixture. My class was full of the smell of Uncle Nash's Brylcreem, of Mrs. Nash's Jean Nate Eau Du Toilet, and the feel of good things all around.

Mrs. Nash, wearing her very best Sunday dress and a bugle boy style white hat with matching white paten gloves, poured generous portions of lemonade into Howdy Doodie Dixie cups. Like old King Belshazzar and his nobles, with my concubines and wives, with my gold goblets, booty taken from the temple of God in Jerusalem, I toasted the gods of gold and silver, of bronze, iron, wood, and stone (Daniel 5). Once, twice, three times, I defied Beelzebub until I was inebriated with the spirit of the Lord!

Then one early May Sunday morning, a few days before my tenth birthday, on the way to church in our 1957 blue-and-white Chevrolet Caprice, my mom spoke to my dad with reverent solemnity, excessive even for the Sabbath. Dad was driving fast because we were delayed by a telephone call.

"Who was on the phone?" Dad asked.

"Magnolia Cook," Mom, noticeably upset, replied. "Last Wednesday afternoon, Bo tripped over a T. M. Jackson grocery display of Kraft grape jelly, and caused Tilley Nash to stumble. They both fell hard to the ground."

"Oh no. . . " Dad grimaced.

"Tilley broke her right hip." Mom continued.

Dad replied, "Velma Jane told me that Tilley broke her hip, but I did not know Bo was responsible."

"He wasn't responsible." Mom quickly responded, "It was an accident!"

"I know, honey. Continue."

I heard everything because I sat in the hateful middle portion of the back seat where the transmission precluded any possibility of obtaining a comfortable ride. My older brother was on my left and my younger brother on my right—enjoying the advantages of being the oldest and the youngest in our family. To cushion my tailbone, I sought the soft aperture on the front edge of the Caprice back seat.

Mom continued. "Bo immediately called for help. T. M. phoned for an ambulance."

With increased urgency, Mom spoke, "The emergency crew took Tilley from the store but she cried, 'Bo pushed me!'"

"Oh, no," Dad groaned.

"It gets worse Martin. Tilley, in obvious pain, cried, 'And then Bo touched my breast!'" Mom frowned.

"Bo, who was unhurt, knowing the accusation was his death warrant, tried to soothe her, 'No please Miss Tilley, I didn't mean to touch you.'" Mom continued.

"On Thursday afternoon Dr. D. T. Stamford at Jefferson Memorial Hospital told Tilley that she would never walk again."

My Mom, with deep emotion, finished, "Everyone knew that Evan would not let this go."

"I thought Evan didn't even like his Aunt Tilley," Dad said.

Mom starred at Dad with obvious irritation.

"Right after sunrise today, Evan and the Klan, woke up Bo, Minnie Lou, and Little Tommy. Bo sent Little Tommy, wearing his Buck Roger's pajamas, to Buddy's house. Minnie Lou refused to leave."

I smiled. I wore Buck Roger's pajamas too.

"The boys tied Bo to a weeping willow tree, beat him nearly to death, and then skinned him alive, Martin," whispered Mom.

To make sure Dad comprehended the full perfidy of this heinous crime, Mom repeated, "Skinned him alive."

"Minnie Lou saw everything."

Dad said nothing.

Closing her eyes, Mom continued, "Buddy and Magnolia, and no doubt Little Tommy, heard Bo first screaming, and then squealing like a wounded rabbit."

"When Evan and the boys left, Bo was still alive. Tied to the weeping willow tree, in mortal agony."

Mom paused for effect. "Minnie Lou took Bo's Savage double barrel twenty-gauge shotgun, and put him down."

"God have mercy on Evan and on us all," Dad responded as he drove the Caprice to church.

# 5

TWENTY YEARS AGO, when I moved to this farm, the yard and pasture were overrun with sharp briars and wiry thistle. I declared war on both. In a year or two, with sickle, bush hog, and Kaiser Blade, and the help of my children, I wrestled eight acres of rolling hills from my adversaries. I left a couple of acres of trees and small bushes to sustain visiting deer and rabbits, hoping, I suppose, to divert these gluttonous carrot eaters from my one acre vegetable garden. It succeeded to a point, but briar and animal demanded more.

Five years ago, with the departure of my last child, I called a truce with hedge, briar, and thistle. These rascals, however, refused to negotiate. In slightly less than a year I lost most of what I had once won. Now, on my 59th birthday, I looked out on the only part of my ten acres that was still graced with lawn. I played soccer with my four children on our slopping front turf. We knew that errant soccer balls rolled to West Virginia or beyond so from the inside of our feet we kicked with circumspection and care.

The other eight acres were overrun by grasping briars, and, in some cases, gentle apple trees. Marauding deer, sensing they owned the whole homestead, regularly ate my Macintosh apples and then marked their territory with feces coated Macintosh apple seeds. With such a fortuitous beginning, apple trees sprung up everywhere. Ironically the deer stole from me any hope of an early fall apple pie, but gifted me with countless future apple pies, if I could live long enough to enjoy their juicy bounty.

This morning, as I walked into the backyard, I could see that I was probably going to lose another one-half acre this summer. Already, the blooming briars were grasping for more of my lawn. Like Hun spies, they peered hungrily from the edge of my lawn, waiting until the last frost occurred, so that they could wage their grisly campaign on fescue and Bermuda grasses.

I closed my eyes, as I remembered Bo.

On the morning that Bo was murdered, we reached church in time for Dad to have a cigarette or two and a cup of coffee.

Religion in white Pedlam, Arkansas, was both hedonistic nihilism and theocratic fatalism rolled into one. The supreme act of worship was an approximately two hour rendezvous between humankind and God, garnished with ample amounts of cigarettes, black coffee, and sugar donuts. All this metaphysical experimentation resulted in peace and joy among all the communicants.

Almost every white person in Pedlam attended at least one weekly church function —the Pentecostals and Baptists two or three. While our religion was more or less devoid of emotion, it was full of symbolic rituals that kept at bay any metaphysical apparitions.

Sunday morning was full of unspoken protocol. We wore our best clothes to church. Dads cleaned vehicles, children washed their hair, and moms put on make-up. We left the best parking spots for visitors, pregnant women, and old people. We spoke softly in the church sanctuary. Almost everyone smoked, but the women mostly smoked at home, and never in a public place. Men smoked in the kitchen or an obscure grassy area behind the Christian education building and afterwards chewed gum to hide their smoky breath.

Our church was a cabaret dinner theater. The master of ceremonies, the pastor, introduced sequential performances and fed the ravenous congregation with vast quantities of liturgical Protestantism. The call to worship, hymn sings, prayer, the sermon, all thoroughly entertained us with their flirtatiousness solemnity. Devotees gathered at Asherah poles, and cavorted with the gods of racism and violence. White Protestantism was the perfect garb for our ghoulish reverie.

Or, at least it felt that way on my 59th birthday.

On the pinnacle of our community totem pole was white supremacy, whose arms reached prophetically over the entire region. At its feet was the black community, with its deficiency of power and prestige. The Pedlam apogee totem animal looked out, looked around, looked everywhere, but to the place on which it depended: down to the insignificant lower totem appendage that had no decorative quality and could actually be a rock or log or other nondescript object.

Over time our ritual totems lost their power: my community lost the ability to sustain itself through our totemic and religious symbols. Just such a moment had arrived at First Pedlam United Methodist Church on the morning that Bo squealed for mercy at the hands of at least one church member.

Brother Krandall Star served communion to the saints at First Pedlam United Methodist Church. We called our pastors "Brother" or "Sister" not "Reverend" or "Pastor."

It was the first of the month, communion Sunday. Brother Star began his communion homily, "The Lord Jesus, on the night he was betrayed, took bread, and when he had given thanks, he broke it and said, 'This is my body, which is for you; do this in remembrance of me.' (1 Corinthians 11:23-24). The first Lord's Supper occurred the night before the Crucifixion. But that first Lord's Supper called Communion by Protestants, was part of a larger production—the Jewish Passover. 'Let every person in every generation think of himself as a former slave, free from bondage,' the oldest continuous meal in history begins (i.e., the Jewish Passover)."

Brother Star stretched forth his arms and brought God and white Pedlam together, and, honestly, they seemed to get along nicely.

It felt very much like I was drowning. When I was five, while swimming in the Gulf of Mexico, I was caught by the undertow and cast into the abyss. The harder I dog-paddled, the farther I drifted out into the Gulf. Only with the extraordinary intervention of my dad, who rescued me, would I overcome the supremacy of the omnipresent Gulf of Mexico.

"Stop struggling," Dad admonished. "Stay still and let me take you to shore."

My five-year-old head dipped beneath the surface. I saw the pristine expanse that was the underwater Gulf of Mexico and I wanted the vastness to absorb me.

I was drowning that morning and I had no one to save me.

While accompanying Dad on a quail-hunting trip one of dad's hunting dogs found a nest of rabbits. As the canines massacred the baby rabbits, I heard them squealing in torment.

Dad and I often skinned and dressed rabbits for Mammy Lee to cook. We carefully removed the fur. Residue from the fur could not easily be removed. A skinned rabbit was a gluey, grey, ineluctable affair, as the memory of a skinned Bo hanging on a weeping willow tree stuck in my mind.

While Sheriff Cletus Compton was wrapping Bo in a makeshift shroud made from burlap Kent Feed sacks, Uncle Evan convened my Bible class with prayer and lemonade. Uncle Evan, preferring word-for-word textual hermeneutics and offered an inspiring exegesis of Esther 4.

Meanwhile, Minnie Lou and Little Tommy, at the Tiberius Wade Funeral Home had some faith, but no joy on this first morning without Bo. Last evening began with anticipation of a Spirit inspired morning at Holy Ghost Church. The evening ended with their husband/father's sticky, tortured body slumped next to a weeping willow tree.

While the Tiberius Wade funeral home placed Bo's remains in a closed pine box and propped a picture of Bo on the top, Sunday school was dismissed, and the men drank coffee, smoked cigarettes, and ate Dolly Jane's homemade donuts in the church kitchen. The smell of menthol cigarettes and brewing coffee comforted the souls of all who lingered at the door of Pedlam self-confidence.

Mr. Gould, in one of his rare appearances at church, confronted Uncle Evan with indignities, curses, and accusations.

"Well, Evan," Mr. Gould said, as if human skinnings occurred every day. "Why did you have to kill my nigger?"

"That nigger lamed my Aunt Tilley, Enos."

"Evan, I don't care what Bo did, you killed my best boy! You owe me!"

Later that morning, during Morning Worship, The Holy Ghost Church enjoyed the Holy Sacrament of communion too.

Cries of lamentation and grief punctuated the beautiful spring Delta morning. Doubt and hopelessness, strident and tempting, competed with the promises of God, solid and true.

"Shadows, thick and dark," Brother Star continued, "gathered in the Upper Room that last night before Jesus died on the cross."

Brothers Williams and Star, and their congregations, at the same time, distanced by race, united by Christ's sacrifice on the cross, heard the same words, "On the night that our Lord was betrayed He took bread, and after giving thanks, broke it and said, 'Take. Eat. This is my body that is broken for you.'"

In both congregations, the Lord's Supper was sustenance to weary pilgrims, who found it increasingly difficult to maintain an effectual life in the midst of a hostile world. We all looked forward to communion Sunday. The difference was we went to the communion rail expecting great things from our God and from ourselves. Brother Williams' congregation could only trust in God.

Central to the Lord's Supper was the notion of the "individual conversion." Every believer had to have a very personal conversion experience. Not everybody was allowed to enjoy the Lord's Supper.

Only Christian believers could enjoy communion. That must have excluded ugly Beverly Montana, the church bully, hosting on her person all species of cooties. She had no right to kneel at the Lord's Supper after she kicked me in the groin on confirmation Sunday.

A few minutes later, on that Sunday, as we stood in front of the congregation, Brother Star asked me, "Who is your Lord and Savior, Jake?"

Doubled over in pain I groaned, "Jesus Christ is my Lord and Savior."

Brother Star, thinking I was overcome with emotion, patted me on the shoulder.

He then served us our first communion.

Presumably Uncle Evan, like Beverly, was converted, or, in southern vernacular, saved. Or he would not be taking communion. We were there to help him in his Christian walk and he was there to help us in ours. It was a community thing.

We went to Pedlam Falcon football games with lots of people; we took communion only with other believers.

On the night that our Lord was betrayed He took bread, and after giving thanks, broke it and said, "Take. Eat. This is my body that is broken for you."

Red Fork Spirit Filled Holy Ghost Church kneeled and wept. Their praise labored for a few moments in clouded hope. Again, one of their brothers was murdered, as others had been for generations. Some were merely beaten, but others were castrated, or lynched, and this time, skinned alive. Those who lived, lived in fear of a regime that ruled with ruthlessness. They knew that Sheriff Cletus Compton would not investigate the affair. No charges would be filed. It would do no good to appeal to anyone because there was no one to appeal to. Except to God. And that was what the Holy Ghost Church would do this morning.

On the first Sunday morning after Bo screamed for mercy and Minnie Lou blew his brains out with a shotgun, as usual, Evan Nash sat in the sixth pew from the back, two seats from the end of the row, left side. We sang: Oh, for a thousand tongues to sing/My great Redeemer's praise. In less than six weeks Tilley would return to her pew, the fourth pew on the left.

Brother Star ended: "This is the feast of victory for our God. Alleluia, alleluia, alleluia. Worthy is Christ, the Lamb, Who was slain, whose blood set us free to be the people of God. With what shall we come before the Holy One, and bow ourselves before God on high? God has shown us what is good. What does the Holy One require of us, but to do justice, and to love kindness, and to walk humbly with our God? (Micah 6: 6, 8)

I loved kindness, thought I did justice, and was sure I walked humbly with my God as I kneeled beside Uncle Evan that Sunday morning at the communion rail. I sat right next to him. At the table of the Lord. For the first time I understood the terrible price that racism had exacted on our white southern souls.

After a half a century, I have never had a windshield as clean as Bo's. His old trotlines still stand limp, and neglected on Bayou Macon. I see him in the rising mist of the Laurel Highlands morning. I hear his cries for mercy in the shadows of eventide.

Like so many of the ones I loved and those, who loved me, Bo took me with him when he died, and I had no taxi fare home. I squatted in the cool mountain dawn, and I held my breath, and I waited. I tried to ignore the agony of a man, who found time to speak to me no matter how hot the day or arduous the task. Who shared an unfiltered Camel with Dad. Who let me hunt wood ducks in his slough. Who tripped over a grocery store weekly special display of jelly and mistakenly grabbed Tilley Stuart's shriveled breast that no man or beast had touched in a decade and none would intentionally touch again.

Brother Star finished, "This is the feast of victory for our God. Alleluia! Alleluia! Alleluia!"

It was my 59th birthday. I could not escape Uncle Evan or Bo.

Psychic pain, however real it might be, did not necessarily gift me with perspicuous insight, nor did it ordain me with lofty goodness. Morbid pain percolated through decades of experience did not generate wisdom.

Now, 50 years later, I remembered.

"I kneeled at the Communion rail with Uncle Evan. Yes I did. I kneeled, bowed my head, and looked over to my brother in Christ."

"The grace of the Lord Jesus be with you," I smiled.

"And also with you," Uncle Evan smiled back.

Until I went to college, nine years later, twelve times a year, I shared the sacred host and poured out blood of our Lord with the man, who skinned Bo alive. I held the hand that made Bo, so full of life, scream and beg to die. I kneeled beside Uncle Evan. I smelled Brylcreem and the residue of Chesterfield cigarettes. I grew to hate Uncle Evan, Pedlam First United Methodist Church, and, for a season, even God.

While everyone else was created in the Imago Dei, in the image of God, was Evan Nash the exception? Was he the first man, who was never good, never had a chance to be good, because he was not a man, really, but a monster?

And even worse, if Uncle Evan was a man, how could a man be so bad that he would do such a thing to another man?

I desecrated the Body of the Lord. I both loved and I hated the man, who gave me lemonade, and skinned Bo, all in one weekend. I partook, and now, as a Presbyterian pastor, I administered, the Holy Sacrament, and since Bo's demise, I wondered if I had defiled the same.

In the $9^{th}$ year of my life I still believed in Santa Claus. I was sure if I found a leprechaun and his rainbow, there would be a pot of gold. My favorite television show was "My Friend Flicka." I loved to run into the arms of Mammy Lee, who was of such a size, and I was of such a girth, that we fit perfectly together. I loved others and knew others loved me. I went on a quest for King Solomon's Temple and the three Kings from the Orient, but instead I found Bo, hanging on a weeping willow, skinned alive on the side of the Red Fork Road.

6

I WALKED TO THE EDGE of my property where there were seven springs. My farm originally included over 400 acres. My house was built in this location because of the abundant availability of water, at all times, all year. Over the years, parts of the farm were sold to adjacent landowners until all that remained was my ten-acre parcel.

The seven springs were too much for Anna and for me to consume. Two substantial overflow pipes directed the excess water, first to a cistern that overflowed through an ancient brick culvert that transported the surplus water under my property. Then, the water tumbled down a sandstone cliff to Ben's Creek. Over the years the brick culvert sprang leaks and, literally, the soil on top of the culvert, leached away, and a significant indention in the middle of my property, one hundred yards long, appeared. Someday I will have to do something about it, but I hoped to wait at least another decade.

Memories of Bo slowly eroded the center of my being and there were places that now were sagging. I ignored this wearing away as long as I could.

Since the perfidy on Red Fork Road, my life had been a quotidian commute with Bo meeting me at every station.

The Delta dawn was mine in memory, but not in substance. I, Jake Stevens left Arkansas 40 years ago, but it lived in me still.

By now it was lunch and, being of the old school, I deferred to Anna in all food preparation.

I left my springs and my sagging yard and went on safari for better things in the kitchen.

When Anna took her frequent consulting trips, she left me Tupperware bowls full of meals carefully marked with dates and times that they should be consumed. Anna perceptively observed that I was too dumb to know when to eat them and it made me nervous to have to decide.

I went upstairs to her office.

Anna preferred a 13 inch Apple Pro Mac. She could afford a desktop, but wanted to maintain consistency. She wanted to create and then later present her power points from the same tool. Anna hated thumbnail drives and borrowed laptops. She would not even share with me! She typed about 24 words a minute—it always amazed me how she could write so little in so long a time and yet it said so much!

"Are you hungry Anna?" I sheepishly inquired.

Harvard Ed grads do not like to be distracted by capricious divinity school students—even one, who loved her.

"No."

"I am hungry."

"I am so surprised to hear that," she sarcastically responded.

"I will put on the tea kettle."

We had tea with almost every meal.

Later we sat down for celery sticks and hummus.

"Gosh, honey. Do I have to eat stuff that is green on my birthday?"

"Not entirely. I have some carrot sticks too."

There was nothing green or orange in Anna's menu that I liked.

"Anna, I was just thinking about Bo again this morning. You met Uncle Evan once, didn't you?"

"Yeah. What were you thinking?"

"I was thinking that long ago I believed in Peter Pan."

"You still believe in Peter Pan."

Ignoring Anna, I continued. "Today I seek passage on the Pequod and wonder what it will be like to serve under insane Captain Ahab. Call me Ishmael. I am a pilgrim. I am a wanderer. I am a man without home, without land, without security. I crew on the Pequod under mad Captain Ahab and like Ishmael, it may be that I shall survive the wreck: 'The unharming sharks, they glided by as if with padlocks on their mouths; the savage sea-hawks sailed with sheathed beaks.'"

Anna said nothing.

"I was born into a community on a mad voyage chasing an unbeatable white whale. Like the children of Israel, we were wandering in the wilderness, but not lost. We knew where we were going. We were headed to the Promised Land, the giants be damned! We meant to get the milk and the honey."

"This morning, this first morning of your sixtieth year, I am guessing you did not make it to the Promised Land. Or maybe you did, Jacob, and you just don't know it," Anna said.

By this time the tea was ready and having abandoned the hummus and rabbit food, we spread bright, sticky orange Marmalade on whole grain bread. That was as close as I would get to a birthday cake on my birthday.

On this day I was acutely aware of the Gibeonite foreigners—Joshua's perennial enemies—who also wanted to drive me from the land and the promise.

The Laurel Highlands meandered north to Lake Erie, south to Frank Lloyd Wright's Falling Water, from the frigid rust belt to avant-garde art. My farm lay halfway between both. Renegade protruding Allegheny ranges punctuated the Laurel Highlands. These bandit ranges drew the cold air of the Great Lakes to the balmy artistic community of the Alleghenies.

Our bodies were refreshed with luxuriant mineral-filled spring water chockablock. Practical Anabaptists, who had no use for inefficient fireplaces, ornate porches, and Calvinists built our 1880 Pennsylvania farmhouse. Nonetheless, the land, the water, the farm, and the woman, have been this Presbyterian's companions for one-quarter of a century.

In the land—gift, promise, and risk—was found the essence of our existence. It was a place for gathering our hopes, the hopes of the covenant people.

Pennsylvania was my Newfoundland, my present home. My first land, the land of my mother and father and their forebears, was the South.

"Do you remember the last time we visited Arkansas?"

"All too well, honey," Anna responded with a hint of sarcasm.

The South of Uncle Remus and the Suwannee River belonged to people, who never lived there, or lived there at a time other than when I did. The South I knew was the South of Flannery O'Connor. My South was full of grotesque characters: a mass-murdering Christian misfit; a deformed lying delinquent; an insane backwoods preacher; brutal Klan demonstrations. The South I remember was full of violent hyperbole.

We married, had our average of two point five children, and lived our lives in expectation and hope that things would turn out all right, and that we could live in peace and prosperity.

We played the harlot. Like Attila the Hun and Lucy in the Peanuts comic strip, we thought we could somehow separate our morality from our cognition. We thought we could replace our probity with epistemology and "tiptoe through the tulips" of human existence with reverent knowledge replacing Judeo-Christian ethics. It was as if God had given us a free pass because we were sincere about our religion and our sin. We thought that somehow our earnestness and feigned naïveté enabled us to escape the consequences of our actions.

Western European ethics have a foundation in the writings of Plato and Aristotle plus some influence from the Bible. Middle Eastern ethics come from a mixture of Judaism, Islam, and Zoroastrianism. In the Far East, Confucianism and Buddhism weigh in. In the southern United States, we harvested our ethics from cultivated self-actualization and conservative Protestant Christianity, garnished with racism and violence, and supposed that it was all good. Like wanton Amsterdam whores, we stood in the windows of the universe and seduced unwary patrons with our malodorous mirages.

Plato described the Sun as the child of the form of the Good. The Good, in that sense, was ubiquitous and provided life to all. Plato further argued that knowing the form of the Good assured ethical praxis. In other words, if people just knew the Good, they would do the Good. Our morality was so firmly welded to our knowledge, and we were so taken with the milk and honey of nihilism, that we were completely deaf to any discordant note that might echo from Sodom and Gomorrah, north of the Mason-Dixon Line.

"Where are you, Jacob?"

"Anna, we were confused about violence and power. We used the former to preserve the latter. However, violence and power were antithetical. Power came from the collective will of the white South. As long as there was no opposition, there was an uneasy peace in the land. However, opposition—mainly from what southerners called 'Northern agitators' and 'uppity niggers' eroded black acquiescence. We then resorted to violence to maintain our hegemony over our world."

"There you go using big words, Jacob. And don't use the N word even in jest. Have you forgotten about our three children and four grandchildren?"

"I know, I know. I just wanted to remember again how it was."

"The absence of power, then, not the presence of power, was at the heart of everything southern. As our southern paradigms and institutions lost their compelling legitimacy, violence was necessary to maintain control. Ironically, then, as the South lost power, we resorted to violence. The heart of southern parochialism and racism was weakness—not power."

"That was why the South you knew as a child had a shrill and often irrational voice," Anna interrupted.

"Yes, pouting and screeching with blind fury, we stumbled into the last half of the twentieth century. It was not power, but weakness that drove our violent nature. Like an old, angry, impotent man, we acquired youth and vigor by violent intimidation. Or like a panting vampire, we sucked blood from our people and thereby reclaimed new life."

"Insightful, Jacob."

"Jacob," Anna continued, "I can't get out of my mind the discussion with your mom when she said 'right or wrong, that is just the way it is.' How do sane people watch insane things happen without changing it?"

"That is part of my dilemma. We were not deranged. In fact our actions were controlled and deliberate. No, we were quite sane, reflective and intentional in everything we did. The problem was, somewhere along the line, perhaps when General Pickett failed to capture Cemetery Ridge, or when we lost the court case Brown vs. the Board of Education of Topeka, Kansas, we lost our equilibrium. We thought we lost control. At that moment, we separated our actions from our ethics. Or perhaps not. Perhaps we thought ourselves righteous. Like all autocratic societies, we sought to alloy our chicanery with virtue."

"Oh Jacob, do you have to think about these morbid things on your birthday?"

"Anna, I think about them every day."

# 7

VERY QUICKLY, all visitors, and residents alike, realized that water, not land, was the preeminent topography of the Delta. Water brought flourishing growth unmitigated by intemperance. Soft hope shimmered in Delta conception and application. Squatting robins enjoyed pungent, decomposing flora and fauna, as they extricated vigorous earthworms from Sabbath loam. The Delta was an epic battle between life and death. Gratuitous warmth and abundant water, brought sudden, sustaining life, but, just as quickly, violent death. The flooding bayous yanked thriving pin oaks from their antediluvian nests, and cast them into the grasping shallows where catfish lay eggs and water snakes discarded leathery casings. Life and death in the Delta were pernicious and indiscriminate. The Delta, though, demonstrated a brawny propensity toward overgenerous life.

Fierce cottonmouth snakes ruled. They bit the careful and the reckless alike, in water and out of water. Delta exuberance encouraged this nefarious species to thrive. Cottonmouths taught a vital lesson: a charitable environment must not produce softness. Successful species must be proportionately ruthless to the same degree as the land was charitable. Cottonmouths and Homo sapiens, for that matter, prospered because the suppleness and the promise of the land did not make them puny or remiss.

There were buoyant witnesses in the Delta. The gentle breeze over a bayou. A tentative fawn following its mother on the edge of a canebrake. The dance of a magpie on a rotting cypress limb. One imagined a better day was ahead, a new world in the making. It was the land, the living, and the dead that met all at once on the same stage every single new day.

All this water was the gift of the St. Francis, the White, and the Arkansas, who all emptied into the Mississippi River in about the same place.

Like a sleeping alligator, the jagged snarl of the Delta began at the eastern rim of the Mississippi River. At first it was simply a slimy demur of the watery periphery of the muddy River. Suddenly, it optimistically rose westward through the rolling piedmont to the pristine Ozark Mountains north and to the pine barren Ouachita Mountains south. The tail lay somewhere near the Sabine River.

Gar filled bayous sluggishly meandered through snowy cotton fields and sugar cane brakes. Everything was moving. The fish and snakes moved down and up the rivers and bayous; the rivers and bayous moved down to the Mississippi River. Across the River, water flowed from the East to the West. In the Delta, it flowed from the West to the East. This peculiarity created contrariness in its land and in its people.

The Arkansas Delta ran from Eudora north to Blytheville and as far west as Little Rock. It was mostly the creation of one phenomenon: the mighty Mississippi River.

The Mississippi River encompassed everything that was American. With its many tributaries, the Mississippi's watershed drained all or parts of 31 US states and two Canadian provinces between the Rocky and Appalachian Mountains. The Mississippi River began as a 20 foot tributary in Lake Itasca and ended as a mile wide juggernaut flowing through 10 states into the Gulf of Mexico. It was the epicenter of the nation, indeed, most think of the world. Some historians and theologians argued that the world began at the Tigris and the Euphrates or the Nile or the Indus, but they were wrong. The world began somewhere between Lake Itasca and New Orleans along the 2,530 miles of the Mississippi River.

Native Americans long lived along the Mississippi in the Arkansas Delta. Most were hunter-gatherers or goat herders, but some, such as the Mound builders, formed productive agricultural societies. Europeans in the 1500s brought horses, cattle, and small pox. Life was never static along the River. Annual flooding and spotty drought constantly transformed the land.

The River was at first a boundary, a limit to what was and a start of what would be. Its frothy water formed the borders of New Spain, New France, and the early United States – then became a vital transportation artery and communications link among them all. In the 19th century the Mississippi and its diminutive cousin, the Missouri, formed pathways for the western expansion of the United States.

Gifted with thick layers of this river's silt deposits, the Arkansas Delta was one of the most fertile agricultural regions of the world. From the moment Noah's Ark landed on Mt. Arafat, decaying plants and animal life consorted to create a massive Garden of Eden for those fortunate enough to live there. The Delta grew everything. Exuberant cotton, prolific soybeans, and sturdy corn warred with Johnson grass, boll weevils, and canker worms for the right to rule this exotic kingdom. Friend and enemy alike thrived in this verdant Eden.

The Arkansas Delta was bisected in the North by Crowley's Ridge that served as pathway and refuge for Native and

European Arkansans during the flood season. The region's lower western border followed the Arkansas River just outside Little Rock down through Bluff, where the border shifted to Bayou Bartholomew stretching south to the Arkansas-Louisiana state line.

The Arkansas Delta was not monolithic. Like any connoisseur dish, it exhibited diversity with its five unique sub-regions including the St. Francis Basin, Crowley's Ridge, the White River Lowlands, the Grand Prairie, and the Arkansas River Lowlands.

Heat came from the sun and from the ground. Centuries of profuse mornings and protracted days oozed from the land. A millennium of death was resurrected. Seductive, sticky Delta affection thickened all moisture, and the moisture gave the land a sauna-feel. Crane and man unfurled their wings in the dense humidity. At times the sun prevailed and the Delta became a foggy mass diced by delicate sunlight. But, it was obvious to all that the sun would win this campaign.

Yet, lurking in the background, in all parts of the Arkansas Delta, were the bayous, sloughs, and rivers...

"Are you ready for our afternoon stroll?" I asked.

Daily Anna and I walked down what we called "the lane." Cutover oak and maple trees absorbed the sunlight and charmed us with a shadowed, emerald opacity.

"Sure Jacob. But, I thought your arthritis was acting up?"

"It is, but I am restless today. Let's take a walk to the mailbox and circle round back to the tire swing. I feel like talking more than walking."

And so we did.

I loved visiting the tire swing. It was an altar of nostalgia, so to speak. It was Taoism in reverse. The basic aim of Taoism was to live in harmony with the "Way (Tao/ Dao) of Heaven" by reverence to absent family members. Rituals to honor ancestors were extremely important and must be performed in precise ways. By carrying them out properly, by pausing occasionally and remembering the echoes of my four children laugh, and sing, on the tire swing, I regained a measure of their presence.

Anna was a dedicated realist but I had no problem imagining and pretending.

The tire swing was an old Michelin tractor tire that was the perennial barracks to stinging yellow wasps. I attacked the tire swing quiescent interlopers with Black Flag wasp killer and respectful trepidation.

My foresight enabled my four children to mount the Michelin stallion like seasoned rodeo riders. They taunted pretend furious Indian warriors who circled and charged the demure homestead.

This was not the MacDonald's playland swing or the tame, Swing-and-Slide at church. No, the tire swing was visceral, feral, and dodgy. One could do real damage to person and the cosmos on a Michelin tire swing. As if a tornado struck, when my children gathered at the swing, limbs shook, leaves fell, history quivered.

My children went much farther than Kansas on this tractor tire. They launched into opportunity. They learned that they could soar to the end of the firmament and yet return safely to the sedentary loam. They enjoyed the thrill of infinity and the caution of similitude.

Empty of bouncing children, this discarded tired surrogate mistress was once a wild bucking horse, a twirling UFO, a charming Casablanca prince. Its shredding manmade plastic rope twirled and charmed my world. It hung from a massive sugar maple tree that a lumber company once offered me $3500 if I would let them cut it down for maple kitchen tables with stylish faded scars of maple tapping. But I would not surrender my tire swing, even for a pot of gold.

Thankfully, once, for many years, actually, they depended on me to launch them into perpetuity. One could not pump hard enough, push away energetically enough, to break gravity's grasp. Astronauts, rodeo riders, cavalry militia needed someone to cast them from the tug of sedateness into pandemonium.

I liked the fact that they needed me. I wanted to keep it that way.

It could not be. From that old tire they moved into antiquity. They moved beyond the mendacity of their restricted world and found their way into Middle Earth where there were new beginnings, new hopes. They gracefully wriggled their toes at passing mourning doves and plowed furrows through sensual alfalfa pasture. They laughed at late summer zephyrs and frowned at interloping grasshoppers. They dodged descending maple leaves and smiled at gathering thunderclouds. From my tire swing.

From the cerulean heavens they caught a glimpse of a world that was beyond Ben's Creek. They saw the distant Galleria enticingly gracing the horizon. On their tire swing they were taller than I, they saw more than I saw. And they no longer needed my tire swing, and, me.

At first I launched them into their dreams but as they matured and their legs grew longer and stronger, as their mass drew them to the steady loam, they pushed away in new fury.

They pushed their ship away from Cyclopes to escape one-eyed, but now blinded, Polyphemus. They ignored old angry Poseidon, who no doubt would avenge his son's angst, and steered their ship into the azure Aegean.

Alone, they invaded the twilight below the tire. They took solo trips to the horizon. They differentiated themselves from time, and me, and pushed away from certainly and poise into a reckless iconoclasm.

I did not hold back. I pushed my kids as high into the Highlands sky as my body and arms could reach, and then I let them go. We challenged the gods of the age to a duel. We won.

I closed my eyes and I saw Emma, our middle daughter, pumping her pudgy legs in futile pursuit of lofty heights. She never quite understood that the tire swing was not the playground swing, and no amount of concentrated effort of knee motion could coax the Michelin to heavenly thrills. Our bohemian daughter never willingly submitted to constraint and order.

Grace, our oldest daughter, was more careful. She understood limits imposed by gravity, motion, and force.

Nathan our oldest son was a reckless daredevil like his sister, Emma. But, while she violently but purposely attacked the universe, Nathan soared in blissful anarchy and often injured both himself and those around him.

Our youngest, Joseph, our birth son, a pale white boy, often invited to innocent perfidies by Emma, trusted us all to offer limitations to his globe and therefore felt free to experiment in grace and joyfulness with all that was around him.

One thing my four children could not do: twirl. They needed me to do that. All four of them, Nathan standing on top, defiantly holding on with one hand, and leaning to the right, Emma, legs grasping the tire on the left, to balance her brother's silliness, Joseph in her lap, and Grace pushing into the right, grasping Nathan's legs and the frayed rope lifeline. All gleefully squealed in anticipation when I wound them tightly on plastic rope, and let them go. A whirling tempest of mischievous devilry feigned mortal peril.

I wanted them to stay on my swing and let me twirl them forever, that thing that I alone could do. But they had seen the flashing light of the Pharos behind the mountains, a pristine suitor drawing them into adulthood and away from the tire swing. They knew about Lilliputian, Utopia, Troy, and Acadia. They wanted to see those places but I wanted them to stay on my tire swing.

It was my 59th birthday and I was tempted to phone my children and to ask them if they wanted one last ride. The rope and the dad were frayed, but sturdy, and there were rides remaining in one, and pushes in the other.

I walked pass the empty chicken coup across the magic bridge and I am again twirling the tire swing. But with no children shaking their feet at the fates. They had decided to risk losing twirling to explore Timbuktu.

Something of their youth was captured in that old tire swing. It was there still. Something of them was resurrected as I walk to that tire swing and for one fleeting moment our untroubled souls kissed again. The grass grew wildly underneath the tire swing; there were no protruding appendages plowing my pasture. Where once pudgy starfighters attacked the universe, caterpillars wriggled through worn tire threads. I did not need the pasture but I still wanted the toes.

I ran my hand across the rough edges of a discarded Michelin tire hanging from a giant sugar maple tree.

I am the man who twirled his children into adulthood, and for one introspective day, on my 59th birthday, smiled, and I twirled the tire swing once again, and remembered one more time the unforgettable days that were gone. Anna understood that I was daydreaming and gently touched my arm.

Anna interrupted. "Jacob, let's keep moving. Can you walk and talk at the same time?"

"With some concentrated effort—remember I don't have an M. S. Just an M. Div."

The Arkansas Delta had been thoroughly conquered only once. During the Civil War Union general Ulysses S. Grant's august legions marched southward to besiege Vicksburg. Since then, the Delta progressively wrenched retribution from Northern enemies, the eroding hills of Pennsylvania, Ohio, Illinois, and Minnesota.

The only real Civil War battle fought close to my hometown, Pedlam, Arkansas, was the Battle of Ditch Bayou, a tributary that ran across Choctaw County into Chicot County. Broken trotlines littered the banks. Snapping turtles and base water snakes sunned themselves on ancient charred oak logs, discarded from campfires.

Being an ambitious boy, I hoped that my toes would drag across the remains of a human skeleton. But as time advanced and I spent more days swimming on Ditch Bayou, I lowered my sights. I now looked for spent cannon balls or broken bayonets or even a rusty belt buckle—anything! I found no relics in Ditch Bayou. But on a field trip to nearby Vicksburg, I bought a mine ball that I threw into the shallow edges of Ditch Bayou. Then I retrieved it, hoping and imagining that this spent relic would somehow call from the deep another cousin, willing finally to reveal himself to this little boy, who earnestly sought to harvest history between the shambles and dirtiness of Ditch Bayou.

"Anna, do you remember Ditch Bayou? I took you there once. It is on the way to the Greenville, Mississippi Bridge."

My birthday was in May, and May in Western Pennsylvania was still late winter. We both put on our light jackets and L. L. Bean Wellies.

"The silence is intense, isn't it Anna? Can't hear a thing. Wonderful isn't it."

"Well . . . not really Jacob. I hear noise everywhere—cars, birds, and our neighbor's tractor. You must have forgotten to put in your hearing aids."

"You are right! I did forget honey."

"Well, don't expect me to talk much to you then! Speak away Jacob! I can at least listen to you."

"Well, Anna, in the interminably long humid summer evenings before air conditioning, I lay on my bed and listened to my Western Auto AM radio. It picked up only a few radio stations after 5:00 PM, when KTFA, the voice of Southeast Arkansas, our local AM radio station, signed off. When I was older, after midnight, I listened to WLS, a Chicago radio station, and I wondered what life was like so far north of my axis. Frequently I heard of "passing cold fronts" and "chances of snow" that were not to be mine. For the first time I heard Mick Jagger:

I can't get no satisfaction,
I can't get no satisfaction.
'Cause I try and I try and I try and I try.
I can't get no, I can't get no.

"Oh, my Jacob, that was awful."

"But oh how I love to sing!" I responded. "And it is my birthday!"

"You are taking advantage of that birthday thing!"

"Speaking of which, what special supper have you planned for the birthday boy?"

"You will see, Jacob. You will see."

"No Tilapia! Please! I hate that stuff.

"Well, I could take you out to a first class restaurant," I offered. I knew there was no first class restaurant within 100 miles from our farm.

"Into the early morning I would listen to the Chicago Cubs playing West Coast teams. I could not go to Chicago, but I counted pitches, until I finally fell asleep. It was my first visit up North. It would not be my last."

"Really, Jacob, after living up here for 34 years I think you can now call yourself a Yankee."

Ignoring Anna, "Remember my old house, Anna?"

"Was it the house that your grandmother built?"

"Yes, and it had a big yard. When I was five, I sifted the rich Delta soil through my hands. It was bursting with earthworms, dormant seeds, Indian spearheads, and broken pottery. This was a rich land, full of life past, present, and future, life that was still to grow from its fertile bowels, and life that once thrived and then was discarded into the rich loam. Once I found a 1923 worn Buffalo (or Indian Head) nickel and imagined that a little boy like me lost it two generations earlier, wondering where it had gone and if it would ever be found. I found it. The little boy missed his nickel; since it was hard to get nickels in 1958, I imagined that it was even more difficult to get them in 1923. He could not buy his ice-cream cone or candy bar, but now I could. I would. I did."

"Anna, too bad we don't have rivers like the Mississippi around here. The Monongahela is a joke. The sky was limited by the heavens that the Gemini missions had showed me was above the stratosphere; the River was illimitable. It both seduced us with its brazen concupiscence and frightened us with its rapacity. We loved the river, but would only hazard its water in the most desperate or reckless of times."

"Jacob you think everything is better in the South than it is in the North."

"Did I tell you about the trips we took to the River?"

"Several times."

"Do you mind if I tell you again?"

"No go ahead."

We stopped. Anna fed our two barn cats.

They were well taken care of, but had no names. We rescued them from the animal shelter. We called them "Cat One" and "Cat Two." Cat One and Two seriously diminished the rodent population on our property. They lived in our German barn with long slopping shingled platforms that doubled as siding and a roof.

I told Anna about my time on the River.

My father would take my older brother, Little Martin, and me on boat rides on the river. The Mississippi River was more foreboding up front than from a distance. One felt vulnerable and in harm's way, much like I felt when I once climbed the Pedlam Water Tower. One fatal mistake and one descended into the abyss.

I half expected that I would die on the River like Tommy Makin did. Tommy was boat riding with his Uncle Buddy and the boat capsized after hitting a sunken log. Neither Tommy nor Uncle Buddy survived.

We took our flat boat to enormous sandbars and pretended we were Beau Geste Foreign Legionnaires protecting innocuous French ladies from nasty Arab raiders.

"Anna, do you need to be protected from the nasty Arab raiders?"

"No, but I wonder if the Arab raiders would stack the firewood like I asked you to do six months ago?"

"Not on my birthday."

"Jake, you can be the filthy Tunisians. I am Beau Geste!" my brother Little Martin said.

My brother and I thought our land infinitely good, and our culture perpetually sustaining.

The history of the city of Pedlam and the history of the railroad through Pedlam were intimately connected. In 1872, a vision of this town was birthed when a railroad was constructed from Pine Bluff southeastward through Bakersfield and on to Chicot County. In April 1923, the Gulf Coast Lines and the International-Great Northern merged, forming the Missouri Pacific Railroad.

Important in the history of the town of Pedlam was the Pedlam family, which came to the area from Alabama in 1857. Benjamin Pedlam; his wife, Sarah; a son, Abner; and daughters, Laura and Mary, settled on land that was now a part of Pedlam. Abner Pedlam, son of Benjamin and Sarah Pedlam, purchased 240 acres of land on March 1, 1876, on which the town of Pedlam was later to be located.

When the railroad came into Pedlam in 1878 and continued south and southwest, people began to move into the area. Abner Pedlam constructed a large country store and profited from the new arrivals. He created a dynasty that would massively enrich our ethos and pocketbooks for a generation.

"Speaking of supper, Anna, don't I get to choose the menu or if we go out, the restaurant?"

"Sure. But no Shanghai Buffet."

I loved the Shanghai Buffet, an Asian fusion restaurant run by Slavic immigrants. Only in Western Pennsylvania would you find such a thing.

"Ok, ok. No Shanghai Buffet. Quantity, but no quality. I won't pick the Shanghai Buffet if you don't cook Tilapia for a month."

"I don't negotiate with terrorists, Jacob. Besides you eat too much at buffets."

Anna has had me on a diet from Hell and the thought of committing gluttony with Sesame Chicken and egg rolls was tempting.

"Keep talking, Jacob. Tell me about Pedlam."

"During World War II, on the outskirts of Pedlam was a Japanese-American relocation camp. Daddy Ray, my grandfather, owner of Pedlam Laundry, profited handsomely from government laundry contracts associated with this camp, as well as nearby prison camps for Germans and Italians.

"I never met your grandfather. But, who could forget your grandmother!"

"Mamaw loved to stop in colored town, where all Asian-Americans lived, to purchase Ginseng roots that she put in sun stewed ice tea."

Our oldest son, who worked in Asia, constantly sent us some. It was foul stuff.

"Legend says it is an aphrodisiac," Anna was fond of saying.

"Not working," I sighed.

"Mamaw," I continued, "warned me, though, that Chinamen—Mamaw called all Asians 'Chinamen,' no matter what the true nationality—ate dogs and rats and so forth, and I should never buy or eat any meat from their markets."

"Let's pick up the pace, Jacob, and burn some calories!"

The problem was, one could not walk more than 50 paces without walking up some sort of hill. Hills were everywhere and it fatigued me even to look at them.

The hills around my house were a curious mixture of alfalfa, the intentional gift to cows that once lived on my rolling hills, and now to dandelions, unwelcome interlopers who had taken advantage of my benign neglect to colonize all my hills. On the perimeter of this erstwhile pasture, vicious briars framed and protected my hills as surely as log fencing guarded Fort Apache.

I discovered that the hateful briars in appreciative gratitude blossomed with beauty that more than compensated for my obstructed hill paths. At first, I bush-hogged the intruders but, for at least a decade, my tractor had been broken. It turned out that all these years of mowing did not destroy the core but it did destroy the blossom. Now in orgiastic rapture I lived in a fiery storm of profuse beauty. I had hills to spare but I wondered how many more halcyon days I had to walk in this wild kingdom of unruly briars gifting me with extravagant, redolent charm whose *raison d'etre* tracked very close to mine on this nippy spring afternoon when I ceased fire on the briar bushes: we had yet to sign an official treaty. At least for now.

But enough said. I was on a walk with Anna. I could not mow the hills anyway. I enjoyed this languid détente I have crafted with my disreputable briars, when left alone, bloomed in rapturous beauty on the surrounding hills!

"Anna, I think I will wait for you here. You can finish your walk and come back and pick me up."

"Ok. See you later Jacob!"

# 8

IT WAS NOT UNCOMMON for Anna to walk without me. She walked with determined purpose, and her purpose was to burn calories. I walked with determined repose, being careful to examine every discovered treasure—a red leaf or a fawn hiding in the underbrush. Anna saw nothing, but had a vigorous walk. I saw everything and moved slightly faster than a comfortable stroll.

Anna's walking was exercise but I mostly exercised at the local YMCA. I was the youngest member of a weight reduction, health accountability cluster called Guts and Butts. We regularly competed with the Silver Sneakers who flaunted their Blue Cross and Blue Shield PPOs.

We periodically competed to see how many pounds each group could lose between Thanksgiving and Christmas. The SS champs lost 150 pounds. We gained a net 9 pounds. They received gift certificates from Weight Watchers. We gave ourselves a Taco Bell party.

We competed in the swim-the-most miles contest too. We were on an honor code and wrote our daily mileage on a poster board behind the life guard, who very carefully scrutinized both pool performance and log in totals. Once I logged a mile. The life guard scowled at me.

"Well, if you consider the back strokes, it was a mile," I sheepishly offered. Of course it took me about half the life span of the teenage life guard sitting on his exalted lifeguard throne, to accomplish it, but I did it. Really.

We logged a whopping 150 miles. The Silver Sneakers soared at 350. They got free tickets to the Pirates. We made Rotel Dip and watched the Pirates on television.

An 82-year-old Amazon, Margaret, whose sagging breasts were slightly smaller than her husband's, led us.

"This is our year," she prophesied.

Our opponents had little red roses embroidered on their matching navy blue swimming suits. Jimmy the Whizzer—we called him that because that was how he breathed after even the most moderate exercise—had a naked mermaid on his left forearm. That was the only swimming motif we could manage.

The Silver Sneakers had the newest rental lockers sporting top-of-the-line Master combination locks. The Guts and Butts could not remember our combinations, so we put our stuff in the broken lockers hoping that potential brigands would ignore broken lockers.

I swam my laps with no destination, no pressure to perform. I loved my swimming and I loved my God. And in the YMCA pool, I found my way again to the sublime perpendicular line on the bottom of the pool that told me again, one more time, good and faithful servant, you have reached the end and needed to turn around. I could not flip over like the Silver Sneakers, but I knew how to turn around and go back in the other direction when I touched the wall. And that was enough.

Not that I would win any coupons to Wendy's. But, this I knew—I would enjoy my time with friends, old and infirm, faithful and unpretentious, which, if we couldn't win a contest, still would laugh along the way.

I knew that no matter what happened, at the end of the great swim I was going to party with my brothers and sisters—and no doubt a few prideful Silver Sneakers too—at the end of the long swim. The God of the YMCA was faithful and true. "I have fought the good fight, I have finished the race, I have kept the faith."

Thinking of swimming and of Wendy chocolate shakes, I sat under a birch tree and waited for Anna to return.

A tension that existed in my hometown from its genesis concerned whether Pedlam would be a farming community or a railroading hub. It turned out to be a mixture of both.

The first slaves entered the Arkansas territory in about 1720, when settlers moved into the John Law colony on the lower Arkansas River, occupying land given them by the king of France.

John Law's concession was established in August 1721 and was located at Little Prairie, just over 26 miles from the mouth of the Arkansas River, next to Choctaw County, and about 40 miles from Pedlam, in present-day Arkansas County. The colony was located near the Quapaw city of Kappa. Its failure slowed the growth of Arkansas as a European colony, although settlers continued to live at French-held Arkansas Post throughout the eighteenth century.

Already by the summer of 1686, Arkansas Post was an important French trading post between New Orleans and Michigan, but no serious efforts were made to establish a permanent settlement. The French government realized that, to compete with England, it would need to establish profitable colonies, but it did not have the resources to extend all the way down to Choctaw County.

John Law, a Scottish economist, came to the rescue. Law was given a 25-year charter to settle the Louisiana Territory for France in exchange for exclusive trading rights. Law settled 6,000 colonists and 300 slaves in the territory and set aside a 12-square-mile concession for himself near Pedlam.

Life was hard for these early immigrants, especially for the enslaved ones. They had to clear sturdy Arkansas white oaks, pampered by bright sunshine and excessive rain. They splashed around in bayous and sloughs infested by water moccasins and malaria, clearing centennial cypress trees and their intrusive root knees. It was a horrible life, really.

The Civil War changed little for most blacks. Most of them stayed and entered a form of serfdom: they farmed alongside former white masters as sharecroppers. These blacks traded their freedom for cycles of acute poverty.

By the beginning of the 20th century Pedlam, Arkansas, was emerging as a promising town. The largest structure in Pedlam was the Yellow Brick Hotel. The Yellow Brick Hotel looked like what one imagined a Little Rock or Vicksburg hotel to be: it was a four-story white-brick structure. We were proud of the Yellow Brick and were glad that it greeted visitors as they disembarked from the train.

The Pedlam Motel, on the other hand, was a one-story row-house structure looking like most of the houses in which we lived. This motel offered each room a vehicular parking place and a rusty metal rocking chair. Every chair, every parking spot, every hotel room was the same. The Yellow Brick was admittedly more glamorous. But many visitors found Pedlam's modern facilities, with a toilet in each room, more appealing than the Yellow Brick's shared washroom facilities, duly segregated by gender.

Although both the Yellow Brick and Pedlam were of approximately the same species, the Pedlam Motel with its Pedlam Falcon Restaurant had bragging rights. Every Friday night the Pedlam Falcons, our high school football team, ordered steaks, fries, and milkshakes before the big game. This blessed dispensation assured the proprietors of the Pedlam Motel that they would have a steady stream of customers. If the apex of Pedlam power and prestige chose the Pedlam Restaurant, who in the general population would disagree? To show solidarity with the football team, scores of residents would wait in line to eat black-eyed peas, gumbo, collard greens, and fried chicken before the game. They wanted to stand beside their heroes in body as well as spirit.

Anna never understood how a civilized people could be so excited about a stupid football team. And even worse, our favorite state football team was the Arkansas Razorbacks, whose mascot was a rabid pig.

More fortunate classmates got to be Razorbacks; I had to be a Commodore or Crimson something-or-other—whatever Harvard students are. I once took Anna to visit Fayetteville, Arkansas, "Mecca" in Arkansan parlance, the home of the University of Arkansas. The town square featured the holy shrine of Arkansas pathos: a bigger than life statue of a wild hog.

Anna, though, offered me no commiseration.

"You have got to be kidding, Jacob. You people worship an anatomically correct pig statue?"

"Would you rather be a girly Rutgers Red Knight?"

Anna smiled.

As the football team departed Pedlam Hotel, before the gods descended from Mount Olympus, the adoring fans offering a departing cheer. "Falcons! Falcons! Let's go Falcons!"

In addition to our two places of accommodation, there was one drugstore that gave credit and dispensed viscous chocolate sundaes to waiting patrons. The great attraction of the drugstore was the proprietor's daughter, whose bosom was the lodestone for dozens of excessive-testosterone-driven Pedlam male youths.

This was the world in which I grew up.

When I took Anna down for a visit, being the barbarian Yankee that she was, remarked, "I am not impressed Jacob."

Pedlam was the very essence of diversity. It was not reticent, however, about maintaining distinct boundaries among these diverse groups. Pedlam adjudicated its court cases, educated its children, and defined its social policy according to color lines. There existed in Pedlam a "paradox of pluralism."

Mid-twentieth-century America in general, Pedlam in particular, engaged in discussions about pluralism and its inherent value. The American people in general, a nation of diversity, were unequivocal about the value of pluralism. America was full of cultural diversity and we celebrated that fact. Pedlam, however, was not so sure that pluralism, equality, and justice were the most edifying social impulses a healthy society should manifest. Homogeneity, even the illusion of homogeneity, was preferable to pluralism. The maintenance of homogeneity created a tension. From this tension flowed the quintessence of the Pedlam character.

It was not until the 1960s that anyone in Pedlam really talked about "racial equality." We thought about it, and then we rejected it—even though the Bible and scientists told us that all humans came from a common set of ancestors.

Anna once observed, "Only in white Pedlam would a group of people create a language to describe divergent people groups. First, there are white people. Then, the Chinamen, who are forced to live in what you call colored town. Next, the 'nigras'—whoever heard of such a word?—blacks, who accepted their white determined place and life and caused no problems. Then, there was a deprecatory term for blacks who, in the estimation of the white controllers, caused problems."

By this time Anna joined me, and we continued our walk home.

"Anna, do you remember the time we filled out the census form in 1990? The United States Census Bureau instructed that 'one-eight black person should be classified as black.' Not biracial."

Our adopted children had biological white mothers and black fathers.

"True," Anna responded.

No matter what the percentage of blackness to whiteness, any hint of black 'blood' classified someone as a 'black' person. In fact, with racist purism, Pedlam refused to accept the category 'biracial.' One was white or one was black. Losing one's white homogeneity was akin to losing one's virginity. One was not partly a virgin and was not partly a white. But black or brown—it was all one ball of wax.

"Billy Joe Burns looked whiter than me, but he could not use the bathroom at The Spirit of Red Fork Lion gas station."

"Colored bathrooms. Colored water fountains. That was so asinine."

"Asinine——now that is a Harvard Ed School word——go girl!"

"Do you remember when we came to Arkansas to visit my mom in the 1980s? No restaurant would serve us and our kids could not use the restrooms unless they went to a 'colored' bathroom."

"Oh yes, I remember. You commented that we were driving on the 'sacred soil of Arkansas.' It turns out, since no roadside gas stations would let our mixed race family use its nasty bathrooms, our kids peed on the sacred soil of Arkansas. Wooeeeee pigs soeeeee."

I was not going to deign a reply to this overeducated Yankee!

"Donny Ray was half white and half black. Everyone knew that Jim Bob Mercer was his dad. No one talked openly about it, but everyone knew. Donny Ray lived with his unmarried mom on Railroad Street; Jim Bob Mercer lived with his wife and other son on North Fourth Street. Donny Ray was even called 'Donny Ray Mercer.' But he never dared to enter his father's world. Nor was he invited. Jim Bob regularly visited his boy—even bought Donny Ray a St. Louis Cardinal all-star Ken Boyer autographed baseball glove. But in Pedlam, white trueness was more important than paternal care. We kept our colors separated and thought it best to do so. When Jim Bob Mercer died, Donny Ray was not allowed to attend the funeral at the white Assembly of God Church, where Jim Bob worshiped."

"I don't remember Donny Ray, but I remember the Assembly of God Church," Anna said.

"At first Donny Ray stood at a respectful distance next to a wax myrtle tree, and quietly wept as they took Jim Bob to the altar and commended his soul to Jesus. Then he pushed his way into the church to say good-bye to his dad."

"'Now Donny Ray,' Deacon Crooked Eye Ellis said as he blocked Donny Ray's path. 'You all stay back with your nigra people.' "

By this time Anna and I had reached our house.

"Jacob, I have a few more things to do. I will see you later."

"Bye."

I sat before my computer, but I was not ready to continue working. . .

As white Pedlam learned to name minorities, so also a system of control arose. Racism was a justification for control. Racism with all its stereotyping components evolved into a sort of Gilligan's Island. We were a bunch of castaways, who lived in a cornucopia of abundance, with social stability untouched by the Supreme Court and President Eisenhower.

The truth was I had no problem with this. I did not particularly think deeply, nor did I reflect upon an alternative world. I simply accepted my world the way it was, just as Mom had stated to Anna. It was just the way things were.

There were moments when I lost my equilibrium—like when Bo was murdered—but I was able to forget, or at least not think about those things. I existed in a sort of Götterdämmerung, twilight of the gods. The gods were dead, or were dying, and a sort of late 20th century chaos descended on the land. I denied Plato's ideas of being and becoming, the world of the forms, and the fallibility of the senses. I had no intention of refuting the senses, as Plato did. What seemed right according to others——religion, Yankees, even God Himself—were ignored.

By the fifth grade, I hated Yankees, and other expansive do-gooders.

When Mrs. D. W. Higginbotham told us that the Yankees attacked our people at Central High School, in Little Rock a few years before, I wanted to join the National Guard that rallied around Governor Faubus to battle the U. S. Army.

Mimi Delilah Davis' mom was a Yankee. Her dad was stationed at Fort Dix, NJ, during the Korean War and he married a Yankee. Poor Mimi was teased. We all wondered if her mom really killed puppies and so forth like we had heard.

I wholeheartedly thought that Malcolm X should die. I joined my classmates and applauded when Martin Luther King was assassinated. By the time I was 14 years old I was an Übermensch, a superman, rejecting all abnegation and mortification of the body. If I raped, pillaged, murdered, and intimidated it was for a higher good, a noble cause. Like a terrorist in a training camp in Yemen, the 1950s and 1960s made me a willing recruit for the butchery that would soon follow.

# 9

I COULD NOT JETTISON Pedlam, Arkansas, from my brain and, when I was bothered, I inevitably bothered Anna.

I wandered upstairs to bother Anna.

Her office had a bay window with a view of the Laurel Highlands Trail. The Trail traversed the Allegeheny Mountains from Johnstown, PA, to Ohiopyle, PA, via Eight Springs Ski Resort. It was arguably the most beautiful walk on the East Coast. Anna, I, and our four children spent many Sunday afternoons skipping from rock to rock like Russian ballerinas on a quest for the Holy Grail. The midday sun caught the glimmer of a World War II plane crash, at the crest of the Trail, in the right corner of Anna's window. I often put my hand on the window where the crash flickered on the soft sheen of our double pane window. Without taking one step, we could see, and if we wished, touch, life and death, the past and the future.

I stood quietly outside Anna's office door. Unaware of my presence, Anna was focused on what she was writing; nonetheless, I was comforted by her closeness.

There were some, who did not and do not understand the South. Outsiders, who do not have the advantage of growing up in mid-twentieth-century white southern society. One of these deprived souls was my Anna.

In August 1976, while sharing a turkey club sandwich at Elsie's in Harvard Square, Anna and I fell in love. I was at Harvard Divinity School translating Ernst Troeltsch and Anna was a student in the Harvard Graduate School of Education.

We had met a few weeks earlier at Thursday night Intervarsity Fellowship. The magnetism of our relationship went beyond the obvious physical attraction between male and female, truly in this woman I met my opposite. South met north. Our life experiences couldn't have been more different. My compulsive, hyper uneasiness met a gentle stream of calm and stability. I by nature was a talker, she a listener. Yet, she drew me into new worlds with question. Anna questioned everything. She didn't settle, she questioned until she found peace even in the unanswered. No one was more surprised than myself as I came to understand that I had fallen head over heels for a Yankee. I was drawn into her query. We were not on a quest for truth, but found a common excitement in the treasure hunt for life's meaning and purpose. For Anna life was not to be accepted as is, but with strong determination she aimed to gain joy in the journey of discovering more.

During the next few weeks we met for lunch in Cambridge Commons, a convenient half point between the Ed School and Divinity School. When we did not have an afternoon class, we would enjoy lunch at Elsie's.

Elsie's sandwich shop was a Harvard University favorite. It was an unexpected slice of Americana in the midst of Harvard Square, which had the feel of a plaza in Paris, France, not a square in Cambridge, Massachusetts—which by the way was really not a square anyway. The Square was an olfactory battleground — sweaty unwashed homeless men warred with cinnamon mocha lattes. The Square was crowded with cramped bookstores, outdoor coffee shops, movie houses running artsy movies no one could understand, and, of course, the mother lode, the COOP. I loved going to the COOP—as a Harvard student, I was a stockholder. It was an exclusive store for Harvard-types. It was my store. I loved the COOP.

When my visit at Harvard Square ended, I often entered the Johnston Gate, an ornate gate designed by famed architect, Charles McKim in 1889-1890. The Johnston Gate allowed entrance to the Old Harvard Yard from Massachusetts Avenue. It seemed just about right to satisfy my ample ego.

Anna mostly avoided Harvard Yard.

"More pompous asses per square yard than anywhere else in America," she sneered.

Eating an Elsie's turkey club in Harvard Square was memorable, but it paled in comparison to the first kiss Anna and I shared under a Kentucky coffee tree in front of Widener Library. I was in the shadow of one of my lovers and in the arms of another. Later that evening we shared a yellow spread blanket while listening to the Boston Pops at the Hatch Shell near the Charles River. The juxtaposition of the glittering John Hancock Building and the deepening twilight of the Charles River basin added just the right amount of ambience to create eternal love. The next day we quietly contemplated the grace of God and one another in rapture and gratefulness as we stared at each other in the shadow of Revere Beach.

Anna grew up in New Jersey.

New Jersey in the 1950s was about as different from Pedlam, Arkansas as possible. Her house was above Route 22, which was a conduit of chaos that flowed from the spires and cathedrals of old Newark to the foothills of the Pine Barrens.

Anna lived in the hardwood-forested Watchung Mountains and attended a mostly white school full of driven kids. Blacks lived in ghettoes across Route 22, and attended mostly black schools. But this was not de jure segregation; it was de facto segregation. The fact is nobody in Plainfield was being skinned alive or castrated because of race.

Anna's family was a very pious, devoted Christian family. In fact, Anna was converted when she was five and had virtually no memory of a pre-conversion life.

From a multi-cultural, multi-racial family, Anna had one biological brother, six Korean American siblings, one black mixed sister, and four siblings that really couldn't accurately be labeled. Represented however, was Native American, Vietnamese, Italian and Russian strains. To say the least, Anna was pretty outspoken about the hypocrisy of racial and ethnic prejudice.

"Do you remember the night I asked you to marry me?" I now interrupted her concentration.

"Yes," she turned and smiled at me.

"I was cool, calm, and debonair, right?"

"I would not use those words, but yeah it was special, Jacob."

"Are you glad you married me?"

"Yes."

"You can kiss and hug your spouse anytime you like you know. It is allowed—after 34 years of marriage. You want to now, like we did under the Kentucky coffee tree?"

"Sure big boy. Come here."

On the night I asked Anna to marry me, we took the Redline to Pier 4 for dinner. On the rocking platform that stood only a few paces from the historical site of the Boston Tea Party, a perfunctory receptionist—who had no idea that she was standing in front of a Harvard man——made us wait where we were lavished in the twilight of a Boston sunset that reached across the sky from the Western horizon East to where Anna's parents were born—Scotland. It felt like a historical moment.

At the same time I was growing increasingly sea sick on the bobbing platform and wondered why I opted for a floating restaurant.

"Window seat, please." I confidently informed the receptionist.

She placed us near the kitchen. The deprived soul did not know the credentials of her hallowed guests.

I sat with my beloved and waited for the popovers to arrive.

This was the night I would ask Anna to marry me. Not at supper; no, I wanted to pop the question at ground zero, at Harvard, but this meal was to be memorable enough. Anna would be so dazed by the menu and my poise that matrimony would be a real possibility.

"Remember the waiter?" I asked Anna.

Chuckling, she recalled, "I'll never forget Jacob. You really got yourself in a pickle there. Certainly a red flag there, I should have broken up with you."

"You choose the wine tonight!" I had instructed the middle-aged waiter.

"I wonder if he thought you were an ignorant country bumpkin or just a pathetic 'God's gift to mankind' Harvard scholar? In any event he got you!"

He was the sort of waiter, who clearly grasped the fact that I was a somewhat out of my element, a wine newbie reaching to make this a special occasion. Calculating the increase to his tip possibilities he took no pity on this poor boy flaunting pretense.

The waiter chose a 1970 Baron Philippe de Rothschild Chateau Clerc-Milon, Pauillac, Bordeaux, France: the $58 price in 1976 was real money. That was not the first time I had to borrow money from my sweetheart to pay the tab, but probably the least propitious one.

"And I don't recall that you ever repaid me Jacob Stevens, 58 bucks!"

"I am good for it Anna."

Later that evening, when we returned to Harvard I asked Anna to marry me in the Divinity School Chapel, where Ralph Waldo Emerson had presented his 1838 Divinity School address to graduating seniors.

The Ed School had a paltry, pathetic history compared to the Div School.

Anna sarcastically observed, "Harvard Divinity School is devoted to preparing Unitarians to be Christian pastors. Really Jacob, how does one do that?"

Being the insecure sort, I had practiced the marriage proposal in several different forms many times before this historic occasion.

I would infer, "If we got married, where would you like to live?" or "If we got married, how many kids would you like?"

Now, if she was silent, that was good. If she said, "I will live wherever you want to live and have as many kids as you like if you will only marry me," that would be better. If she laughed or said, "Are you kidding? Get married to you? I hardly know you," I was toast.

Fortunately Anna never answered my practice questions—Anna can be silent in about seven different languages—but at least she did not tell me to go and read Troeltsch. So I was reasonably optimistic that the answer would be satisfactory on this evening.

On one knee, I began my proposal by quoting the first few lines of Emerson's address:

"Anna," I began. "In this refulgent summer, it has been a luxury to draw the breath of life. The grass grows, the buds burst, the meadow was spotted with fire and gold in the tint of flowers..."

Before I could finish, Anna burst out in laughter—which was not my anticipated response—but I knew the time was right. If she was not inspired, at least her defenses were down.

"Will you marry me?"

Even then I was thinking, "Oh my God, I'm asking a Yankee to marry me. What am I thinking! Has Harvard bewitched me?"

"Yes," Anna's eyes all, but disappeared in a full smile, "As long as you promise me you'll never burst any more buds or burn any more meadows!"

That first Christmas after we were engaged, we took a sky-blue Braniff Airlines Boeing 737 from Logan to Memphis, rented a dark green Chevrolet Chevette, without air conditioning, and drove down Arkansas Highway 1 to Pedlam. Highway 1 runs like a thread through the heart of southeast Arkansas. We crossed a ferry on the White River—Anna's first ferry ride. The rusty tugboat spewed toxic off road diesel fumes into the air and deposited disconsolate passenger cars onto the riverbank. Then we followed a gravel road along the Arkansas

River levee to the McClellan Bridge, which crossed the River at Yoncopin, Arkansas. Anna thought it odd that a rutted dirt levee road met one of the most modern bridges in America. She immediately discerned that it was a fitting metaphor for Arkansas.

Arkansas, with Fulbright and McClellan in the U. S. Senate used "graft" and pork barrel power to obtain funds for phenomenal, relatively untraveled bridges over every conceivable bayou, swamp, slough, and river. The federal government paid for the bridge; the state paid for the road to the bridge. Ergo, awful gravel roads lead to exceptional bridges.

Whizzing down Highway 1, driving like Yankees that we were, dodging road-killed armadillos and squashed country dogs, we approximately replicated Grant's march to Vicksburg.

"Are dogs dumb down here?" she asked amazed at the prolific road kill. "Or do you southerners hit them for sport?"

We stopped at The Spirit of Red Fork Gulf Station for overpriced gasoline and a nostalgic visit to the bathroom. I immediately felt sad knowing that Bo would not clean my windshield. But the Lion gas station offered some opportunities. It was the iconic symbol of everything southern. It occurred to me that Anna needed a little orientation to southern noir ambience before she reached Pedlam.

Store shelves featured exotic offerings such as pickled pigs' feet, fried pork rinds, and beet-flavored hard-boiled eggs. Unfortunately, Anna was not hungry, but I made up for both of us—pigs' feet were in short supply at the Harvard Danforth House.

When I kindly offered to buy her some Red Man Chewing Tobacco, Anna wrinkled her nose in disgust, "Jacob, if you use, or have ever used, the stuff, our kissing days are over and, in fact, this engagement is on hold."

I quickly lied that only today did I discover the awful stuff.

I drove by Bo's old house. I told Anna about Bo. I had to. It would be like marrying someone without knowledge of your undisclosed deformity or something and never owning up to one's mental or physical challenge before it was too late. The story of Bo poured out like a pent up flood.

Yet, I hated to tell Anna about Bo. No doubt she would have enough trouble acclimating to the Promised Land without this acrimonious digression. Moreover, I knew that Uncle Evan would be in church on Sunday when I introduced my bride-to-be to Pedlam First United Methodist Church. Uncle Evan and Bo in one visit—along with my mother—might be too much. Anna might abandon the South and me.

Bo's old house had debris strewn across its front porch and into the front yard. Old lard cans, broken soda bottles, and discarded farm machinery littered what was once a tidy front yard. Buddy Cook and Raleigh Parker now stored small farm implements inside the house. A muddy cultivator jutted from the master bedroom window. Lily pads and dense algae chocked the once thriving fishpond and duck preserve. Voracious carp, primordial bull frogs, and angry water snakes inhabited the murky dissoluteness.

"Anna, it is sad. The only thing thriving is the weeping willow tree. It has doubled in size since the last time I saw it."

"When I was 16, and I could drive alone, I could never travel down Highway 1 without taking a detour down the Red

Fork Road. The weeping willow tree was thriving then too. It always seemed wretched to me that there was no historical marker to honor Bo. Less than a mile away was an historical marker commemorating Napoleon, Arkansas. From 1840-1860 Napoleon was a thriving riverboat town at the confluence of the Arkansas and Mississippi Rivers. But it had washed away into the rivers. It rated a marker, why not Bo? Napoleon lasted only 20 years, but Bo was a vital human being for about 32 years. He had a wife and child; he was my friend. But there was no marker for Bo. In fact, only the cypress slough, the cackling wood ducks, and the weeping willow remained."

Anna, observing that I was visibly upset, mostly held her fire. But she unleashed one short inquiry.

"Jacob, what is it that you love about this place?"

She did commiserate with me by holding my hand. I was thankful she did not hitch hike back to Memphis and catch the next flight to New Jersey.

Near Pedlam we arrived at my parent's rented farm. The roomy farm full of deep shag carpets was a far cry from the mansion in which I grew up, but was quite satisfactory for my empty nest parents.

"Oh, this is the Yankee." My 40 something blond mother smiled as she hugged Anna.

Mom could do that: inflict painful insult and dispense polite affection, both at the same time. By Anna's accent—socially acceptable, delicate New Jersey speech, not the Bayonne "Youse guys" slang, but more like the Princeton "Sir and Madame" type of accent—Mom knew darn well that Anna was from somewhere foreign, perhaps Turkistan, but surely not, Mom hoped, from New Jersey.

"Oh, but Jake tells me you're Scottish."

I had said no such thing. I said that Anna's parents were from Scotland. Anna was an American citizen although, to Mom, American citizenship was judged, like grades of meat, according to age and what part of the cow the meat or citizen came from.

"Now Anna," Mom sweetly asked, "in the War of Northern Aggression, did any of your relatives fight with the Union Army?"

Mom hoped that no distant cousin of Anna—and presumably her grandchildren's relatives—had fought on the wrong side during the Civil War. A New Jersey fiancée was bad enough, but a New Jersey fiancée whose ancestors were Union soldiers, a polite euphemism for "damn Yankees," was intolerable.

Anna had no relatives in the Union Army, of course, since her family had not yet emigrated from Scotland.

"What is a Yankee?" my sweetheart asked.

The cat was out of the bag. Poor Anna was being handled roughly. She was introduced to southern white garish narrow-mindedness. I hoped that her inherent disdain for hypocrisy, and therefore all things southern, arose from some deep-seated sin nature, such as I had read about in Calvin's Institutes, but such a thing was not in my beautiful Yankee. Naïveté, yes. Indigenous rancor, no.

My mother was fishing for reasons to dislike Anna. It was hard to do. But Mom rose to the occasion.

"Anna, I understand that your parents have adopted a beaucoup amount of children. What possessed them? I can't imagine having mixed races in your family."

"Yes, Mrs. Stevens. I feel blessed to be part of such a large family. There is rarely a dull moment!" Putting a positive spin on the intentional digs, that was my girl!

"Down here we do not do that sort of thing—mix the races." My mother retorted, not trusting Anna's intelligence to catch the intended insults.

I was hoping Anna would not say, "No shit. I certainly did not know that." But sweet Anna held her fire.

"Mrs. Stevens, I can see that. Even in New Jersey it is uncommon."

Alone later that evening, though, Anna let it rip. "Thanks Jacob for the heads up! Your friends and family are just down home, friendly folks, whose only quirks are eating frog legs and stuff. Seriously? Who are you and to what planet have you brought me? This Yankee animosity is out of my experience."

Mom was not done with Anna. Not by a long shot.

Hatred was something that could be engendered even where there was no cause, like spontaneous combustion. My mother's hatred was a type of combustion that was self-generated: bogus fears and specters increased by paranoia, followed by thermal runaway, so that fear bred more fear, and finally ignition.

But Mom had met her match in Anna. Mom would not conquer this woman.

The main problem was that Anna was so different from other people, even other Yankees. My mom disliked Anna because she was different. Mom insisted that people be categorized. They had to belong to static categories. Under Mom's category 'fiancée,' for instance, were words like 'Southern,' 'quiet,' 'subservient,' 'unimaginative,' and 'docile.' Anna met none of these criteria.

"Jake," mom asked, "Where did you find this Yankee?"

Mom hated everything unrehearsed and spontaneous—people who did not meet any of her known archetypes.

Anna was the most nonconformist person I knew. She was the consummate radical. Anna believed that the universe was orderly, that humankind's senses were valid, and as a consequence that our proper purpose was to live our own life to the fullest. But we had to do this with self-honesty and not even a hint of fraudulence. Like Pythagoras, Anna required some standard of behavior from her followers.

One can imagine what a great threat Anna's views were to my mom: Anna held that a worldview would require a commitment in ethics as well as in philosophy. To Mom, with absolutely no malfeasance, ethics would be applied only when they were to one's practical advantage to do so. Goodness, morality, and ethics were a reflection of exigency and culture rather than vice versa.

Anna defied convention. And, I must admit, Anna's genuineness, authenticity, and sincerity could be a tad bit irritating at times. Anna was, in short, an anomaly.

The African albino was revered as a god. Flowers displayed roadside after an accident marked the end of a tragedy. Flowers placed on gravestones created nostalgia in visitors. Holy water sprinkled on infants at baptism promised future efficacy.

An invasive and intense notion of reverberation abounded at the heart of this whole matter of infectivity. Anna was a dangerous person! Her sense of meaning touched everything, interconnecting everything in an unseen web of links between events, places, impressions, substances, practices, and persons. Anna, in her articulateness, in her lucidity, embraced the whole creation. Nothing happened without a cause, and everything affected everything else. One Yankee could leaven the whole loaf. One Yankee could transform the entire Stevens clan for generations to come.

There also was danger that Anna might become an icon that draws others away from the altar of Southern mendacity. I owned a baseball that former, famous San Francisco outfielder Barry Bonds once threw to me from left field. I had no way to prove it was really his. I had only the memory and the feeling, and that was more real than the event itself. By the millions, people visited Elvis Presley's home to touch the stone and concrete of the master. Many claimed that George Washington slept at their house—as if the notion of his false teeth resting on their bed stands would make them president someday.

Anna brought us our moment of hopeful greatness. Anna did that to us. She made us dream of a better world, and made us very uncomfortable in this world. We, therefore, loved and hated her both at the same time. Anna was an anomaly—stimulating a superstitious mode of thinking that we all innately possessed, fervently believing that if we possessed a certain power, we would always possess it, and that we could anoint ourselves with it somehow, and so sanctify our lives. We wished to touch the Shroud of Turin and be in close proximity to perfection.

'Love' to Anna was a 'form' from which virtue flowed. Honest, sincere, loyal Anna was indeed dangerous to Mom's world. She would blow it apart. Mom was right to fear Anna, to dislike Anna.

In a lucid moment Mom once shared with Anna, "Anna, you are right, and I am wrong in my views about nigras. I will never treat them as equals. You are right. I am wrong, but I will never change."

I once told Anna, "Silly Yankee. You thought that was an apology, an admission of guilt, a confession of sorts. You were ready to announce absolution!"

"Yeah silly me. I should have married my former boyfriend the Harvard Medical School student from Connecticut."

I ignored Anna.

But it was not anything of the sort. Mom wanted to remain safe in the majority—in this case, the majority of her friends and peers. Mom was not admitting guilt or repentance or even a desire to change. She was merely stating a fact. Mom, the skeptic, maintained that human beings could know nothing of the real nature of things, and that consequently the wise person should give up trying to know such a thing. So Mom launched the last serious philosophical campaign to undermine the human will as a determining factor in decision-making.

It was very disconcerting to Anna when she realized that some people—mostly southerners — would admit something to be truly wrong, and then neither change the definition of 'truly wrong,' nor renounce the wrong action. We chose to do what was wrong and to feel good about it. To Anna, this anomaly was unacceptable, illogical, and immoral. Knowing the good called for doing the good.

"Yes, Anna, my Yankee wife, you caused problems of epic proportions. It was like striking a match near spilled gasoline. No one escaped the conflagration."

"Remember what mom said? 'Why can't you have problems like other people your age—like drug problems, white-collar crime or even shoplifting? No, you have to marry a Yankee!'"

"Ha, ha," Anna replied, "I think she was still hoping for the possibility of a divorce scandal. Her friends would have rallied round the Steven's boy, who regained his senses."

"And do you remember what you did after supper?"

After supper, making things worse, Anna helped clear the table and went to the kitchen to assist the black help in washing the dishes. She wasn't about to participate in the charade of having a person subservient to her because of the color of his or her skin.

"Get the Yankee out of the kitchen, Jake!" Mom bluntly ordered.

The black "girl"—an appellation for all minority help, of all ages and ability—was embarrassed by Anna's well-intentioned interference.

"You should do what she says, Miss Anna," the sagacious young lady advised.

I doubted Anna would do what mom said. And so she didn't. War was declared.

I, Jake Stevens stood helpless.

"Oh, my Beloved. That is why I had to have you. Why I have enjoyed every moment of these 34 years with you. You are absolutely, positively iconoclastic. And if you are sure something is right, nothing will stop you from doing it. When justice is involved your obduracy knows no bounds!"

"Thanks, Jacob. I think there is a compliment somewhere in there."

I was so changed by, inspired by this woman, that after we were married, Anna and I adopted three children and never considered race to be a category to determine their choice. We now had four beautiful chocolate colored grandchildren. Milk chocolate or dark, Anna loves chocolate. This certainly added to my mother's angst.

# 10

BIRTHDAY OR NOT, we both had to go back to work. Rather, Anna had to work; I just fiddled around with the computer.

Routinely, I spent my morning visiting social media sites.

Generally I did not wish to be anyone's "friend," nor did I want "to follow" or "to be followed." Yet I felt I must. I yearned to have a publisher like Charles Scribner, but alas, authoring required other things than merely writing inspired prose. I was stuck with Bright Blossom Publishing, a B publishing company, who nonetheless sold well to my niche market. Bright Blossom's real moneymaker, unfortunately, was not Jake Steven's works, but a three-volume polemic against Communism. I was always embarrassed to think my serious literary works were on the same website as my fraternal anti-this and anti-that authors.

My young publicist, with a perfunctory tone unmitigated by the exigencies of aging, urged me to promote my books on social media. I was there now. Promoting my books. Sort of. Mostly staring into the Mac universe and wondering why my reading about my Facebook friend Irma Louise's grandchild getting a new Schwinn bicycle was going to help sell my books.

My publicist reminded me of Fred Rogers of Mr. Roger's Neighborhood. My first church calling was in Pittsburgh, Pennsylvania, and I was in the same Presbytery as Fred Rogers, who was also a Presbyterian pastor.

"Hi, Jake," he said each time we met.

I fully expected to hear him quip, "It's a wonderful day in the neighborhood, Jake, and will you be my neighbor?" But he never did.

However, Fred greeted me with the same tone and demeanor as he did my children on television; he even wore the same sweater. Yes, Fred was the genuine article.

Fred was on the staff of Sixth Presbyterian Church, and I pastored Fourth Presbyterian Church, so I was two church ranks ahead of him. Never mind that his church had more than five hundred members and mine had eighty.

I always wanted to put a tack on Fred's chair and my publicist's chair and see if they would say, "Oh, ouch, that hurt," or perhaps some other expletive.

I preferred the basement purgatory to the den of iniquity in my second-story farmhouse. In the dingy, spidery abode of the damp basement, I was all earnestness. The dense humidity gave my keystrokes a snappy ring.

My grandchildren decorated my office with Strawberry Shortcake © coloring book pages of Cimmerian Crayola lines and wispy crayon shadows. I often touch their pictures and wished they would visit.

Today I was not feeling like much of an Übermensch. I was thinking of Bo and Uncle Evan.

I stared into my computer screen, imagining the world outside, the real world, but felt deeply the unreal world of the past. I was glad I had no windows to distract me from the painful nostalgic marauders torturing my soul. The pain was real and cleansing. I wanted to feel bad. I was fighting an urge to pour myself a glass of lemonade.

A significant hill was next to my springhouse. The slope, extravagant in its trajectory and festooned with early spring alfalfa, quickly angled up over five hundred feet. I started to climb that hill yesterday, on the last day of my 59th year. I turned back.

In the winter, when I was hardly three decades old, my children and I swaggered upward. Nathan pulled Joseph on a sled and Grace pushed Emma on another. We climbed Mt. Nebo and looked over into the Promised Land. Like Achilles, we defied irate Neptune throwing thunderbolts at us. On bright plastic chariots we dodged barbed wire and defied fate, relying on gravity and providence to propel us into glory and our unmowed neighbor's pasture and God's grace to stop us before we crashed into a diminutive pond.

On my 59th birthday, my children were gone, there was no snow on the ground, we never made it to Canaan, Troy had fallen, and the springhouse was secure in concrete.

"Why should I climb that hill?" I muttered to myself.

The fickle western Pennsylvania spring added to my melancholy. In the 20 years I had lived there, I lost three crops of tomato plants. I suspended disbelief, so to speak, and put the tomatoes in the ground right before Memorial Day—the Yankee Memorial Day, the last Monday of May, not the Confederate one I celebrated in late April—and three times frost ambushed my tomato plants.

When I was nine, at approximately the same time I planted my doomed tomato plants, I visited Eudora Welty with Mamaw, my paternal grandmother. Mamaw, with curly dyed brown hair, drove her yellow Buick La Sabre convertible down

Highway 144 through Eutaw, across the Mississippi River, and gunned the engine as she drove into Miss Eudora's antebellum plantation near Lake Ferguson, Mississippi.

"Come with me, Jake," Mamaw drawled. Mamaw never asked. She commanded.

Mamaw took me along to keep her company, which meant I mostly sat quietly and let her talk, something she did incessantly. One could not get a word in edgewise.

"Jake, keep your hands off the leather interior," Mamaw warned.

Mamaw and Miss Eudora had been friends for twenty years, since meeting at a Garden Club convention in Jackson, Mississippi.

A wealthy Jackson scion Gertrude Prewitt protested, "Well I'll be. Mrs. Stevens and Miss Welty were such a peculiar pair. And both fallen women!"

Later Mamaw said, "Mrs. Prewitt was just jealous and her orchids looked like they were dowsed in cow piss."

Mamaw, nor Miss Eudora, mixed their metaphors.

It turned out "fallen" meant Mamaw was divorced, and Miss Eudora had Yankee parents, both egregious offenses. Camaraderie blazed vibrantly between these two elliptical eccentrics whose orbits were different from all those around them. Often their colossal worlds collided, but each grew stronger through the skirmish.

Mamaw would bring a brown sack of black-eyed peas, a six-pack of Budweiser, a bright pink azalea bush, and her grandson in her Yellow convertible. Mamaw and Miss Eudora would drink beer in jelly glasses, eat San Marino olives, and curse Orville Faubus. Miss Eudora was the most unattractive woman I have ever met, but this fit her bohemian nature. She wore low-cut house dresses with Texas bluebonnets embroidered on her lapels, drawing attention to her minuscule breasts, losing vigor in inverse proportion to her prose, which blazed in robust potential and expectation.

"Jake, would you like a Coca Cola and some peanut brittle?" Miss Eudora asked. She always put salt in her Coca Cola to add fizz and flavor.

"Yes ma'am," I responded.

Miss Eudora's "girls," as she called them, brought me these things and if I had missed dinner her girls would also give me cold corn bread with buttermilk and sugar poured on top.

In Miss Eudora's short story "A Worn Path," an elderly Black grandmother protagonist, Phoenix, went to the doctor to obtain medicine for her grandson. But because of senility, she could not remember why she came!

The nurse tried to tease out of Phoenix her reason for coming. "You mustn't take up our time this way, Aunt Phoenix," the nurse said. "Tell us quickly about your grandson, and get it over. He isn't dead, is he?"

At last there came a flicker and then a flame of comprehension across her face, and she spoke. "My grandson. It is my memory has left me. There I sat and forgot why I made my long trip."

"Forgot?" The nurse frowned. "After you came so far?"

Like Granny Phoenix, on my 59th birthday, I must not arrive at my destination, but forget why I came! I have come so far.

During the week I wrote curricula, magazine articles, and novels. On Saturday I prepared my sermon. On Sunday I preached at a country church consisting of a few extended families, which I loved. They didn't require much and were always grateful for what I did.

I peered into my electronic demise. This sterile wasteland told me the time and corrected my spelling, however, it did little to assuage the discomfiture of this afternoon.

I cut and pasted, spell-checked, and grammar-checked my way to syntax coherence. Thomas Aquinas tried, but, with my computer I acquired Aristotle's Golden Mean (in Nicomachean Ethics). My orgiastic moment came at a price. Symmetry, proportion, and harmony were mine. This triad of nirvana infused my life with moksha. The click, click, click of the keyboard immersed me into exquisiteness as an object of love and something that was imitated in my life. Unfortunately, though, Dionysian passion replaced good old common sense. My computer replaced my sovereign autonomous will with anarchic, collective, anonymous experience. Like Icarus, I built feathered wings for myself so that I could escape the clutches of King Minos. I did not wish to remain in the middle course, and the sun melted the wax off my wings.

I was lord of the rhetoric. My IM replaced good old American syntax and diction. My tinkering did more damage than good. My computer, in short, promised more than it could produce, and often got me into some sort of trouble.

The computer-writing life transformed me into a collage of subjectivity—really the antihero. I had opinions about everything. I was god of the digital universe. But my power required no great courage or astute permutation.

These tangential reflections, however, merely masked what I knew I must confront.

Before puberty, considering my fondness for Uncle Evan, I wondered who the real heroes were in my unfolding life narrative. Already, before I had lived a decade, my heroes exuded empathy, not goodness. My heroes were persons who liked me, were kind to me, but committed all sorts of atrocities. This emerging dialectic drove me into melancholia.

Chase Bank reminded me that I was nearing my credit limit. At the turn of the millennium, I was near my credit limit and have more or less paid enough to keep the dogs of Chase at bay ever since. Chico Department Store was having a late spring sale that I did not want to miss. I would miss it, and I was hoping Anna would too. Dorothy wanted to be my friend, and all I had to do was dial 1-866-BeMyHon. I put that one in the spam folder. The Vanderbilt Alumni Club wanted me to attend a $1,500-plate fundraiser. The Vegan soiree would show solidarity with California broccoli pickers. Would skip it. Grow-a-Hummingbird-Vine Company wanted me to buy a hummingbird vine, also known as a trumpet vine. I would forward that to Anna. She liked hummingbirds.

John Bartholomew, a fellow pastor, sent out a public e-mail extolling the virtues of his "Honey Bunny."

"Happy 42nd Wedding Anniversary, Honey Bunny! I Love You More Today Than Yesterday, but Not as Much as Tomorrow. Love, Your Hubby, Blue Eyes." I wondered how Honey Bunny reacted to the sobriquet and gut-wrenching, embarrassing show of emotion that her Blue Eyes so gratuitously shared with his Internet friends. One hopes she did not mind—or Blue Eyes might not have a happy forty-third!

I paused for a moment to think about Honey Bunny. There was something wholesome, real, and invigorating about a love that engendered such awkwardness among its hearers, and perhaps for its recipient. It was extravagant love, love that didn't care what others thought. Love that went beyond appearances and etiquette that forced the recipient to respond. That love was not ordinary, reserved, controlled love. It was generous love that was full of risk. Blue Eyes simply did not care how people would react—perhaps even Honey Bunny—because he had to tell the world, or at least his e-mail list, in no uncertain terms that he loved his Honey Bunny. He loved his Honey Bunny more today than yesterday, but not as much as tomorrow.

I tried not to be too critical. I had that tendency. John often embarrassed me the same way old senile Miss Marcia Dalton embarrassed me by kissing me on the mouth after every church service. After pronouncing the benediction, I sprinted down the aisle. But Miss Marcia inevitably blocked my path with an open mouth kiss that never failed to amuse Anna.

I would refer that invitation to Anna too. She was, after all, my Honey Bunny.

Next was an e-mail from Mindy Sue Shank. Mindy Sue was the informal Pedlam Class of 1971 secretary. Mindy Sue told us when people get married, die, and so forth. Occasionally she slipped in information we really want to know—like who was divorced, had a sex change, and so forth. We all liked and appreciated Mindy Sue's unselfish, tireless effort on her part to keep us informed about the quickly aging Class of 1971.

She was inviting me to my 1971 high school class reunion. Technically I should be in the Class of 1970, but I was sick with whooping cough most of my kindergarten year, so I started the first grade when I was seven. During Falcon Fest—Pedlam chose the majestic falcon as its mascot—no one ever saw one, but the idea was noble—the Class of 1971 was going to enjoy its 40th reunion. Flacon Fest was Pedlam High School's annual orgy of nostalgia, the first Saturday in October.

The reunion was to be held at Mandell's Café. Joey and Raylene Mandell hosted high school reunions since John F. Kennedy was assassinated. Mandell's Cafe had no jukebox or television. Patrons were entertained by raw open altercations between Joey and Raylene that only embarrassed the rookie customer, who had not witnessed the wrangling before.

"Joey, fart brain, get your butt out here and serve these folks!" Raylene ordered. This was one of her milder epithets for Joey.

The truth was that the arguing meant something: these two really did hate each other, which never to them nor to us seemed to be ample reason to abrogate the marriage nor to close down the Café—both of which were affectionate icons.

Moreover, the Mandells served the nectar of the gods: Miracle-Whip-coated greasy hamburgers caressed by cheap dill pickles and Sunbeam hamburger buns dripping oleomargarine. The more adventurous humbly—the only way anyone could talk to Raylene—asked her to add some cheese, which meant Velveeta cheese since everything else was either made by people in Wisconsin or by foreigners. Joey and Raylene had high regard for their patrons and high standards for their cuisine.

My interest was piqued.

We were to meet at Mandell's on the anniversary of the day former class member Bubba Rogers died while fighting a fire at Barnie's Department Store. Drinking sweetened ice tea and consuming lard-fried catfish, we would remember former times and take one more macabre step closer to Bubba.

Mark Davis was coming. No surprise there. He loved parties.

"Where is the action?" Mark always said.

Likewise Tyrone was coming too. He loved eating.

"What is the menu?" Tyrone queried.

And Dottie asked, "Where is Tyrone?"

Dottie was coming. Dottie loved Tyrone. Although both had married other spouses, they had had a child out of wedlock. Dottie went to Greenville, Mississippi, and put the baby up for adoption. Both regretted that decision made even more nugatory by the hellish marriages both were presently experiencing.

The buxom Cindy Talbot was coming. Mr. Talbot, a local farmer, would hire us Pedlam boys to pick up wood limbs from newly cleared land. Pulling a wagon into which we were to throw the wayward branches, Mr. Talbot placed his gratuitous Cindy on the back of his John Deere tractor and we would stumble along picking up things we could touch and imagining things that we couldn't. Little Mo was coming. Little

Mo married a girl from Pocahontas, Arkansas, which to us was equal to marrying a Yankee as I alone had done.

Debbie Sue was coming. During a thunderstorm, Debbie Sue married Ricky Joe in 1972 on the bank of Boogie Bayou. Debbie Sue left Ricky, when he hit her and married Bubby Joe in 1976. Debbie Sue was presently married to Jim Boy, who in 1982 changed Debbie Sue's flat tire on Possum Fork Road and they fell in love. All four were planning to attend. I would try to stay away from Debbie Sue.

Noticeably absent were Susie Lou and Martha Anne. They had disappeared into the Ozark Mountains after graduation. Susie married a Primitive Baptist pastor, who handled snakes and drank venom. Susie was a Southern Baptist—not a Primitive Baptist—something she neglected to tell her husband, Jubal Rochester.

"Jubal, keep those things away from me," Susie Lou warned her rattlesnake-waving husband. Apparently though, he offered other virtues since they had three snake swinging boys. Jubal, I heard, eventually died when he picked up a backsliding copperhead.

Martha Anne married Ronny, an Annapolis graduate. There were no naval bases in Arkansas, so she left Pedlam until Ronny retired. Martha Anne religiously maintained her allegiance to Pedlam, and when she described her education on Facebook, it was "Pedlam High Graduate," even though she was a Rice University cum laude graduate with a degree in civil engineering.

Little Willy never graduated from high school, but was still invited. And he would attend. Little Willy hoed rice levees for

Mr. Amos Joseph Sinclair, and carried home four-foot moccasins that he barbecued in a cooker converted from a fifty-five-gallon DDT chemical drum.

"They taste best dipped in butter," Willy explained.

Mary Ann was not coming. She married Bubba Don from the class ahead of us and, feeling superior, claimed that she belonged in the Class of 1970. In addition, they both had converted to Roman Catholicism.

My stomach felt uneasy.

I enjoyed the notion of seeing old friends. We played on the same baseball teams, joined the same scout troops, and attended the same churches. We worried about Sputnik. We crawled under our desks and pretended that the Russians were bombing us. We were afraid of polio. We went to see Elvis when he sang at the old VFW Lodge.

We made out in our parents' Pontiacs. Our young hands explored heretofore-unknown environs. We experienced the anguish of unrequited love, and the dangers of gratuitous coitus, stimulated by passion and curbed by religion. Our confidence was the confidence of Achilles. We all supposed that we were immortal and could not be slain, even by brave Hector's capable sword.

But something or someone was missing. At first I was not sure who it was. Zula Mae Gray was a night clerk at Mickey's Liquor Store and could not get off. Pratt Purnell would be picking cotton for five to ten years at Cummins Prison Farm for robbing the Milligan Bend Piggly Wiggly.

Tallulah Quinn would not join us either. Every post prom morning, for those sober enough to attend, Tallulah Quinn's mom served us squirrel brains, scrambled eggs, and deer sausage—all liberally anesthetized with Louisiana Hot Sauce. Mrs. Quinn would have young squirrel craniums ready, thoroughly cleaned, heads intact. They gave the brown Sciurus carolinensis eyes to their Siamese cats, which were obviously grateful for their gifts. To preserve freshness, Mrs. Quinn would decapitate the progenitor of our breakfast at the very last minute. One little critter's head was offered to each weary patron.

As sprinkles of bacon grease solidified the flour droplets tumbling through the eyeholes, she rolled the sacrifice in a flour-buttermilk batter. Next Mrs. Quinn would drop the head into the hot greasy skillet, where it would turn into a golden dark-brown mass that looked much like little shrunken human heads that I saw on Saturday morning Tarzan movies. Then she gingerly dropped the rodent cranium upon a bed of fried eggs garnished with blanched grits and deer sausage. Oily melted oleomargarine bubbled up through a glacier of coarse corn bliss.

Blessed recipients used knife handles to tap the skull right between the eyes. "Whop!" Hungry prom pilgrims were rewarded with oozing squirrel brains that tasted somewhat like lobster.

Some impatient squirrel-brain eaters would simply put their lips on the right or left eye and forcefully sucked the brains into their mouths. Yet that approach was compromised if Tallulah had overcooked the delicacy: brain matter, especially the cerebellum, became lodged between skull and mouth. More than one dedicated squirrel-head sucker had to backtrack, grab a knife handle, and choose a more, cautious orthodox path.

In thirty-four years of marriage, Anna has never served me squirrel brains. "It would make a nice 59$^{th}$ birthday meal," I thought.

I returned to the task at hand. Who was missing at the reunion?

Then it hit me. "We were not going to invite any black class members to our reunion!"

Fifty members—46.4% — of my class was not invited!

# 11

AND THEN, I LAUGHED INCREDULOUSLY. "We never wanted to be integrated and by golly we managed to "unintegrate" ourselves 40 years later."

The truth is, even though we had almost 50 black members in our class, I only remembered the name of one black classmate: Theodis Murphy. Theodis was a taciturn boy with gappy front teeth, who gratuitously flashed smiles to all who looked. At first, we thought he was being disrespectful, even mocking. But it was not a scornful, derisive smile, but an inviting smile whose good-naturedness was not reciprocated.

I met Theodis in 1966 when he and six black classmates desegregated Mrs. Harper's math class.

They were obviously terrified——as well they should be——before the day was over they were accosted by verbal, and in some cases, physical threats that heretofore they had not known.

We called them Sambo or Uncle Tom or Louisa. We never bothered to learn their real names.

Our white teachers encouraged us in our wickedness. Ironically, our indignation unified all whites, across all social strata. Hatred of desegregation was a cleansing stream that washed over white Pedlam.

School desegregation was strange. Blacks were forbidden to sit in the same waiting rooms in doctor's offices, to use the same gas station bathrooms as we did, and to sit in the same place in the theater (blacks sat upstairs; whites downstairs). They attended different churches, ate at different restaurants.

In short, our world was completely segregated except for one place——the public school. It was maddening.

We took care of that at our 40th reunion!

Black students segregated themselves in our school. They sat together in class, in assembly, at lunch. They went to the bathroom together, always choosing the one most distant at the end of the hall. Informally, whites stopped using those bathrooms and we enforced a sort of *de facto* segregation.

Ironically desegregation of the public schools inflicted more prejudice than ever more. The NAACP saw desegregation as a necessary step in racial progress; to the young people who participated, it was Dante's ninth level of Hell.

In effect, these black students were both the beneficiary and the victim of laudable social engineering that encouraged racial warfare. Twelve and thirteen year old boys and girls were the front line soldiers in an epic social revolution.

Previously, racial prejudice was covert, hidden, and systemic. Privileges were withheld from blacks; the Klan isolated and intimidated individual blacks. But, for the first time, in a wholesale fashion, injury, carnage, and perfidy were inflicted overtly on young blacks.

"You don't like me," Theodis once said to a white boy, who had just squashed Theodis' peanut butter sandwich under his white Keds, "because you do not know me."

I did not think much about those things when I was in my teens.

I did not know our black classmates in 1967, when we won the state football championship with the help of recruited black linemen.

In 1969, when we opened the new modern school, and the NAACP initiated judicial lawsuits (against the expressed wishes of whites and blacks) that precipitated full integration immediately, I made no effort to meet any of my new minority classmates.

Desegregation occurred in stages. For five years one class at a time Pedlam public schools were integrated. Lamar Sturgis, esquire, whose offices were in Pine Bluff, Arkansas, filed a complaint in federal court that the Pedlam High School District was dilatory in its implementation of federal laws requiring integration.

C. T. Starnes, the school board attorney responded with a straight face: "Your honor we are doing our best."

"Sixteen years is your best?" NAACP Attorney Sturgis responded.

"We are doing our best, your honor, and, also, everyone except those Yankee agitators like things the way they are," C.T. laconically concluded.

Later, Judge Cutter Smith scolded C. T.: "You knucklehead! Couldn't you do better than that! I had to rule against you or Starnes would win on appeal."

So, our schools were finally integrated. Completely.

Still, some blacks dropped out, and others simply never came. Even after classmates poured Aunt Jemima Pancake syrup down Theodis' jeans, he persevered. For the rest of the day, enduring the jeers of cruel classmates, he wore clown pants procured from the principal's office claim box. Even when Stanley Burton urinated on Theodis' earth science book, Theodis opted to stay.

In 1970, the Falcon talent show, Christmas party, and spring formal were all moved to the all-white Choctaw County Country Club. I never socialized with, did not even learn the names of, any my black classmates in 1970.

I surely did not know them in 1971, when we graduated.

During senior year graduation practice, Pedlam school principal Dunlap Donnally reminded Black graduates that they did not actually have to attend the graduation ceremony to obtain their diplomas.

"Some of you colored children," he offered in a soothing voice, "may prefer to have us mail your diploma to you."

Moreover, the white members of the junior class posted sentries in front of the Pedlam football field's bathroom facilities, where the graduation service was held, enforcing a whites-only policy.

On my 59th birthday I still did not know my black classmates. I didn't know how to know them. I could look at their pictures in old yearbooks and I recognized their faces, but I still would not know them.

White classmates Larry Starnes and Dubby Mays were killed in the 1968 Tet Offensive. The next Wednesday issue of the Pedlam Times included a six-page insert of pictures and memorabilia about our heroes.

To honor Larry and Dubby during the November 11, 1968, parade, Pedlam veterans walked silently in steady cadence—including alcoholic Earle Ray Arbutus, a World War II Anzio Beach veteran, whom no one could remember being quiet or walking in a straight line for more than five minutes—marched in sober deference from the City Laundry to Hambone Bonnet's Welding Shop.

It turns out that there were two other Vietnam War Pedlam heroes.

On March 2, 1968, Willy Joe MacPherson picked up a booby-trapped baby doll just a few hours after he arrived at Da Nang Air Base. What remained of his body was shipped home the next day.

No mention was made of his death in the Pedlam Times—not even in the "Colored News" section.

Ophelia MacPherson, mother of Willy Joe, asked if Willy Joe could be buried in the VFW cemetery.

"Whites only," Mayor Stuart responded. Willie Joe was buried next to his dad, a World War II veteran, on the bank of Kelso Bayou.

Likewise, on May 14, 1968, Biggun Barnes was killed near the DMZ when his helicopter was riddled with lethal AK-47 shots. Biggun was the side gunner, and he died as .50-caliber tracers arched into the Dong Xoai night sky. The Army awarded him a Bronze Star. The Pedlam Times never mentioned Biggun.

The Barnes family knew better than to try to have Biggun buried in the veteran cemetery so he was interned at Arlington Cemetery.

We stood in silence during morning announcements for Larry and Dubby at Pedlam High. Neither Willy Joe nor Biggun ever made the morning announcements. In fact, no public accolades were offered for these minority heroes. Never.

As a town, as a society, Pedlam chose its war heroes as it picked ripe tomatoes from Little Marty Edgar's tomato patch—with discrimination. Willy Joe and Biggun were listed on the Vietnam Veterans Memorial in Washington, D.C., but in Pedlam, Arkansas, no one, but their family remembered them.

The Supreme Court desegregated our class, but we de-desegregated it. We ignored the whole Civil Rights era like we ignored Willy Joe and Biggun. The Class of 1971 began its public school experience segregated, and if we could not end our senior year segregated, we would be at our 40th reunion! We were not going to invite 46.4 percent of the Class of 1971, and we were going to do that with not so much as a pang of conscience.

The Pedlam Class of 1971 was rewriting history to create our own new version, not of what was, but what we thought it should be. We were anarchists, who recognized no authority from God or human. We were not subject to the laws of nature or history. We were nihilists—judges of the world, not as it was, but what we decided it ought to be. We were supermen and superwomen; we were in power. We did as we pleased. We insisted that history discard its rough draft and embrace our rewrite.

With cheerful pride and gladness, we managed history to suit our purposes.

Our confidence in our own virtuousness was unbounded. Guilt, remorse, and sin were so absent that we planned a weekend of celebrative and nostalgic activities while ignoring almost half the people, who ipso facto were part of those memories. White Pedlam owned the country club, the baseball fields, the city swimming pool, the police force, the school board, and other places of influence in Pedlam, and now we owned the history of Pedlam too.

We the Class of 1971, or at least the white portion of it, reserved the right to invite whomever we pleased, to ignore whomever we pleased, and to do so with virtue replete with goodness. The mistakes and foibles of our history were ascribed to imperfect social institutions and to naive ignorance, not to a flaw in character or to general perfidy. Like a virgin unjustly assaulted, we reclaimed our virginity, our purity, by nullifying all that we judged as being unjust. Or perhaps we didn't care about justice at all. We did all these things because we could do them. We were still in charge of Pedlam, and we could do as we pleased.

Words, to us, had no permanent address, no solid and irrevocable meaning. Our pragmatism expressed itself along two main axes. One axis was negative: a critical diagnosis of what we discerned as surely at the heart of our society's evil. The other axis was positive: an attempt to show what intellectual culture might look like once we freed ourselves from the governing metaphors of mind and knowledge, in which the traditional problems of epistemology and metaphysics were rooted.

My 12$^{th}$ grade physics teacher, Mrs. Chardonnay Dubois said "Language was the essence of authenticity. In other words, if something was said and presumably not heard, it was not real. If a tree fell and was not heard, it did not produce sound."

If it fell and was heard, it was sound and had meaning, according to the pragmatic results of its falling. Thus, to a squirrel it might mean the end of an acorn factory. To a squashed ant, it might mean the end of existence.

We felt wholly comfortable with this dialectic, having reached what the old Sophists called *aretē* (Greek for "excellence, virtue") as the highest value and the determinant of one's actions in life. For a season we struggled with this black-and-white thing and reached a sort of excellence that brought us both enlightenment and harmony.

I couldn't wait to tell Anna about my 40th Reunion!

# 12

ANNA AND I SAT on the front porch swing.

The porch swing was an antique wooden affair hand built by a local farmer, who asked me to help his son prepare for the SAT. We bartered. I got the better deal.

A corroded chain held the swing to the roof of my porch. We tried not to touch the chain, because it inevitably gifted us with an oxidized reminder of our porch swing interlude. But occasionally, to steady ourselves, we were forced to grab the chain and hazard the rust.

The problem was, I forgot myself, and I swung too high. As a result, the wooden swing banged the grey wall of our house. Anna cautioned me to be less ambitious in my swings. She was constantly moderating me and, and on this afternoon, I was grateful for her attention.

"Are you accomplishing much?" I asked.

"Not really. I answered a few e-mails. How about you?"

I told Anna about the class reunion.

Cat One and Two joined us on the porch competing for owner approbation. Two loved to lie between us, to offer us its back for our rubbing pleasure. Knowing that I often brought kitty snacks to the porch swing, Cat One, hoping to be rewarded for its modesty, employed a more cautious approach.

"Anna I must confess, when I received an invitation to the reunion, I had an overwhelming urge to rewrite history again, to act as if John Lewis had not been brained on the Edmund Pettus Bridge. I was ready to head down South, eat a double mayonnaise Charlene burger with fries, tell a few innocent black/white jokes to show who's on top, and fit right in."

"Wouldn't take much Jacob——for you to backslide."

"Ha ha."

Cat One curled around Anna's right ankle claiming ownership before Cat Two contested. As I pushed back with my feet, Cat One was caught on Anna's ankle and somersaulted to the carpeted porch floor. With feline determination, One returned to claim its human once again. I thoughtfully rewarded its tenacity with a treat.

"No really, Jacob. You are thoroughly a Yankee now. You whine when we have two consecutive days above 80 degrees."

Ignoring, Anna, I continued.

"The triumph of nefarious racism in the South and the resulting collapse of common sense left a huge vacuum in my life. The history of the South and of my life is in great part the history of how that vacuum was filled. Adolf Nietzsche was right, when you gaze long into an abyss, the abyss also gazes into you."

"It is Frederick Nietzsche, Jacob. Lighten up. Let's watch Pay-per-View tonight."

We enjoyed the cool hush of a Laurel Highlands spring afternoon. The porch enclave curved wind and rain but in no way diminished the omnipresent exquisiteness of late afternoon daylight. It curled around hedge rolls and trees. The cold sunshine, uninhabited by spring insects, was life giving and clean. It promised a bright future and hopeful tomorrow. Laurel Highlands spring sunbeams did their best to compensate for the frosty, lingering, winter night that never quite disappeared until late June.

"Sounds good, Anna. But I think I will read tonight."

I began reading seriously when I was twelve.

The Choctaw County Library was a twenty-by-forty-foot single-room brick structure behind the First United Methodist Church. Even from my twelve-year-old perspective, it was unimpressive. This library was actually smaller than the tiny apartment in which my Mammy Lee lived above the dog pen.

But to me the Choctaw County Library, Pedlam Branch, was the Palace of Versailles, the Taj Mahal, the Pharos lighthouse in Alexandria, the Hanging Gardens of Babylon. The library took me far beyond Southeast Arkansas and Uncle Evan and everyone I knew and introduced me to people and places I wanted to meet and to see. Although I did not actually meet Henry Fleming and Jane Eyre and Reverend Gail Hightower, my books took me into their worlds, even if it was just for a week or a few days—as long as it took me to read a particular book, poem, or play. I was on a safari to view the animals, not to touch them, not to kill them, but to look at them. Perhaps to pause and watch them live.

T. S. Eliot, William Faulkner, Richard Sheridan, Katherine Anne Porter, Willa Cather, and many others changed my life.

In spite of the fact that I stuttered and as a result was banished to the Bluebird reading group in school, obviously the B Team, I could read silently with intense comprehension. Reading was a fever. It consumed my soul. Like an addict, one book made me want to read six more.

The cold, heartless librarian, Mrs. Eagleson, was a hybrid of the Wicked Witch of the West from The Wizard of Oz, and of Mr. Rochester, the grumpy master of Thornfield Hall in Jane Eyre. I avoided all books authored by "G's" because they were located behind Mrs. Eagleson's desk.

I read Albee, Bronte, Cervantes, Dickens, Eliot, and so forth. Systematically moving down the alphabet, I reached the Z's by my sophomore year.

Walking into a library always felt like I was coming home. As an undergraduate, on an average day I spent thirteen hours at the Vanderbilt Joint University Library (JUL) and six hours sleeping in my dorm room.

To complicate matters, Vanderbilt University offered weekend entertainment to on campus students. In particular I remembered a Grateful Dead concert. My freshman dorm room—Vanderbilt freshmen lived in single rooms — was on the 4th floor of Kissam Quad. The Dead proposed to build a platform outside my room to descend to their audience. Knowing I was not a believer, as a peace offering, Jerry Garcia gratefully offered to sign my program. I declined and quickly escaped to the new JUL James K. Polk collection, which was staying open to accommodate Dead Head phobics like myself.

Not that I was completely unsociable. When Bill Monroe brought his Blue Grass Band to campus, I hid my backpack in the classical section—no one went there—and enjoyed a few lines of "Blue moon of Kentucky, keep on shining."

In graduate school at Harvard I hit the jackpot. For two years I migrated from library to library—there were seventy libraries at Harvard—each one evoking grateful raptured awe! Widener, though, with its dark black-walnut desks was the mother lode. In 1976 there were no computers to distract me. I had the real thing. I touched books whose checkout cards had the signatures of John F. Kennedy (Fanny Hill) and Franklin Roosevelt (The Wealth of Nations). The exchange between man and book was clean, virginal, unadulterated by pedantry and sophistry. I became so distracted that I forgot to welcome the tall ships that visited Boston Harbor on Independence Day.

Whatever I did, wherever I went, I took my books with me. Every life situation reminded me of something I read. I supposed I had to write this book eventually, to reclaim my personhood, as it were, or I might be absorbed into biblio-oblivion like Keanu Reeves almost disappeared into computer-oblivion in The Matrix.

The porch swing banged the house.

"Jacob!"

"Anna, I was thinking about how much I want to attend the reunion. I—the righteous one, the social critic, the enlightened zealot, the father of three racially mixed children—intend to move my tents next to wicked Nineveh. Like Gregor Samsa in Kafka's The Metamorphosis (1915), on my $59^{th}$ birthday, I woke up to discover myself transformed into a noisome creature. Like Samsa, I looked at the wall clock and realizes that I had overslept, and missed my train for work. Looking very much like a cockroach, I was now embarrassed, and didn't want to open the door to either friend or foe alike. The fact is that I still saw Pedlam, Arkansas, as my home."

"Jacob did you really read Kafka? Because most of us just read Cliff Notes."

"No I read every word. Enjoyed every word."

"I believe you, sweetie."

"I don't think that was a compliment dear!"

"Anna, I want to attend my reunion!

Anna took my hand.

I loved it when Anna took my hand. It meant, usually, that I was a bad boy and she was going to ameliorate me with her fifth grade teacher voice.

"Jacob, the truth is that you were disowned by most of Pedlam, Arkansas, many years before. First you lost a few friends when you married me. Then we adopted mixed race children! Honey, don't take this personal—but nobody wants you to bring your Yankee Harvard educated wife and your liberal racial views to his or her reunion."

Anna was right of course. I contemplated Anna's insight.

My obstinate embrace of the delusion that I still was welcome at a place I so thoroughly rejected was a testimony to my penchant to embrace a Jungian dream complex. My dreams were not attempts to conceal my true feelings from my waking mind—as Freud believed—but rather they were a window to my unconscious. They guided my waking self to achieve wholeness and offered a solution to my perceived problems. In other words, I chose to embrace the dream, in this case a delusion—that Pedlam, Arkansas, loved me more than its ideology—to conceal painful realities from my waking mind.

But I was not finished with my delusion.

"Anna, my class knows this and still invited me!"

Anna remained silent.

I changed the subject.

"Speaking of delusions and leaving home, do you remember what Mamaw told me before I came north to graduate school?"

Anna smiled.

On the last evening in Arkansas, before I departed to Harvard, Mamaw drew me aside and offered me some advice.

Mamaw pointed her index finger at me and warned: "Jake, be careful."

"Mamaw, air travel is safe in the 1970s!" I assured her.

Ignoring me, she continued, "Be careful of Yankees."

"Yes mam," I deferentially responded.

"Be careful, especially, of Yankee women!"

I had heard rumors that Yankee women never shaved their legs, never wore bras, and in general were catty, disrespectful creatures. But I had had a Vanderbilt girlfriend from Milwaukee, and she was nothing of the sort—although she did not wear a bra—a laudable habit, as a matter of fact.

"Jake, you are a naive southern gentleman."

I don't know about the gentleman part, but I certainly was naive and southern.

"Yankee women are smarter—much smarter than you," Mamaw warned.

I didn't doubt it.

"They will seduce you."

I fervently hoped so.

"And marry you. Stay away from them."

Yankee women, in Mamaw's estimation, were facile, amoral shrews whose capacity for fraudulence was unbounded. Her favorite calumny for everything born and bred north of the Mason Dixon Line was "asshole." Knowing that she was in the company of the future clergy, however, Mamaw held her fire.

Nonetheless, she shot the Yankee race in toto with birdshot and she hoped that a few stray pellets would hit unmarried northern women.

She called Troy David Marcus, a juvenile delinquent bully, who lived two doors down, an "asshole" but everyone knew he deserved that sobriquet. But Officer Kimbro, who did not deserve that appellation, was perennially called an "an asshole" since he regularly stopped Mamaw for speeding on the Masonville Highway.

"Miss Jane," Officer Kimbro demurely offered, "Your license is suspended."

"True," Mamaw responded, as she put her Buick into reverse.

Officer Kimbro, confronted by punctilious reasoning, was struck with a sudden taciturnity that persuaded him both to ignore the crime and the criminal.

On our second date I asked Anna, "Do you shave your legs?"

"None of your business, Jacob! Why do you ask?"

"How about under your arms!"

Anna hit me with her manuscript edition of Carol Gilligan's In a Different Voice.

On this 59th birthday, I really wanted to be a part of this reunion.

My farm enjoyed the praiseworthy advantages of being on the southeast side of a fairly significant hill. Howling wintry winds whirled over the top, but barely reached, the bottom of the house. However, the payback was that sunset came at least one-half hour before my neighbors, who were not graced with the warm appendages of the Highlands. So, even now the sun was sliding below the northwest mountain horizon.

"Jacob, it has been nice, but it is time for supper. Do you want me to take you out for egg rolls?"

"No, Anna, if you don't mind, let's eat in. I will help you. But would you mind if I sat here alone for a while? Then we can prepare supper together—or at least I can set the table and you can prepare dinner. Is that ok?"

"Sure Jacob. I will see you later."

As Anna grabbed the rusty chain to ascend out of the porch swing, we saw a huge buck move out of the border briars on our property and move toward the lawn.

For two years, almost every evening a ten-point buck invaded our yard to enjoy our apples. The majestic buck finished by trimming our rhododendron. He greeted us with a slight nod. It was ironical to me that I spent my whole childhood looking for such a trophy buck only to have one walk daily into my front yard to eat my apples and bushes. It seemed wrong to kill him, wrong even to name him. Naming implied ownership and kinship that would never be ours. Our buck would be no one's pet or familar thought.

Anna kissed me and moved toward the kitchen.

# 13

MAMAW WAS MY DAD'S MOTHER, but, in a real sense, Mamaw belonged to all of Pedlam.

Dad was born in 1932, in the Great Depression that afflicted others, but not Dad. He was the youngest son of Raymond and Jane Stevens, whose company was the largest employer in Choctaw County. Ray Stevens, Daddy Ray, my grandfather, was married to Jane Parsons, Mamaw, my grandmother, in 1927. They raised Varner, Mamaw's son by a previous marriage, Uncle Varner to me; Ray Stevens Jr., my Uncle Ray; and Martin Hancock Stevens, my dad. My Dad's middle name, Hancock, was the name of Mamaw's favorite in-law, Hancock Stevens, Daddy Ray's illegitimate mixed-racial half-brother, my great uncle Hancock, who lived in Tennessee. I met him once. He was a curly haired version of Daddy Ray. Both had dark Bavarian skin, but Uncle Hancock had pronounced black features.

Uncle Varner was one of the most prosperous landowners in the area. Uncle Ray went to Tulane and became a chemical engineer. My dad, who loved Pedlam and black-eyed peas on New Year's Day, stayed at home, and eventually, Daddy Ray gave his business, and his home to his youngest son, Martin.

My dad and mom had three boys, Martin Junior (whom we called Little Martin), me, and Henry (whom we called Henry).

If Pedlam was the center of that generous domain, my grandmother's home was the apogee.

Built during the 1920s, the House—so named by Mamaw—reflected my grandparent's unbounded optimism and deep pockets. Pedlam was kind to its elite. No one questioned their credentials—especially when my grandmother imported bricks from New Orleans streets, painted wicker chairs from ornate shops in Havana, and displayed crystal chandeliers from abandoned Liverpool, England mansions. The bricks that enclosed the fireplace and floored the kitchen evoked a faint smell of horse manure, which increased in strength as winter fires were stoked. The Stevens enjoyed their corn bread in the ambience of horse excrement.

The House was a testimony to both my grandmother's generosity and her eccentricity. Flaunting five thousand square feet, six bedrooms, five full baths, and a full basement—the only full basement in my below sea level community—the House appeared in Southern Living in 1928 and 1930. The servants' quarters were above the kennel. There were two kitchens: the winter kitchen, leading to the dining room; and the summer kitchen, attached by a walkway.

Mamaw was a forward-thinking woman. With remarkable lucidity, Mamaw saw a good deal and bought a huge section of uninhabited Pedlam. Then, over the next few years, being careful that no lot was equal to her own, Mamaw sold ground to other less savvy latecomers, who sought the solitude and prestige of the Pedlam suburbs. Eventually, old Wiley Pedlam himself, the richest man in town, built a mansion two lots down from the House. My family made a fortune on land speculating.

Mamaw was also a freethinker—she was the only white woman in Pedlam to vote for Franklin Delano Roosevelt, but her progressivism should not be misunderstood. In the basic corpus of Pedlam ideology, she was a reactionary, as radically conservative in her social theories as the most ardent racist. Her racism was a blue-blooded paternalist variety that expected the whole world to know and to accept that blacks were inferior to the whites.

Mamaw was a master magician. Her fictions were adopted as truths by willing Pedlamites. Mamaw created illusions that shaped perceptions so thoroughly that participants adopted them as their own. Thus, Mamaw did not merely "like" or "hate" or "judge" people or groups of people. Mamaw created concomitant ideologies to go with her opinions about humankind and society alike. She judged people with elaborate social theories attached. These ideologies justified her caricatures and played to Pedlam fantasies. Mamaw, a purveyor of hope, was the fairy godmother, dispensing dreams, visions, and expectations. Pedlam all felt better after spending time with Mamaw.

In short, Mamaw was no Civil Rights activist, nor did she pretend that she had any high moral standards. Tactically, Mamaw claimed no ground that she could not hold. She avoided all grand social-reform agendas. She abhorred grand philosophic schemes, however correct they may be in principle. Mamaw was satisfied with piecemeal change. And she observed no one's law but her own.

Once Anna and I took our family to visit Mamaw. Driving her yellow Buick with no concern for pedestrian or rider, she took us on a memory lane tour.

As we moved from house to house, Anna obtained incredibly important information. Verna Beck grew giant privet shrubs beside Judson Cornwall's pigpen to keep wayward pigs from eating her daffodils, but this attracted cats whose defecation invigorated the privet hedges beyond Pedlam decorous good taste. Dorothy Sue put a scandalous statue of a naked Greek goddess in her frog pond, but Dorothy Sue's neighbor Bessie Craig, who had three little boys, put duct tape on the Greek goddess's boobs. Bobby Sue Jones found a Civil War cannon ball on her property and used it to weigh down her Lake Quapaw catfish trotlines. Sissy Markham kept a life size rubber oily jade alligator with cat eyes in her rock garden to keep inquisitive little boys away from her tulips.

Suddenly braking, "Look!" Mamaw cried. She pointed to a stately, red brick mansion with windowpanes flaking flecks of white paint to the wind.

"That used to be Prissy Lou's house," Mamaw continued.

"Prissy Lou was having an affair with Troy Allen at the same time Troy Allen's wife Twila Beth was having an affair with Prissy Lou's husband Vonnie Mach. No one knew the other partner was cheating, until Vonnie Mach found two used WWE Wrestling match tickets in Prissy Lou's apron pocket. Vonnie Mach had never been to a WWE Wrestling match, even though Prissy Lou knew that Vonnie Mach loved the WWE. Meanwhile, Twila Beth found a pack of Chesterfield Lights in Troy Allen's shirt pocket and she knew that Troy Allen had been seeing Prissy Lou on account of the fact that Troy Allen hated Chesterfield Lights and Prissy Lou loved them. It turned out Troy Allen had syphilis, which he got from a one-night stand with Yettie Lee, which Troy Allen gave to Prissy Lou who gave it to Vonnie Mach who gave it to Twila

Beth who probably had it already since she was married to Troy Allen. So, they all had to go to Greenville to get treatments together!"

"Jake and Anna, are y'all getting all of this?

With great distress Karen looked at me. "Sure, Mamaw."

A few doors down, Bud Taylor often argued with his shrewish wife Priscilla. Bud had an awful temper and more than once Mamaw comforted Priscilla while Daddy Ray went over and talked to Bud.

"Now Bud," Daddy Ray scolded, "Use your words, not your fists. Your words!"

Bud did not listen.

One early spring day Priscilla disappeared. When asked, Bud Taylor explained that Priscilla had just taken off. She loaded up their green and white 1950 Studebaker Champion Starlight coupe and just vanished.

One particularly low water mark a few years later, the green and white Champion Starlight appeared in the shallows of the Mississippi River near Milligan's Bend. Priscilla Taylor's skeleton was chained to the steering wheel.

When Sheriff Cletus Compton confronted Bud, he categorically denied having anything to do with this tragedy. The fact that his wife was insured for $500,000 was coincidental.

Eventually, Bud was brought to trial and acquitted.

After the trial, and after he had spent most of the $500,000 on a new International Harvester tractor and gambling trips to Hot Springs, Arkansas, Bud admitted that he had murdered his wife. Of course double jeopardy prevented Bud's indictment for this murder. Bud, though, brazen in his sin, and in his contempt for neighborhood approbation, continued to live next to Daddy Ray and Mamaw. He was later elected to a vacant deacon position at the First Baptist Church.

"Jane you had better be careful," Daddy Ray jested when Mamaw gave him trouble, "Our Buick sinks faster than the Champion Starlight."

Without missing a beat, Mamaw returned to her story.

Lillie Rose had tolerably acceptable azalea bushes, but the deer massacred her lettuce patch until Lillie Rose placed Lifebuoy soap squares with fishing monofilament on stakes next to the lettuce. It worked.

When we reached the black section of town, Mamaw turned to my Yankee wife and with great empathy yet great pride announced, "Look at those poor coloreds.

"My niggers never dressed like that. They were the best-dressed niggers in Southeast Arkansas," Mamaw boasted.

I thought Anna was going to jump into the front seat. I held Anna until she cooled.

Mamaw really was unflappable. We all hoped she was just mischievous and not malicious. She could be both at the same time.

Mamaw begged old man Hiram Parker, the chief loan officer of First Pedlam Bank, to lend her money to build her house. No bank would lend her money for construction because her chosen location was redlined: it was squarely part of the black section of Pedlam.

"Hiram," Mamaw, with her most pronounced, helpless Arkansas female-beguiling tone, began, "Do you remember that pecan pie I brought you last Christmas?"

Daddy Ray had only solvency and prosperity to offer. My grandmother had other assets—like her pecan pie, which was worth more than the entire First Pedlam Bank's material goods.

"Jane, you know I want to loan you money, but do you have to build a mansion in colored town?"

Daddy Ray wanted to build his house in the new Golden Gate Estates, where all sensible, prosperous, blue-blooded white Pedlam citizens lived. But, no one in Pedlam, including Daddy Ray, denied Mamaw anything she wanted.

Against the wishes of the Veterans of Foreign Wars and the Daughters of the Confederacy, Mamaw successfully persuaded the Pedlam City Council to plant 45 Mimosa Trees along Taylor's Drive to honor the boys, who were killed in World War II. The VFW and Daughters of the Confederacy, correctly, it turned out, opposed the mimosa trees because they shed vast quantities of flower blossoms, which clogged vehicle air filters and damaged vehicle paint. Even today, no one parks on Taylor's Drive, which, to Mamaw, was exactly the point.

To Mamaw, everything southern was excellent. The converse was also true: if everything in the South was good, then everything else was good, or bad, depending on how similar it was to the South. Thus Manchester, UK, was a better place to live than Manchester, Connecticut because it was more "southern" than anything in Yankee Connecticut.

New Hampshire, Wisconsin, and, especially, Illinois—why would anyone want to live there? Moreover, being full of rude Yankees they also contributed to the general moral decline of America.

To Mamaw, things and attributes were always such that

any reality, any social theory, was either true or false, but not both. To Mamaw, each thing or attribute was logically and ontologically independent of every other thing or attribute. In other words, Mamaw did not compromise.

Only gradually would she espouse general principles, so that the miniscule goodness or badness that might emerge could be controlled. Thus, Civil Rights legislation was bad because it was excessive. It could be good if it were trimmed down—like perhaps letting blacks have equal schools, but not the same schools. This made perfect sense to Mamaw. Her excursion into the appearance never mitigated her passion for utility, although she used it positively, not just critically and destructively. What all this meant was that Mamaw had the rare ability to violate all your rights, to steal you blind, and you would thank her.

Mamaw was no hypocrite. A hypocrite would have to believe something and act in the opposite direction. She was consistently in pursuit of her own agenda. Mamaw was the only woman, who consistently answered the question "why" with "because I said it is so" and really meant exactly that. She was a cold realist. Her egoism was unalloyed with any idealism.

Mamaw knew an auspicious place to build a house and was not going to let the absence of money or Jim Crow laws stop her.

Old Man Parker eventually loaned her the money at no interest. The deal was sealed when Mamaw promised to bake him a Christmas pecan pie for the rest of his life. And she did. Parker ate pecan pie every Christmas until he died (in fact, it may have killed him: when he died, he weighed a whopping

330 pounds). Only once did Mamaw fail to live up to her bargain: one season the pecan crop was abysmally bad, and she had to substitute Vermont walnuts.

"Sorry, Hiram, no pecans this year. Even the Cajuns did not harvest a crop. I regret both the walnuts and that they were grown by damn Yankees."

Mamaw's unapologetic insulting expletives and slurs were piercing and ubiquitous, but not uncommon in the place and in the time.

Mamaw did not like to cook, nor did she need to cook: she always had servants. But when she did anything—cooking, building a house, playing hide-and-seek with her grandchildren—she played and cooked to win. She was the only grandmother I know, who used loaded dice (which she obtained from my Uncle Charlie, who owned the Pool Hall) when she played Chutes and Ladders.

"Mamaw, you cheated," I cried. "No one can get twelve moves six times in a row."

Mamaw retorted. "Done be a poor loser, Jake."

Married when she was fifteen, and divorced when she was sixteen, Mamaw was truly a rebel. She was the first unrepentant divorced woman that Pedlam had ever known. The few divorcees that existed, inevitably left town to start life over again. But Mamaw, like Hester Prynne in The Scarlet Letter, wore her sin on her bosom with pride. Her first husband, Rosco Wayne, after their first son was born, hit her once, and she nearly killed him. In fact, she would have killed him, but the shotgun she grabbed was loaded with number 9 birdshot and only lamed him for life.

Mamaw was never charged for any crime.

Mamaw walked away from the marriage and the man. She never filed for divorce——but Judge Murphy knew what she wanted, so he filed and granted divorce for her without Mamaw even going to court. The divorce was probated and made official when the county clerk forged Mamaw's signature.

Rosco never remarried and limped through life in ebullient regret. For penance, he became a Nazarene pastor. Mamaw never spoke or thought of the man again. Nonetheless, out of respect we all called him Uncle Rosco. He was to remain quietly in the background of my life all through my childhood years, still in love with Mamaw. He never remarried.

It seemed natural to live in a community with a confessed murderer——Bud——an assaulted spouse——Uncle Rosco——and a sadist/murderer——Uncle Evan.

She had her enemies. Mamaw was divorced and she had to be punished. Pedlam high society banished Mamaw from the country club.

After she was banished from the country club, most felt that she was sufficiently castigated. But Mamaw was not penitent. In fact, when she married my grandfather, the wealthiest and most eligible bachelor in town, that high society was only too happy to invite my grandmother back into the country club.

My grandfather was willing, even anxious to do so.

"Come on, Jane," Daddy Ray pleaded, "Why can't we join the club?"

"Never."

"Well I am," Daddy Ray stubbornly responded.

"Like Hell you will."

"Why, Jane, can't we join?"

"Because I said we can't."

So, Mamaw, Daddy Ray, and all her offspring, and the following generations grew up as pariahs, without the benefit of southern country club amenities. On my 59th birthday I still did not know how to play golf.

Mamaw never again set a foot in the Choctaw County Country Club, however she hosted garden parties and social events in her house that rivaled the most impressive country club soirees. The proprietor of the Natchez Botanical Gardens once visited one of Mamaw's parties and instructed fortunate Pedlam socialites in the particulars of growing rare orchids.

And of course Miss Eudora was the special guest at a literary society meeting at the Choctaw County Library where Miss Eudora read the first chapter of Golden Apples. Miss Eudora stayed at the House and the Arkansas Gazette featured a two-page spread on the event in its Sunday society section.

Pedlam high society was both scandalized and remorseful in one fatal blow.

Mamaw was good at that.

# 14

MY DAD WAS ONLY 19 when I was born. When I was 19, I was a sophomore in college. He had two children, and he owned the largest, most prosperous business in Southeast Arkansas.

I grew up before Dad did. I understood the benefit of reading a good book and experiencing delayed pleasure; I accepted reciprocal exchanges between desire and pain, and the necessity to endure the pain to gain the desired goal. Dad never quite grasped the fact that he was not the center of the universe, and he never willingly felt pain. Accepting necessary pain was heretical and superfluous. He endured nothing of the sort, and if this meant that he languished in a sort of perennial boyish irresponsibility, then so be it.

Dad was raised in Mamaw's house. He loved his mother, but he was a shy boy and found the whole ordeal of living with Mamaw to be disorienting. She was bigger than life, and Dad wished nothing more than to remain anonymous.

> Mamaw hired a "girl" named Oleander to nurse and to raise him. Dad loved Oleander as though she were his mother; indeed, she was his mother, for he rarely saw Mamaw. To my discerning eyes, he was the most relaxed and happiest during visits to Oleander, who had retired to her family home in colored town.

Dad was a natural athlete. He was the first Pedlam quarterback to use the I-Formation. Dad was a shortstop on the Pedlam baseball team. He had football scholarships to attend the University of Arkansas, and an offer to join a St. Louis Cardinal farm club, the Springfield Eagles. He chose baseball, but after only one spring training, he came home to marry my mother. Dad had no college degree and no signing bonus, but he had my mother.

My mother, a natural blond, was almost two years older than my dad and the president of her senior class. As head cheerleader, she risked obsolescence by dating a younger boy with dark blue eyes and black hair, even though he was a football star and his family was one of the most prosperous in town.

Completely out of character, and perhaps in one of the most courageous acts of history, no doubt the most courageous act in Dad's life, he defied Mamaw and married Mom. In fact, it was as if he used up all his courage for this one act and would never do such a thing again.

Mom and Dad were married one May evening and settled in Mamaw's House because Mamaw had bought a modest two-bedroom bungalow behind her mansion and did not think it right that my dad raise her grandchildren, in something as pedestrian as a house in downtown Pedlam. Moreover, Mamaw had already planned early retirement trips to all of South America and parts of Europe. Once Mamaw lost a fight, which was rare, she was quick to turn defeat into victory by rewarding herself with vacations and other indulgences that mitigated the sting of conquest.

Dad was Mamaw's baby, and, in her own way, she adored him. Mamaw's approbation was always contingent upon her own self-aggrandizement, not his subservience. She could accept the latter as long as the former was not compromised.

In some ways Dad was his mother's son. Like an oriental potentate, he ruled his own kingdom with aplomb and poise and demanded that his whole family show homage to his plenary myths and deities. He wished to rule though, with the minimum of melodrama.

Still, some melodrama was inevitable—Dad was 17, married, and the proprietor of the largest employer of Choctaw County.

My dad, though, was the idealist, the romantic, the dreamer. Everything about him was arcane. He was not complex. His raison d'être was monolithic and quite unfussy. His expectations were colossal, but his needs were simple. Even though he had been to world fairs and had vacationed in celebrated places, his fondest memory was rolling himself into a frayed quilt sewn from discarded army surplus fatigue jackets and sleeping on the bank of Bayou Mason. In the morning, when he fished in the Bayou, he would cast a chipped, wooden Lucky 13 fishing lure into the turgid late-summer frothy water of the Bayou. The young boy's faith in the felicity of his Lucky 13 was undeterred either by the rapid approach of darkness or the meager catch. The essence of the moment, the prevalence of the moment, and the possibility of the moment— they all satisfied my dad's unstinted optimism.

His hero was not Douglas MacArthur—my mother's personal favorite—who ruled the world in epic finery and splendor. His hero was Willy Earle, whose four-pound stuffed black bass was eternally gaping at Sporting Center patrons; they were brothers in worshiping at the bighearted altar of human benevolence. Willy Earle was a metaphysical vagrant, a man whose only allegiance was to the game and fish that adorned the outdoors of Choctaw County. Time was an immutable object that Willy Earle gladly shared with his disciple. He instructed Dad in the virtues of concupiscence and bounteousness. Willy Earle was a kindred spirit to my dad, a hero he always emulated, and a willing companion in his perennial forays into the universe of munificent self-centeredness.

All these things conspired to make Dad a terrible provider. He was a god-awful businessman. What compelled his dad, my grandfather, to trust his business empire to his youngest 17-year-old son, was one of the fractious ironies of our family history. Daddy Ray supposed that Dad's unreliability would be cured by responsibility, much as penicillin would quickly cure a sore throat. One supposed that the soreness would go away in time, and surely the host would survive. But how much better for all if medicine could hasten the curative transformation.

Ungrateful with Daddy Ray's gift, Dad was nonplussed. Wealth, power, and influence were paltry offerings to a man, who knew the approbation of an all-night fishing trip to King Tut Lake. Dad was the only man I have ever met, who truly was fulfilled, who suffered no existential crises, which knew exactly what he wanted and knew too that he had it. He worked hard at nothing. He had no ambition because he was so ambitious: he would not play the ruse or accept the fake—he wanted nothing less than the unadulterated sublimity of a universe that had no other complicity than to be his pleasure-filled harem.

To many, the most prosperous business in town, the town's largest employer, would be a terrific bequest. To Dad, it was a commotion disrupting his real vocations: hunting and fishing.

Perhaps he was the only person alive, who could take such a thriving business and make it an unprofitable disaster in such a short time. It turned out that he had a real knack for making bad business decisions.

When the business began to fail, as it surely must under my dad's direction, Mom quietly investigated. It was no small feat for a party line southern lady to conduct so complicated a covert operation as to help her husband without his knowledge, or even more, without the knowledge of my grandmother, who shared little of my dad's impracticality and none of his optimism.

Quietly, but determinedly, Mom took charge. She discreetly audited the books. She found no malfeasance, but a husbandly propensity to extend credit to the shadiest of neighbors. Methodically she observed the fatal largesse of Dad, consuming the fortune of his father, his family, and her future. She realized that without immediate intervention, her family's way of life was doomed. His inept managerial skills allied with boundless optimism spelled our kismet, and Mom knew it.

Always the apostrophe and never the exclamation point, Mom struggled now in her mythology of feminine inferiority because she was a brilliant, capable woman, yet shackled to a man equally bright, but with none of her business acumen. Ironically, one of the attractions of the man—his name, lineage, and wealth—would be the unraveling of his character, and all that she valued in this world, unless Mom acted quickly.

Mom had to emasculate the man and save the business, or save the man and lose the business. It was never really a choice to my mom.

Mom would be the helpful little woman, who quietly supported her man behind the scenes. She would not injure his fantasy for safety nor succor. Perhaps that was the greatest compliment one can give my Mom: she loved my dad with a love that constantly afflicted her considerable aptitude. Mom chose the man over her own existence: once she had put on the garment of duplicity, she needed to wear it all her life. With loveliness and poise, she gave her life for my dad. Such a great gift bestowed on a man was a precious thing, but unknown by my dad and unappreciated by her sons. She quietly gave my dad all his selfish dreams while sacrificing hers. It was a quiet and slow death, however, and partly explains her persistent irascibility.

Mom, though, loved to work. She relished the times when she could manifest her ample and inspired intelligence. Few such opportunities came her way.

Dad, on the other hand, hated to work. Work was a diversion, a distraction. He never said, "Oh, I like to work" or "That job is fulfilling." He never worked longer than he had to. Nothing was more important than the things he enjoyed doing. Work was not one of them. What he never understood was that while he could be satisfied with an antiquated fishing pole and a peaceful day on Boogie Bayou, others might want more from life.

Dad 'played' all his life. He was quarterback for the Pedlam Falcons, which gifted him the lovely Marjorie Malone, my mother. He was a shortstop for the Pedlam American Legion Team, which gifted him with a tryout for the St. Louis Cardinals baseball team. He may have thought that being owner of the Pedlam Laundry and Dry Cleaners would garnish similar accolades. I don't know.

His passion was raising hunting dogs and little boys—in that order. Both dogs and boys were prepared at birth for the vicissitudes of a life dependent upon game seasons and fickle weather. A hunting dog was taught to bite lightly on a stuffed brown sock enclosing an opened baby pin, simulating a quail already swallowed by morbidity.

"Fetch girl, fetch."

When the dog fetched, without destroying the safety pin and newspaper filled sock, Dad rubbed the dog's ears.

"Good, girl. Good, girl."

Dad was universally loved by man, boy, and pet. I never met a more loved man.

The boy was taught to replace normal life-cycle mileposts with the hunting cycle, to live on the edge of hunting season. Neither the brown cotton sock nor the hunting trip was real life; each had euphoria and pain captured in the essence of a moment: if the quail was returned undamaged, it was already dead, and dog, boy, and father knew it to be so.

After less than a decade, I knew my place in my father's pantheon. I was never to join the stage next to my dad. No one could.

He was the lead actor, though, and both waited for the other to speak. Occasionally one of us spoke haltingly while the other listened intently, or pretended to listen since the sound of our voices was competing with our own history and passion. We were actors on a stage that was constantly moving, from one game season to the next. We rarely obtained our limit and often killed nothing. But we stayed on stage with zeal and courage, facing the next act, the next curtain call. We did not have a script; we did not wait for the audience's applause. We merely moved quietly from fishing hole to cane brake to cypress swamp. The game changed, our dogs grew older, but we stayed the same. Or rather he did. We all changed. Dad didn't.

"Walk quietly, Jake," Dad said. I learned to walk through life, heels first, quietly, speaking little and observing much.

Every Saturday before Christmas we obtained our pathetic Christmas tree from Four Mile Creek.

"Do you think Mom will like this one, Jake?" Dad sincerely asked me.

It was an anemic Scotch pine that was cursed with too much hot weather and too much water. The pine had no reason to grow hardy limbs or verdant needles. It was spindly and bare.

Our Christmas trees reminded me of Ichabod Crane. Generous silver tinsel, voluminous bubble lights, and fake plastic ice icicles could not redeem these monstrosities.

"I think, Jake," Dad sincerely pronounced, "This is the most beautiful tree we have ever cut."

"What do you think?"

"Absolutely, Dad. Absolutely. I especially like the top." I lied.

Dove season began September 1, squirrel season October 1. Deer season was in late November and early December. Christmas was a necessary distraction, but heralded duck season, followed by a dreadfully dull time when dad had to work at the laundry: no excuses, no game season. But this period was mercifully short and violently ended by Dad's favorite hunting genre: turkey season.

"The season begins in two weeks!" Dad pronounced. With all the drama of a launch from Cape Canaveral Space Center, Dad counted down the days to the beginning of turkey season.

Then by May 15, Dad was fishing for irate female black bass that were guarding their young in stagnant Delta fishing holes.

We would stand in the backyard and Dad would instruct me in the intricacies of fly-fishing.

"You throw the line, not the lure," Dad explained.

"Once you catch the fish, you do not pull him to the boat," Dad said. "You let the fish tire himself and then you snag him with a net."

Even at an early age I learned to let my opponents struggle and tire themselves out as I held firmly on the line.

June 1 to August 1 were the dog days of summer, the nadir of the calendar year, when southeast Arkansas temperatures hovered around 98, and the humidity was never below 90. With sweating palms, we consumed vast quantities of dripping buttered corn on the cob and wished fervently for the slightly more bearable fall. We would begin dove season in our shirt-sleeves and passionately hope that by the beginning of squirrel season there would be a deep frost. There almost never was, so we all learned to walk gingerly through crinkly fall leaves, which were hiding diamondback rattlers and cottonmouth moccasins.

August was devoted to finding dove-hunting locations, and then the cycle began all over again. The truth was that Dad almost never worked.

As an insecure teenager, I remembered arriving home from school and finding him looking sheepishly at me across the hood of his butt-ugly peevish yellow first-generation Chevrolet Blazer, in which he had added a wheezing, dripping external air conditioner.

"Ready to go?" Dad asked.

I wanted to say, "No, I have to study for a test." But I never did. I could never stand to displease my dad.

I'm glad I had a solid education before the ninth grade because after that—on almost every afternoon and without a doubt on every Saturday, and even on some early Sunday mornings (we always managed to arrive at church on time)—we were hunting and fishing. Like Abraham Lincoln, I mostly self-taught myself by reading the classics.

On one Sunday morning, after a moderately successful squirrel-hunting foray, stretched out because I was temporarily lost in the woods (I always got lost), we arrived at church precisely at 9:30 AM, just in time for Sunday school. Dad was visibly agitated—he usually smoked two unfiltered Camels and drank weak coffee before he joined his Men of Galilee class—but he had no time today. Moreover, he was the substitute teacher for Judge Murphy, something he abhorred doing. Dad had to teach the International Sunday school Lesson to the Men of Galilee Class without the benefit of caffeine or nicotine.

To make things worse, Spooky Hill was particularly argumentative during class and insisted that Moses had crossed the

Reed Sea, not the Red Sea, and it really wasn't a miracle at all.

"Spooky," Dad said, "Hold that question for the Judge next week."

Dad, terrified at teaching the Bible to anyone, much less his peers, found himself shaking and sweating as profusely as a junkie.

Yet Dad gained inner strength from knowing that Sunday afternoons could be profitable hunting or fishing events. As long as all participants had done penance in morning worship, saved by grace through faith, they could with clear conscience hunt and fish with reckless abandon.

I managed Sunday school well enough, although twice I fell asleep during Uncle Evan's insightful discussion of the fall of Jericho.

My dad had shaken me awake at 3:30 that morning in spite of the fact that we would spend, as usual, a solid hour and a half in the woods before first light.

During the worship, normally I sat next to Mamaw and cuddled into her fox furs, which had small, dark-red glass eyes. Mamaw was an open-minded United Methodist, perhaps a closet Presbyterian, who understood that little boys were predestined to Heaven—not to Hell. Since I was her grandson, surely I was predestined to the former, so I did not need to be saved by grace dispensed by any Methodist preacher. With no modicum of guilt, I quickly placed my head on the fox fur with the beady-eyed mammal staring at me.

I fell asleep after we sang "What a Friend We Have in Jesus," woke up a few minutes before the assurance of pardon, and resolutely committed myself to slumber during the sermon.

However, during the final hymn, "Amazing Love, How Can It Be?" I was startled and inadvertently threw up my left hand in an apparent abject salute to God. In fact, my arm had fallen asleep, and I was merely trying to reclaim, as quickly as possible, blood circulation in it.

"Praise you Jesus!" I exclaimed.

Mamaw, rejecting the fake adoration, was not deceived. Like a spiteful Donatist, Mamaw pinched my right knee so evocatively that I felt a repentant spirit enter my wayward heart.

However, in my exuberance and feigned religious zeal, I had unintentionally deposited hitherto unknown squirrel entrails on Mrs. M. J. McQuisten's left earlobe—about an inch and a half long, of nickel-size width. Mrs. McQuisten's earlobes were veritable legends in the Delta. They now were adorned with squirrel entrails.

But the deed was done. To add to the growing list of my infractions, I had neglected to wash my hands after cleaning the morning kill. Now, deposited on a substantial thicket of earlobe hair, was a piece of squirrel pyloric sphincter. Mrs. M. J. McQuisten, being a more mature saint, was able to retain her composure even as squirrel guts were dangling from her left earlobe. But she was not amused.

Mrs. McQuisten, who had little Christian charity and no mercy whatsoever, made sure that my mother thoroughly punished me, which in my case meant being grounded. While I was truly sorry for anointing Mrs. McQuisten with squirrel gut, I had to feign disappointment at Mom's insistence that I not go hunting for two weeks. For two glorious weeks I enjoyed the unaccustomed soiree of Faulkner, Hugo, and Goethe. My dad, on the other hand, sulked until I was released from purgatory.

"Marjorie? Don't you think Jake has been punished enough?" he asked.

My two brothers, more practical than I, had abandoned paternal approbation for more palatable pursuits like dating and studying for final exams. It was a sort of parental abuse: Dad was a madman whose addiction to fishing and to hunting was insatiable. I was the innocent victim. I was drawn into his madness as I followed him to every known fishing and hunting location in southeast Arkansas.

On one occasion, in the exuberance of the moment, we took our garbage to the dump and also brought our cane fly rods with light-green fishing line and bright-red popping bugs. Dodging discarded creamed-corn cans and feminine-hygiene napkins, we caught red belly brim all afternoon, which thankfully we had no intention of eating.

"Throw them back, Jake."

Throwing them back only slightly mitigated the joy of catching huge, red belly brim, and holding the frenetic fiery starbursts up to the horizon, before returning them to the polluted deep.

Dad was addicted to hunting almost anything, to fishing almost anywhere, and to watching me snag my jitterbug fishing lure in every cypress swamp from Monroe, Louisiana to Pine Bluff, Arkansas.

Deer Camp Road, River Bend Road, Four Mile Creek Road, Deep Creek Road, Ten Mile Road, Clear Lake Road, and the Arkansas River Road. Thus the Anthrax Hole, King Tut Lake, Possum Fork, the Bar Pits, Whiskey Shoot, and Lake

Quapaw were more common to me than the street in front of our house.

Dad was a wise man. His wisdom was greater than King Solomon's. Indeed, it preceded King Solomon. It returned to the wisdom of Abraham, who was wise enough to trust God for his own good fortune (blessing).

Abraham assumed he was so important that God would not take his son since earlier God had promised Abraham that his children, the heirs of Isaac too, would be more numerous than the stars. Following God's orders, Abraham felt he could march right up Mount Moriah, put his son on an altar, grab a knife—did he know that God would stop him before the deed was done? God didn't stop Abraham only to save the boy; God called a halt also because Abraham was so special. Plus God had made a promise, and Abraham knew that God kept his promises, even if he had to raise the dead.

Dad teased the fates, enriching the pot with great risk because he believed in his star: since he was so special, God himself would not thwart his plans for modest gains like sonorous quail and deer hunts. Dad thought he could have it all, deserved it all; he did not and could not think otherwise. He could do whatever he wanted, and we all helped his dreams come true because he was so earnest in his beliefs—all, but my mother, who like Sarah was horrified at such a faith that would brazenly take her only son to Mount Moriah, to knife to death her only son. All, but my mother, who could only remain silent and wonder what her husband would do next while he so selfishly pursued his own dreams and did not even consider her dreams. Dad did not even think that she might want something more than he wanted, so she acquiesced. We all acquiesced and let him have his way because he held these dreams so devoutly. We let him have his way, but something died in Mom as in Sarah. Sarah lived her life with Abraham after Abraham brought back Isaac from Mount Moriah, but Sarah was never the same. Abraham was the same because, again, he got his way.

After the laundry business failed, we eventually lost Mamaw's House, Mamaw, and all that we cherished: things changed. But Mom lived with Dad, made love with him, raised three boys, and in time understood that his wisdom preceded Nimrod, Esau, and even Adam and Eve, and even preceded original sin. Dad was with God when he created the universe, and no doubt even God wished to please my dad.

Dad placed me alone, with my first gun, under a mature sweet-gum tree at 4:00 AM on the first day of my adult life, which in his estimation was age ten. We were hunting at Four Mile Creek. He left me.

The smell of rank earth and putrid autumn leaves was oppressive. Dew dripped from sweet-gum tree leaves onto my camouflage entourage. My canvas pants, shirt, and game bag, too long the inhabitants of Sportsmen's Paradise, now were my baptism. This was my initiation morning; henceforth, I was a man.

I was not so reflective at that moment, however. The exigencies of the moment demanded my attention. I sat under the sweet-gum tree, wondering what it would be like to see, and then, horrors, to shoot a squirrel.

I was reading The Song of Roland, and I was sure that some evil Saracens would cut my throat. Yet even I could not imagine what the Saracens would be doing at Four Mile Creek in early October.

"When the Saracens struck, I will be ready," I thought, "as brave Roland was ready before the treacherous Saracens overwhelmed him and did him in."

I checked to make sure Little Martin's 4-10 caliber Savage shotgun was loaded. Little Martin had graduated to Daddy Ray's old pump action twenty gauge and he let me borrow his 4-10.

Suddenly, as I looked intently into the darkness I realized I would not survive.

I thought, "Dad would find me in late morning or perhaps tomorrow and say, 'Ah, the lad fought a great fight!' Or, as good King Charlemagne proclaimed in admiration of dead Roland's valor. " 'He has learned much, who knows the pain of struggle.' " (Stanza CLXXXIV, line 2524)

> But it would be too late because fierce Roland and I would be dead.
>
> "Pedlam would put up a marble memorial extolling brave Jake Stevens, who 'fell in mortal combat on the shore of Four Mile Creek.'"
>
> The fourth grade class would come to school to find, to their horror, that brave Jake Stevens had been slain by the Saracens. Classmate Jamie Kay would never know how much I loved her.
>
> "School would be dismissed. Counselors would be called in to minister to my distraught classmates. For the rest of the school year, my teacher Mr. Bunn would leave my

chair vacant to honor brave Jake. Every year, at the beginning of squirrel season, Pedlam Elementary School would have a moment of silence to remember the valiant warrior Jake Stevens."

As the dawn filtered through green leaves impatient to be ravaged by the delayed Delta frost, I glanced over my shoulder and saw my dad hiding behind a black-walnut tree. There he was, with his Browning Automatic Belgium-made 12-gauge with a gold trigger. Charlemagne had not abandoned me to the Saracens. There would be no monuments or moments of silence. I survived my first hunting expedition.

Dad was like that. Just when I thought he had abandoned me to the Saracens, he was watching over me after all.

# 15

MY MOTHER LOVED COMPUTERS. She bought a Commodore 128 in the 1980s, and it sat on her kitchen table for six months until Rodeo Suffrage set it up and showed her how to use it. She would have loved the one I was staring into right now.

She ultimately became a PC lady. She was sure that moving the cursive to the left to delete was a Communist plot. And in appearance and reality, she wanted to go on record, even though the Iron Curtain had disappeared ten years before, that she was an ardent anti-Communist.

Not that Mom would be caught dead staring into anything. To stare was impolite, and my mother was the very essence of politeness. It was her life's ambition: politeness.

My mother would have been happy that none of the black members of my class were invited to our fortieth reunion, good manners or not.

Mom was victimized by racism, and she was a perpetrator of it too. Racism both seduced her with its promise of acceptance and ravished her with its destructiveness.

Racism was her ticket into southern respectability.

"Black people, of course, are not inferior to white people. They are just different. The Doctor B. F. Skinner has shown that to be true." Mom, name dropping, loved to couch her racial profiling in pseudo-scientific language.

Born into abject poor-white-trash poverty, Mom was only too glad to gain prestige through racism. That view of life she held sincerely; racism definitely brought acceptance and, in a word, pedigree. It tied one's bloodlines to southern ethos as surely as belonging to the Daughters of the Confederacy. In fact, she grasped it with gusto and vigor. Her manifestations of racism were particularly full of energy. When Mom lacked ideology for a motive, she compensated with vigor.

Scriptures of various religions claim that the meaning of the world must be discovered outside human experience. But truth to Mom was what all of us white southerners agree was truth, and what we agree was truth was more a reflection of circumstances than it was any absolute or objective reality outside humankind's experience. Mom loved God—although a decidedly ivory and anemic God. In Mom's more candid moments, she had to admit, we were all the result of a purposeless and materialistic process that did not have us in mind. Thus in the larger scheme of things, ontologically, according to Mom, we were all screwed.

Mom felt sorry for blacks, but was glad that she was white. She considered it her responsibility to ameliorate their needy condition. Mom loved the drama, the intrigue, and the superiority that race relations prompted in her life.

Mammy Lee became her cause célèbre, her case in point.

With head down deferentially, Mammy Lee was an experienced and ingenuous lackey to my mom. "Oh yes, I needs your help." Or, "Yes Mrs. Marjorie, I needs those clothes you gave me."

Nonetheless, when white people were absent, Mammy Lee was the consummate, confident leader. She ran the house, homeschooled me, disciplined me, and was the public relations director for the Stevens City Laundry. This was before answering machines: Mammy Lee could network with business contacts better than any of her white peers. She would employ the best black jargon she could muster: "You-all won't be disappointed if you-all let Mr. Ray wash and dry youse clothes. Theys be perfect!" And so forth.

In short, in every way Mammy Lee was the intellectual and social equal of all her white employers, but she made every effort to keep such revelation unknown. Anonymity assured employment and a quid-pro-quo existence. Mammy worked hard to appear stupid and dependent. She needed the whites to think that she needed them.

And in a real sense, she did need them. For employment. Sanguine black-white relations assured housing, food, and most of all, protection from the black-hating KKK. Whites were a vital part of Mammy Lee's life.

In a complementary way, blacks were a vital part of Mom's life. They made her life, her country, and her land nonpareil. Relationships with blacks generated a baffled emotion that fed her fragile ego. She was important if blacks were unimportant.

"Lee is under my employment and on occasions I employ a few other girls," mom was fond of saying.

In other words, Mom "owned" a few and thus felt a need to "take care of my nigras." Mom liked the owning and the caring.

Mom's racism was her own. Like a woman preparing for a debutante party, Mom nurtured it, refined it, and savored it. She was always superior to someone as long as she was prejudiced.

Mom's world was based on delusions. First, she suspended

disbelief. Mom chose to believe in the incredible. For instance, Mom was sure the Viet Cong would place its banner on the Pedlam Post Office's front steps if we lost the Vietnam War. Second, Mom created a narrative and fabricated a world of immoral, even forbidden ideas that were disguised as something socially acceptable. She did this so she could enjoy these ideas and the experiences while denying to herself that she was doing that.

These two delusions empowered Mom to draw herself into invented scenarios that formed the background for her shaky morality. She was both the victim and perpetrator, playing both roles with robust energy.

# 16

SAMMY MALONE, MOM'S GRANDFATHER, refused to celebrate the Fourth of July. He could never shake the memory of Confederate General Pemberton's surrendering Vicksburg to the Yankees on July 4, 1863. He hated Yankees. As a boy Sammy remembered the Yankees' marching through on the way to Vicksburg. They had stolen his only friend, a four-year-old gelding, who was a constant companion to this only son of a Mississippi Delta family, and they had killed the fathers of many of his childhood friends.

Sammy loved to sip cold buttermilk from a crystal wine glass discarded by a passing riverboat patron and discovered when he was exploring the shoreline one cloudy afternoon in 1870.

The Mississippi Delta was wild country. Virtually uninhabited, some of it was even unexplored. Virgin trees crowded between the levees bordering Mississippi on the East and Louisiana on the West. Cougars, bears, and Native American ghosts inhabited this wilderness.

Sammy Malone had given his best effort to conquer this land, but one stormy day, in the middle of a delta winter afternoon, he succumbed to tetanus after a tussle with a wild boar. Sammy gave up the ghost, in his late twenties, when Jesse Malone, Big Daddy was only twelve.

Big Daddy's mom quickly remarried Stanley, who consumed vast quantities of first-rate moonshine, distilled from silver queen corn and cane sugar, liquor that served both as Stanley's vocation and addiction. Sobriety, to Stanley, was an early stage of inebriation.

Moderately intoxicated Stanley was innocuous, even pleasant. Then, as the brew took hold, he was vicious. Right before Stanley succumbed to mental incontinence, he abused everyone around him. Mostly people, especially family members, knew when that would occur and stayed away. But occasionally Big Daddy—and worse, Big Daddy's mother—would happen to be in his vicinity during this inauspicious time, and it was truly amazing how much damage that man could inflict in the little time that it took for him finally to collapse into a drunken coma.

For three years, Big Daddy endured Stanley's abuse. One day, however, Big Daddy saw Stanley beat his mother until she collapsed on their dirty, tobacco-spit-stained wooden front porch. Flopping like a grounded black bass gasping for breath, his mother finally lay in a fetal stupor.

"Stop!" Big Daddy shouted.

Stanley, though, said nothing.

Big Daddy was not finished though. With a discarded hickory limb, Big Daddy bushwhacked Stanley—who even when he was drunk was a powerful man—and inflicted an almost fatal blow to Stanley's ample head.

Sobriety brought a fearful retribution on Big Daddy. Careful not to inflict fatal wounds, Stanley thumped fifteen-year-old Big Daddy with adroit cruelty.

Big Daddy's mom took her husband's side. "Honey, Stanley means well. And he is your father. You must not strike him!"

It was too much for Big Daddy.

He left Stanley, the dirty wooden porch, and his mother forever. He could forget them, but he could not forget the flopping.

For the next two years Big Daddy lived in the woods and swamps in the wild Delta bottoms. Living on the outskirts of early twentieth-century southern towns, he experienced poverty that was sublime in its intensity.

Southern carnivore cuisine and lifestyle were the epitome of conservation and economy. Practically nothing was discarded from any animal: intestines, gizzards, stomachs—it all was eaten. There was precious little left for impecunious orphans like Big Daddy, who ate raw crawdads and charcoal-broiled red-bellied brim.

There was not much that was big about Big Daddy. At seventeen his blond—almost white—hair on his blue-eyed head oversaw a body that was not symmetrical. His hair was so full of tight curls that some narrow-minded dissolute peers suggested there was some miscegenation in his not-too-distant past.

His right arm, a birth defect, was at least an inch longer than his left: when he clapped, his left forefinger landed squarely on the palm of his right hand. Not that Big Daddy had many reasons to clap about anything. It was not easy being a southern rural indigent. Life was harsh and unforgiving. There was nothing remotely symbolic or abstract about it.

Mrs. Gertrude Huckleberry observed Big Daddy rummaging through garbage cans on the outskirts of Monroe, LA. Adolescent orphans were not rare commodities. However, blond haired, blued eyed needy waifs were. So, with curiosity, Gertrude Huckleberry asked Big Daddy to move into her house to help her with chores and such.

"What is your name, boy?"

"Jesse Malone."

"Well, Jesse Malone, how would you like to live with me and Mr. Gertrude?

Big Daddy squatted and spent a minute or two considering her proposition.

"Well, I reckon we can try it," he said.

There was no fatuity in Gertrude Huckleberry. Her 310-pound frame was to be reckoned with. She was everywhere at once and sometimes quite invasive. Gertrude was not a subtle person. However, there was a sanguine generosity about her that made her easy to love.

On top of her chipped, rusty woodstove, she kept a discarded coffee can full of bacon grease that alternately jelled and liquefied depending upon activity in the stove. She liberally deposited bacon grease on everything that moved across her world. Nothing escaped the rich magnificence of her slippery amalgamation. It graced her cuisine; it graced her apron; it graced all that walked in the vicinity of the old woodstove.

Mr. Hugh Huckleberry, Gertrude's husband, owned a bakery, and Big Daddy worked in that shop.

For the rest of his too-short adolescence, Big Daddy lived with Uncle Hugh and Aunt Gertrude, as he called them, and indulged himself in heretofore unknown and exotic fare such as donuts fried in lard. He was too old to be adopted, but in the postwar southern pantheon, he found repose and succor in the Huckleberry cheap frame unpainted house nestled between the locust-humming Ouachita River Delta and the hog-infested Northern Louisiana Pine Barrens. Big Daddy held the Pine Barrens red sandy loam in his hand, and dared again, to call a place home.

He put on weight and met his future wife, Mary Lou Huckleberry, whose father, Nehemiah Huckleberry, was Hugh's brother.

Mary Lou was visiting her Uncle Hugh and Aunt Gertrude and noticed the skinny, awkward boy hoeing the garden.

If Mary Lou was not attracted to Big Daddy, Big Daddy did not even notice Mary Lou.

"Who are you?" Mary Lou belligerently asked Big Daddy.

"Victor Frankenstein," Big Daddy playfully responded.

"Who?" Mary Lou asked. "Are you the neighbor's boy?"

When Mary Lou discovered she had a new cousin, of sorts, she was mostly indifferent.

Gertrude read Big Daddy poetry, history, drama, prose fiction, and even a few nonfiction speeches and essays. She gifted illiterate Big Daddy with a love for literature that he gave his daughter, my mom, and thereby bequeathed along the line to me.

Gertrude loved the British Romantics. Goethe, she felt was obscene; Thoreau and Emerson, supercilious; Poe, talented, but weird. Wordsworth, Shelley, and especially Byron were exquisite! Their grasp of the unassailable was a sublime escape from Auntie's harsh life.

Her favorite poem was Byron's "The Prisoner of Chillon." It was the story of a man, who spent most of his adult life unjustly sequestered in a mountain prison. The young man grew old, but was able to maintain his romantic beliefs in justice, freedom, and goodness. Only at the end of his life, when ironically the prisoner was released, did he lose his hope.

Now that was something that Big Daddy could understand—being in prison. He could not quite grasp the notion of believing in a cause, in any abstract ideology. Yet Byron taught Big Daddy how to love. Byron was punctilious in his rebellion, and neglectful of his ideology. Byron inspired him once again to risk that inferno emotion, which had been quenched by neglect and abuse so many years before. In this face of facileness and superficiality that Big Daddy had so thoroughly grasped into his soul, Lord Byron enticed him again into the burning noonday heat.

In the dusty evenings of northern Louisiana, while Aunt Gertrude read Byron, Big Daddy discovered again the seductive companion of hope. Just as the prisoner of Chillon heard the singing of a bird outside his window, and it reminded him that there's beauty and hope in the world—so also Big Daddy remembered a love he had once, a love freely given him by Sammy and his mom, a gentle minuet whose tune he had long forgotten.

Big Daddy knew that Byron and Sophocles captured his past, but he earnestly hoped that they did not prophesy his future. He had new hope, though, and a later religious experience added to his optimism.

No southerner escaped religion. It was in our DNA. Most Southerners adhered to denominations of Protestant Christianity such as Episcopalian, Presbyterian, Methodist, Pentecostalism, and especially Southern Baptist. The First Great Awakening (1730s–40s) and the Second Great Awakening (1790–1840s) fanned the flames.

Southern religion had an evangelical flavor: faithful followers earnestly sought and fervently passed along a consuming, personal relationship with the Deity, in this case, Jesus Christ. Southern evangelicalism promoted two radical notions: pervasive privatism and omnipresent passion, the latter being alternately evidenced by coy "Amens" to fulsome glossolalia. Faithful followers of Christ barked at trees (to 'tree' the Devil) and smelled Jesus. More stalwart souls even drank poison and handled snakes. There was no equivocation in southern religion. The lukewarm burned in Hell.

It was the nascent metaphysical explorer William Blake and the book of Revelation that brought southern evangelicalism to Big Daddy. With his raw, robust metaphors, Blake infected Big Daddy with fervor and earnestness. In his ambivalence and circumspection, Blake nonetheless drew Big Daddy into the fiery furnace:

> Tiger, tiger, burning bright
> In the forests of the night,
> What immortal hand or eye
> Could frame thy fearful symmetry?

One Sunday, in Monroe Second Baptist Church, Big Daddy heard his pastor preach on Revelation 12. John the Beloved Disciple, John the Divine, pulled Big Daddy the rest of the way into the fold.

> Then I heard a loud voice in heaven say:

> "Now have come the salvation and the power and the kingdom of our God, and the authority of his Messiah."

On that Sunday Big Daddy "gave his heart to Jesus" and believed that he could triumph over the furies, which tortured his soul "by the blood of the Lamb." To southern Christian religion, giving one's heart to Jesus was tantamount to being reborn.

The newly converted English poet John Donne, who gave his heart to Jesus, ceased all obstreperous writing and composed beautiful God-centered poetry. He changed the direction of English poetry toward the sublime metaphysics of the seventeenth century.

Fyodor Dostoyevsky gave his heart to Jesus in the Russian Orthodox Church and created arguably one of the greatest Christian moral tales: Crime and Punishment. The main character, Raskolnikov, has murdered two women and stolen a cross from one of them. Even as he flees from the carnage, God was pursuing him: "Raskolnikov thrust it in his pocket without looking at it, flung the crosses on the old woman's body and rushed back into the bedroom, this time taking the axe with him." God will find him in the person of Sonia.

Early in his career, young T. S. Eliot in bitterness and anger wrote:

> We are the hollow men
> We are the stuffed men
> Shape without form, shade without colour
> Paralyzed force, gesture without motion.

Then, later in life, Eliot gave his heart to Jesus and joined the Anglican Church.

It was a hopeful day for Big Daddy. He had met the God of Abraham, Isaac, and Daniel, the apostle Paul, John Donne, Fyodor Dostoyevsky, and T. S. Eliot. He gave his heart to this Jesus. He also gave up his nightmare image of his mother as flopping around on the cracked, bare wooden floor of his youth. It was not forgotten or overcome by weighty insights; it was expiated by the death of Jesus Christ on the cross.

The odd mixture of Ibsen, Faulkner, and John the Baptist in Big Daddy's fundamental nature was both disconcerting and consoling. It was as if his salvation, his submersion into the Southern Baptist waters of sanctification, supplemented his peccadillo of immersion in Western literature.

He was graced with Byron, Shelley, Goethe, even a little Tolstoy, and thankfully the book of Ezekiel and other Old and New Testament delicacies. He would sit in silent gratitude, listening to Aunt Gertrude read to him about a world that at first was distant and even a little foreboding. As he listened more, and Aunt Gertrude read more, he first grew cautiously enlightened, and then expansively hopeful. It was as if the Western canon and the Gospel kerygma together satiated any remaining soulish doubt.

But, Big Daddy never learned to read, at least not yet. He never wanted to learn to read. He was afraid that if he learned to read, Aunt Gertrude would stop rubbing her fat fingers through his white—not golden—curly hair. It was strange, almost erotic, but Big Daddy always favored having his hair combed and massaged, above all other corporeal pleasures. Yes,

Big Daddy's cup overflowed with goodness and grace.

Only a few years later, Big Daddy left the bakery, he left to join the army. But he never left Christ. Big Daddy had no idea why America was going to fight in Europe and had no quarrel with the Kaiser, but he intended to join before he was drafted.

The army apparently had enough infantrymen, but had a shortage of locomotive engineers, so Big Daddy drove hissing steam engines from the Argonne Forest to Antwerp, retrieving supplies, mail, and other necessary items. When World War I ended, he transported troops across Europe to fight the Bolsheviks. As he drove his steam engine past Switzerland, he recalled ghost stories around a Swiss campfire that would inspire Mary Shelley to write Frankenstein. When he crossed Poland, he wondered where Joseph Conrad was born, and finally, reaching Russia, he pictured Andrew forgiving Natasha before he died in Tolstoy's War and Peace. Having arrived at a sort of literary saturation point, he found himself, not unlike a sugar cube in water, dissolving into everything around him and finding rest.

While in Europe, he practiced meditation and prayer on levels he heretofore had not known. Southern Baptists were naturally dissatisfied with the term "meditation" since it sounded popish and generally scurrilous, like "transcendentalism" or "levitating." And anyhow, Southern Baptists would have nothing to do with anything that was not bred, born, and cured in the Bible belt, whose epicenter was controlled by them. They preferred "the Word" to emotive expressions. Big Daddy was prone to wonder and to love everything emotive. Mystic moments and visions were expressly forbidden in his church. However Big Daddy had touched the face of God, and he would never be the same.

Big Daddy was the first family member, who was a faithful follower of Jesus Christ. He encountered and then loved a forgiving God, who loved him back unconditionally.

Big Daddy returned from the Great War to resume his duties at the Huckleberry Bakery. Such a vocation provided very little remuneration but no excitement at all.

Providentially, though, he became reacquainted with Mary Lou, who by that time was a student at a Bastrop Finishing School for Young Ladies.

Big Daddy was no longer tall and gangly and was heading to a solid job as a locomotive engineer with the Missouri Pacific.

Like so many returning World War I veterans, Big Daddy and Mary Lou, who was Big Momma to me, began a whirlwind romance that would lead to marriage after less than a year of serious courtship.

I thought, "Why did we call them Big Momma and Big Daddy? There was nothing remotely big about my maternal grandmother and grandfather."

It was a southern thing. We preferred to name with size and quantity rather than capacity and longevity. Thus, my dad was Big Martin, his oldest son and namesake, my brother, was Little Martin. Likewise Mom's mom was Big Momma—not "oldest mom" or "tall mom." We thought ourselves to be a generous people and we graced our relatives and loved ones with high-spirited nicknames.

Big Momma, like my mother, her daughter, was an anachronism that was so much the résumé of early twentieth-century southern women. Intelligent, witty, and discerning, she felt cursed above all women. She tried hard to feign docility, to embrace contentment, even when she was convinced that most of the Southern male species lacked both imagination and intelligence. Most of the time she succeeded in the charade, although occasionally the imbecility of her male peers was too much to bear—at which point Big Momma would quietly utter veiled invective and sarcasm. My grandmother found that she had a knack for uttering such oblique reproach and still, after a short respite, resuming her vocation in marriage. The Bastrop Finishing School for Young Ladies showed Big Momma how to run a household, but did nothing to quench the feminist rage in her soul.

To compensate for the hard years in the Louisiana Pine Barrens and crepe myrtle swamps, as Big Daddy matured in the capable nourishment of Henrik Ibsen and Karo syrup pecan pies, his gawky awkwardness was replaced with stunning good looks. In truth, Big Daddy's handsome face for a moment enticed Big Momma away from her controlled cynicism. In short, Big Momma was smitten with this peculiar illiterate boy who had memorized both Psalm 119 and "The Rime of the Ancient Mariner." He was a force to be reckoned with.

One summer day on the bank of the Ouachita River, under a Chickasaw plum tree, the bright, intelligent, and lovely Mary Lou Huckleberry fell in love with Big Daddy while he was describing the shield of Achilles in Hancock's Iliad. Falling in love with Big Daddy was a pure and righteous thing, the most hopeful thing Big Momma ever did.

By this time, Big Daddy and Big Momma were an active members of Monroe Second Baptist Church. The truth was that Big Momma loved a God who was much different from the God Big Daddy loved. Her God was a stern, judgmental God, a God of the Decalogue. This God was just waiting to zap wayward pilgrims with retribution and misery, if they flouted God's law by committing the least sin.

Big Daddy, propitiously, had no access to such assumptions. His faith was fresh, new, and unalloyed with systematic theology, or even church history. He simply heard, believed, and never stopped believing that God loved him unconditionally, and sent his only begotten Son to prove it.

Big Momma came by her vinegary God honestly. There was more judgment in southern Protestantism, and Big Momma, who grew up in the church, was thoroughly infected with the wrath of God.

All Big Daddy could accomplish was a short prayer full of wishful thinking that they shared together after Mary Lou consented to marry him.

"Let us pray. God thank you for gifting me with such a fine woman of God like Mary Lou."

Big Momma married Big Daddy in the middle of the Great Flu Epidemic. They wore sanitary masks as they stood before the altar at Monroe Second Baptist church and exchanged vows, kissed each other decisively (sans masks), and began matrimony with unbounded optimism.

Big Momma called Big Daddy "Daddy" and Big Daddy called Big Momma "Momma" as if they were preparing themselves for parenting.

Big Momma taught Big Daddy to read.

"That was 'read' not 'red' like the color," Big Momma explained.

Big Daddy began by reading The Little Train That Could, but progressed quickly to Defoe and eventually Chaucer. It was a strange thing to Big Momma, to have a student, who was a fair literary critic of some of the most complicated literature in the western canon, but could only read Good Night Moon. Along that line, Big Momma learned to avoid Big Daddy's favorites—he had memorized most of the Shakespearean sonnets so she introduced Marianne Moore to him. He did not much like her, though.

"Daddy," Big Momma gently explained, "You can choose to memorize, or not, certain literature, but reading is reading. You have to read it whether you like it or not.

Big Daddy was not convinced, but nonetheless read what Big Momma required, and, very quickly, was reading what he had always known by rote memory.

There was, then, a certain intimacy that grew between a man and a woman, who shared marital conjugation and Homer, both at the same time.

Big Momma gave Big Daddy the ability to read and much more. The mutual giving was as sweet and energizing as Big Momma's rich, egg white pecan divinity candy. In retrospect, the first year of their marriage was the superlative year of their matrimonial life. It was full of innumerable good things that brought verve and anticipation to both partners.

It was not to be though.

Northern Louisiana's rural poverty stimulated animosity as surely as the June sun matured black-eyed peas. Both human and pea first blossomed, developed a hard shell, and eventually shriveled and died. The resulting fruit in both was dry and bitter. No one really liked to eat black-eyed peas, and no one really liked living in the humid, torrid Louisiana barrens.

The good times were short-lived and replaced with a quiet desperation in both that would never be expressed openly. Before long they stopped reading Ezra Pound together and, eventually, stopped talking with each other at all. They were too tired to be in love anymore. So they gave up all pretenses and lived in the extreme anxiety of the moment. They lived dismal lives in a gloomy place at a bleak time.

What was green and rich and fertile lost its life and turned to dust. Drained of moisture, the red earth turned pink, and the gray earth turned to white dust. The wind swept the rain clouds away and sent dust billowing into the sky.

They kept coming up short. The job, the produce, the weather, and love itself were not enough to sustain life. Humans needed the bounty of the land to survive.

Sublime paucity eroded and eventually destroyed the love that hope and grace had so thoroughly enriched in the first few years of their marriage. It was replaced by a cold silent fury that was never stated, but poisoned the souls of their seven offspring and doomed all to the existential hell so ably described by Sartre in his play No Exit. "Hell is other people." Hell was living with people you did not love.

In fairness to both, while Big Daddy steered his boat close to grace, Big Momma was forced to make sense of their marginal existence in the middle of raising seven children. Big Daddy could escape to the open road; Big Momma had no such escape. Thus Big Daddy, who unintentionally lived a simple, uncomplicated life, complicated Big Momma's life beyond all forbearance.

Big Daddy made very poor wages. This would have been all right in other families: almost all railroad families were poor. Big Momma, an only child of a prosperous Northern Louisiana family, a woman, who had, after all, been to "college"—even if it was only finishing school—now found herself living in a shack like hundreds of other shacks on the edge of an archetypical railroad town.

Big Daddy's readings of Gulliver's Travels were at first entertaining and later immensely irritating. The whole thing was so tiresome and predictable. One character in No Exit never blinks, and he can't blink because he has no eyelids. There was no use for sleep in this Hell, and he realizes that Hell was "life without a break" (line 5). This was what Big Momma felt life was like.

Their problem was exacerbated by the inevitable gradualness of their decline. Within the first year of marriage, Big Momma's Christian charity ran out, and she could no longer cling to even a vestige of her faith. There remained no sustaining motif for her to embrace. She was alone in the cosmos, or so she felt.

Unforgivingness brutalized Big Momma's soul.

Unforgivingness combined with anger created problems out of things that were heretofore not problems.

Big Daddy had a habit of stopping at a local bar and drank whiskey and coke. It was moderate in scope and duration and mostly ignored by Big Momma. However, as Big Momma looked for reasons to hate Big Daddy the problem grew until he was an alcoholic.

"Daddy, where have you been?"

"At the Yellow Brick."

"Doing what?"

"Dancing with Helen Dubrowsky. What do you think I was doing?"

And so forth.

Rancor and sarcasm replaced the previously sustaining air of grace and mercy. Kindness was completely absent.

Big Daddy's demise was more gradual and complicated. Although he never quite felt betrayed by God, he wondered how a loving God could allow such adversity to inflict his existence. He fought off doubt as he fought off the sparks that inevitably blew into his locomotive cab while he sped to Memphis or to Monroe. Mostly he could grab the sparks into his glove-covered hand and suffocate them. But at times, with increased frequency and in direct proportion to the quality of coal provided by Missouri Pacific, Big Daddy had to move away from the wheel and actually fight a small fire precipitated by a spark. Increasing with each new hardship, Big Daddy could feel the inner fire blazing out of control.

The marriage quivered, momentarily shivered, and then collapsed; however, a certain détente emerged, and so did a deep, foreboding silence. Big Momma and Big Daddy became a cheerless couple, and this iciness was visited on their children.

The Missouri Pacific moved Big Daddy and his family across the state line to Pedlam, where my mother and her six siblings were raised. Life was externally improved. They had a better house, and it was relatively far from the railroad yard. Nothing really changed. The move certainly did not change connubial relations. Big Momma and Big Daddy were on a track that had no roundhouse to turn them in the opposite direction.

Across from the train station was the Pool Hall, arguably the most thriving business in Pedlam. Charlie Stuart, who married Mom's sister, owned it.

They were married in the new red brick Pedlam First Baptist Church. My mother was the maid of honor and Big Momma, for a brief moment, was the radiant North Louisiana belle she once was. Big Daddy, in his double-breasted, stripped suit looked and felt absurd, but still enjoyed the wedding.

Big Daddy was delighted with his new son-in-law. Moreover, being one of the wealthiest men in town, and being an inveterate and successful bass fisherman, Uncle Charlie sold one of the best collections of girlie magazines in southeast Arkansas. Also, Uncle Charlie had a small bar and generously sold his father-in-law whiskey sours at half price. In a town where there was no real sin for white patrons unless they wished to cross the color line (prostitution in Pedlam was essentially a black trade), Uncle Charlie's pool hall was a veritable den of inequity. As a young visitor (Uncle Charlie was careful not to let me look at the magazines), I never understood why it was called a pool hall: virtually no one played pool in it. So much of life was like that in Pedlam: smoke and mirrors. The genuine article was hard to procure. The chimera version, however, had an aura of preciosity and latent danger.

# 17

MOM GREW UP NEXT TO THE PEDLAM SEWAGE treatment plant: a feral human odor greeted the Malone household every morning. It mitigated all that was noble, generous, and poetic about human life. There could be no rich motifs, no hope in a place that was so confining and so ineluctable. No heart beat with another.

Man, woman, and child alike manifestly wished to be somewhere else other than at this house. All found a place to go, except poor Big Momma.

Mom understood limitation and constraint. Her home sat on buckshot clay that cracked and buckled every summer. The smell of feces and mildew intensified every hot summer afternoon. Next to her house were Big Momma's fenced pasture and the family's two cows. Behind her house was a woodlot too often the victim of unscrupulous foresters. Enchanted trails and moss-covered paths that would pique the imagination of most children were compromised in my mother's forest by irascible locust trees unimpeded by shade and more congenial oaks. Sunlight was everywhere abundant. Since there was no reason to struggle for sunlight, the young trees grew leafy strong, but selfishly deprived all the other pretty things in the forest of light and life.

The woodlot was a tangle of bush-size trees, hardly a forest, and since it was warm and dry on the western edge, cane rattlers loved to slither in the shadow of the oppressive Arkansas summer sun. On the eastern edge, joining the sewage reservoir, moccasins hissed warnings at mockingbirds, snapping turtles, and inquisitive little girls. My mother learned to measure each step carefully, always looking at what was in front of her, as much as possible controlling where her next step would land. With enlarged caution, she expected little from her world, and thus was more apathetic than apoplectic with adversity.

Not all snakes were my mother's enemies. White-black-and-red king snake Uncle Roy lived under the old piano. No one played the piano but Big Momma kept it around to house Uncle Roy. An aggressive king snake was a valuable boarder. All sorts of advantages accrued to my mother's family: mice were noticeably absent. And no water moccasin would dare bare his fangs near Big Momma's house!

Summer heat caused Uncle Roy to vacate the piano and to rest behind the toilet. This nearly was his undoing, however. Once, when Big Daddy was enjoying a respite and the latest Pedlam Times, Uncle Roy affectionately licked Big Daddy's right Achilles tendon.

Such unfeigned affection was too much for Big Daddy, heretofore Uncle Roy's most outspoken supporter. While Big Daddy admired Uncle Roy's rodent venery skills, which were second to none, Big Daddy could not tolerate this violation of his savoir-faire. With no thought of modesty, Big Daddy, in his entire sartorial splendor, quickly hopped out of the bathroom and into the dining room, where the whole family was gathered for supper. Then, with his pinstriped railroad overalls around his legs, he ignobly fell to the ground, his uncovered derriere signaling his unconditional surrender to human and reptile alike. Uncle Roy, offended by his unreciprocated affection, coyly retreated behind the icebox.

"Get rid of Roy, Momma."

A king snake, however, was too valuable a thing to lose permanently, so Big Momma eventually countermanded Big Daddy's orders and skillfully won Uncle Roy's forgiveness by depositing half-dead, acquired-from-mousetraps mice on the front porch. By this time Roy was comfortably living under a discarded wheelbarrow next to a dogwood tree. Eventually Uncle Roy sullenly returned. He abandoned the piano and the bathroom—which was too bad since eventually rodents, knowing Roy would stay away, made the bathroom into a safe house. Now Roy lived under the icebox—a true icebox, full of Mr. Dinwiddle's block ice contaminated with mice feces.

Dutifully, Uncle Roy magnanimously protected his domicile. Occasionally he protruded his nose from under the icebox, but only rarely, such as when a large roach wandered by. The naturally reticent Uncle Roy could not resist this delicacy. The family hardly knew he was there—but all were grateful for their furtive boarder, although everyone wondered what happened to the new kitten. However, a king snake was more difficult to replace than a kitten, and all was forgiven and forgotten.

Mom was born in 1931 as the American economy imploded. There were no fairy tales to be believed, no myths to enervate her family.

If there was myth or imagination it was to be found in mom's relationship with Big Daddy.

She was persuaded and Big Daddy did not refute this view, that she was his favorite child. It was the first sustaining myth she acquired and it empowered her life. His love was reciprocated. Her love for Big Daddy was a sustaining, sincere, life-giving love.

Mom, in order to protect her dad and in a sense to protect the family, became (what we call in family counseling) a scapegoat. She deflected conflict and tension from her family members to herself and in the process assuaged the stress that was destroying the Malone family.

Mom believed in the power of suffering. She was willing to suffer, to be misunderstood, if this would bring peace to their worlds.

Mom willingly joined Big Daddy in exile and found herself the richer for it.

They would speak to each other in poetic verse. Across Pine Street to South Fourth, past Kimbro's Store to the Wolf Building, and finally to the train station—Mom and Big Daddy would quote Shelley and Tennyson and Wordsworth. Pedlam was never as graced with beauty as it was on those rhetorical treks from Big Momma's house to Big Daddy's Missouri Pacific behemoths.

Later, after Big Daddy died, my mom took long walks, three to five miles long, treks that partly included the sidewalks and paths that she took with Big Daddy to the train station. She again spoke the verses and passages that she once shared with her dad. But she walked alone.

Big Daddy, whose faith had seasoned and matured, graciously offered poet laureates and prodigious dramatists. He did not proselytize. Religion, while a very good thing, was the most private of human affections and should not be forced on anyone or even shared with others. So while my mother received confessional instruction from the Pedlam Baptist Church, she received only a catechism of grace from her dad.

To Mom, if one God was good, many gods were better. Mom's expectations of life with all its largesse and complexity required more than one deity. The polytheistic approach was rich in that it "whooshes up." Whooshing up was the sensation we enjoy at a sporting event when the crowd shared a victory celebration with its home team. It was the spontaneous "wave" that spread across a stadium during an important moment, the seventh-ending stretch when the whole community savored a moment. Whooshing up was communal, it was public, and it was like the experience that polytheism could give contemporary humanity. It invites us to extol great heroes—Lou Gehrig, for instance—whose greatness lay in his ability to let some outside force (the gods) flow through his soul. Their pathos, in other words, merged with their ethos to form a logos.

Mom's faith, then, was anything, but orthodox. But, like Big Daddy, it was a very personal thing and not something she ever intentionally shared with anyone. She might whoosh with you, but she would not talk about her faith.

And as love died in Big Momma's heart toward Big Daddy, it also died in that same heart toward my mom. As debilitating as it was to Big Momma's husband, it was fatal to her daughter. Approval departed like the short Pedlam winter evenings, and Mom was not to know the pleasure of her mother as long as either would live. Mom fell into a dark hole that even Elizabeth Barrett Browning could not draw her out of. She was lost and would not be found in her lifetime.

Most Pedlam houses were constructed on 50-by-100-foot lots, but since Big Momma's house was so near the city sewage, vacant land was abundant. Big Momma, then, was graced with an adjacent two-acre pasture plot. To secure two dairy cows, Big Momma built a property fence. Such construction was not exactly in her portfolio, but she was a resourceful woman, and fences needed to be built. Big Daddy was away most of the time. These fences offered scope and sequence. They promised something more than the austere world that existed inside the cramped house. If someone had fences that meant the person had something to hold inside the fences. Big Momma was expansive with hope at first. She had escaped the poverty and hopelessness of northern Louisiana. She waged one final campaign of hope to reclaim what once was, but now was gone. It was a works-righteousness effort.

Big Momma used no store-bought posts. She herself cut sturdy and strong oak posts and placed them securely three feet into the Delta. Like Christmas-tree lights, Big Momma hung barbed wire around her pasture. Wind humming through nefarious barbs warned coyotes and bears to stay away. Big Momma's fence could not kill, but only injure the offending party. Mom was once impaled on Big Momma's fence when she retrieved a foul ball. The fence reminded her that some things hurt a lot, but were not fatal.

The fence on Big Momma's sturdy posts, however, was not so much to keep bad things out as to keep good things in. More than once her seven children paused on the perimeter of her land before they ventured into dangerous bogs and briars. Yet not all living things were stopped. Cupcake, Big Momma's clever goat, jumped the fence diurnally and trimmed Big Momma's azaleas.

Nevertheless, one day while Big Daddy transported soybeans and cotton to Ruston, Louisiana, Big Momma took her fence down. She had nothing to hold inside her fields. No longer did she expect fence to make things better. What good was a fence if one had no dreams, no hopes of things getting better? The fence became an eyesore or impediment.

Later in life, mom described the terrible day when Big Momma took down her fences:

Big Momma did not take down her fence posts because they were insect ridden: they were not. No termite would hazard the arduous task of digesting these sturdy oak poles. Nor were they rotten. Even the wood in the ground was pure, virginal, and strong. No neighbor wanted her posts. Already they preferred shiny metal posts, which lasted only five or so years, but they were easy to drive into the ground. A farmer could mark and fence his whole ten acres in one day. It took Big Momma with her manual posthole digger over a month to erect her fence. But by now the fence had simply lost all utilitarian value.

The neglected pasture was full of hateful thistles. Ironically, in that spring the thistles blossomed with beauty that more than compensated for her lost pasture. They lavished elegant glory on all around them. In orgiastic rapture, Big Momma lived in a fiery storm of excessive splendor. The gift of nature was appreciated.

Briars or no briars, the problem was that she had no reason to keep fences. She could not hold on to what was not useful. They were no good to her.

I thought about Big Momma's house and her fences. I had fences too. Even when I had nothing to fence I painted them, weed whacked around them, maintained them.

My fences protected my home. I reflected on what home really meant and told myself, "I want to go home to the reunion." What was home? I might see it as a place of sustenance and life, but I was a dreamer, and I did not trust my consciousness. I preferred to explore my memories and to find solace in wistful images of past glories.

Rootlessness and loss were the themes of my life, at least until I met Anna. This was partly the curse visited on me from Big Momma.

My mother's family lost the words and the framework to describe their experience and imaginatively create a sustaining world amid chaos. In short, there was no place of refuge for anyone. No central myth of hope to sustain them in the exigencies of everyday life. Home became a shrill Siren, who consumed and ate her offspring.

Fragmented, living amid the destruction wrought by imagined catastrophes and the collapses of the Great Depression, Big Momma was divided from all others and lived in a society internally divided against it. She built fences and participated in a world that offered bits and pieces of truth full of promises of a better world. But it was a world that invited despair too, and the latter became more real than the former.

When she first married Big Daddy, her life was a self-discovery. Now it was a form of salvage in which she gathered up the pieces of her cynicism and despair, based on the empiricism of life. She collected her remaining idealization and innocence and tried to go on, but all she succeeded in doing was discouraging all those around her.

Big Momma's tragic story was the tale of the self, emerging from the fragments of a ruined world, and it was a story about the kind of family that emerged with it. Big Momma lost her way and tried to build something out of fragments, the raw materials she had to work with. They were not enough.

Big Momma's hope, all our hope, was that empathy and identification with good things that existed would at least temporarily transform them, giving us a vision of a better life. Before long, though, with tiredness akin to cynicism, she gave up hoping. She merely learned to "exist."

# 18

My history was a story of a billion selves, formed and created by God, moving in nature, society, and my own physiognomy, all of which were on a trip to some destination. These billions of selves were caught between meaning and no meaning. All were born into a world whose raison d'être was a mystery: though, they filled the world and themselves with activity and motion, nothing they did between meaning and no meaning could finally solve the puzzle of life. Ultimately an act of God solved the puzzle. Selves needed to reach beyond themselves, to the ultimate other, to find the purpose of all that was.

My life was full of psychoanalytic geography, occupied with images of physical spaces satiated with youthful remembrance. The characters and events traveling through these images took me from the recesses of cognizance into the household of my childhood transformed by recollection and desire. They devoured and banished, ensnared and sheltered, and revealed wonders and hidden truths. My memories were full of mazelike routes, trap doors, secret passageways and lurking dangers.

Daddy Ray and Mamaw gave their house to mom and dad, but they reclaimed their mansion every lunch, the main meal, almost every day.

My childhood house, vast and amicable, was designed to optimize the short tepid winters and to minimize the agonizingly long torrid summers. To that end, my enterprising grandparents built a fairly small high-ceiling dining room with busy ceiling fans. Like furious blackbirds competing for a place to roost in an overpopulated natural aviary, our fraternal ceiling fans drove away unwary mosquitoes, diminutive dust particles, unwearied ladybugs, and ubiquitous Arkansas summer heat.

Our dining room was the inner sanctum, the holiest of holies. It was not merely an appendage of the living room or an extension of the kitchen. No breakfast bar or shuttered divider stood between the dining room and the kitchen. The dining room was ground zero of the Stevens household. Little boys were not even allowed to go into the dining room until they had been thoroughly trained in dining room etiquette.

Eating and drinking were the simplest requisites for survival. Like amoebas or whales, human beings must be fed in order to live. No needs were simpler. Indeed, in most cultures, clothes and shelter were sheer luxuries compared to the need for food and drink; after all, starvation was one of the cruelest forms of death.

Eating and drinking were not simply biological occurrences. They also were human occasions. Practical in origin, they were expressive in performance. Natural needs for nourishment were culturally defined through customs and patterns of behavior. We, for instance, cook and eat according to prescribed rules of etiquette. We do not eat with our mouths full. We do not lick our knives. We do not blow bubbles in our iced tea. Everyone knew that one does not eat with elbows resting on the table—although one might wink if an occasional naughty appendage was surreptitiously placed on the edge.

On rare occasions when we were invited to a meal in the dining room, we employed our best behavior. While we kids were afforded certain amenities in church—crayons and Bible pictures—no such diversions were allowed in the dining room. It was full of calmly loquacious earnestness and purpose. Much business was conducted, every world crisis solved.

"President Kennedy should bomb the hell out of the Cubans," Mamaw stated.

Mamaw was particularly sensitive about Cuba—she regularly travelled there to gamble and Castro had closed down most of the casinos.

"Did anyone notice Saddie Markham's new fake mink stole in Church?" Mamaw continued.

Every meal was graced by Mamaw's Prussian imported silver and monogrammed starched white 1500 count Egyptian cotton napkins. Daddy Ray sat at the head of the table, and we sat as far away from him as Mammy Lee could place us—he hated the way little kids ate. I remember quietly contemplating deeper things about life as I strategized how to get rid of the collard greens on my plate without needing to eat the darn things. At times we stared into the beautiful, cut-crystal chandeliers and for a moment were sure that Vicksburg had not fallen and the Yankees had not pillaged Arkansas Post.

We were tacitly committed to rules and regulations that govern our behavior. As Emily Post reminded us, knives were placed to the right of the plate and, once used, they should be placed on the right upper edge of the plate on a 45-degree angle (so as not to soil the host/hostess's tablecloth). These simple and sometimes picayune rules governed our social lives. According to these spoken and unspoken customs, we judged the worth of one another and conducted the shank of our social interaction.

Our dining room was adorned with four floor-to-ceiling French doors bearing leaded glass with etched art portraying Moses leading the children of Israel across the Red Sea.

The kitchen was strategically placed, close enough to the dining room to make food presentation quick and efficient. It was far enough away to keep the heat from the kitchen, literarily and figuratively, from the dining room.

The kitchen floor and fireplace hearth were made of authentic New Orleans street cobblestones that Mamaw bought from a street vendor. On warm winter evenings, the stove and fireplace heated the dormant horse urine and mixed it with southern cooking and smoky hickory logs to give the House a peculiar ambience.

No one ever worried about dropping food on the kitchen floor. Mammy Lee ignored dirt and grime and spread wet sticky wax over whatever was on the floor. We all felt previous culinary masterpieces shellacked beneath our feet.

In the right corner under the mixer was a stain from a memorable chili dinner last December. Mammy's chili was legendary, the best in southeast Arkansas. On the other hand, the green English peas under the right edge of the icebox were a nightmare I would gladly forget.

Every morning my older brother, Little Martin, had two fried eggs, with yolks broken and grizzled edges. I had two eggs over easy, with running yolks. We both loved thick bacon with heavy rind. My big brother was so good to me: he sometimes shared his precious treasure with his little brother.

"Here ya go Jake," Little Martin smiled as he handed me my gourmet snack.

He yanked that bacon rind out of his mouth and gave it to me to chew. Little Martin was a generous soul.

"Thank you," I responded as I gladly shared the load of chewing bacon rind with my older brother.

On the other hand, my younger brother, Henry, inevitably preferred leftover cornbread, buttermilk, and copious amounts of cane sugar.

Mammy Lee would top everything off with fresh squeezed orange juice. Only when I went to college did I learn of other ways to produce and preserve orange juice.

On the common days, I didn't know what breakfast was like in the dining room, but in the kitchen it was a veritable cornucopia of joy. We were polite to one another. We shared our homemade preserves and bacon. There was a surplus of good feelings and easy talk. And we did not worry about dropping things on the floor. To assure later good memories, we purposely deposited a few memorable items. I wonder if that bacon rind was still where I dropped it fifty years ago.

The kitchen was not the dining room, which taught us that life had limits and ceremony. We did not mind. Life was that way too. The kitchen was not the dining room with crystal chandeliers, but it was comfortable and full of disarming charm.

Second in importance to the kitchen was the bedroom.

I loved my old rusty spring bed with a tight-fitted sheet. I lived in a little room that I shared with my brother Little Martin. Outside our window was an apple tree and an in-ground pond that housed overfed, luminous orange carp. This room remained—even in my memory, even after the room and its house was gone, even on the cusp of my sixtieth year—a place of safety, comfort, and domicile. It was the place to which I came as a child and from which I left as a young man. It was where I learned to know my oldest brother. Two-year-old Little Martin met me when I came from Chicot County Memorial Hospital, and to a growing extent my care was transferred from Chicot Memorial to my brother's tutelage. I learned so much in the eight years that we both lived in that room.

Little Martin and I had our own twin beds.

On these summer mornings in the 1950s, there was something exquisitely exciting about jumping into the abyss of life from my open-spring twin bed. Little Martin, the inveterate fussy, neat roommate, carefully placed his possessions on his own side of the room. On the other hand, I, a poster boy for reckless abandon, placed my possessions wherever spirit and convenience dictated. My property, no less valuable because it was always lost somewhere, was everywhere and nowhere in our shared abode. My plastic soldiers could be under the lamp—boy, those warriors could really attack an Achilles tendon. My used underwear, from last week, might be next to the chester drawers.

My older brother was also very wise. He differentiated himself from my chaos from an early age.

"Jake, stay on your side of the room!"

As I launched out of my bed every morning to visit the veranda, I had no way to predict what dispossessed toy or orphan sock might welcome my invading tiny feet, but I knew that the safest destination was toward my older brother's country since his floor was always free of feet-hurting debris. I learned about grace when I occasionally experienced a clean, cool wooden floorboard and dutifully practiced thankfulness after such a gift.

I rushed down the stairs to stand on the veranda. I opened my toes and pressed them down on the chilly, seductive sky-blue tiles, which militated late-summer Arkansas afternoons. I wickedly pulled down my pajama bottoms and placed my white, virginal butt on the cool, inviting tiles. The world was good, wholesome, and safe when you could put your butt on cool tiles.

There was a problem with Arkansas's chilly vine-covered verandas. Slimy, emerald grass snakes slithered through wooden lattices, graced with creeping blue bonnets. Shy grass snakes, neither dangerous nor aggressive, lingered in our veranda foliage.

Green snakes carefully avoided our scrutiny and yet performed a thankless service, eating bugs, mosquitoes, and even small mice that invaded our veranda. Weak in character, we preferred bugs and mosquitoes to slippery grass snakes with tongues flashing prophetic warnings to their human hosts.

Inconvenient snakes complicated things in other ways. As the summer progressed, I lost more and more precious items in the foliage. A baseball, a balsa wood P-38 Lightning (twin fuselage) heavy fighter aircraft, a deflated birthday balloon—all were inadvertently deposited into the living room of these little scary reptiles. As far as I was concerned, precious things were on loan to the grass snakes until December when killing frost dissolved foliage into a mass of angry, brown compost that littered the entire veranda. Like pieces of discarded hope, forgotten memories, and shed tears, the brown leaves, which once promised such succor and hope, were now only ugly brown splotches on the sky-blue tiles.

I was in despair.

The end of the luxuriant foliage presaged the departure of the nasty grass snakes. Yes, they were gone! The waning winter sun surreptitiously revealed vanished baseballs, marbles, broken kites, and birthday favors.

We found all the good things that we thought we had lost. Some were forgotten; some we expected never to find. Now, with the advent of winter, lostness was replaced with foundness. Our souls rejoiced!

The veranda, though, was on the edge of my life. My bed, my bedroom, and my roommate were at the cardinal point of my existence. They were directly above the hypocenter of my being, the point where my soul and essence originated. My ancient bed, decrepit and old, was to me the defining moment of my young life. I had my own bed and my own brother. Even at 59 I sometimes wake in the night and reach across time and space for my big brother.

I loved jumping on my bed. I loved jumping on Little Martin's bed. This was not play to me: I was in training for the circus.

My favorite Walt Disney movie was Toby Tyler. Toby Tyler ran away to the circus (something I fervently wished to do), where he soon befriended Mr. Stubbs, the hilarious chimpanzee. He had all sorts of adventures and fell in love with Mademoiselle Jeanette, just as I did. Someday I would marry a circus queen, who sailed through the air with the greatest of ease on trapeze poles.

At 59 I still wondered what happened. I gave up the twirling life of a highflying trapeze artists for the earthy calling of writing.

I checked on Anna.

Anna was standing over our stainless steel propane stove. She was humming choruses. "What can wash away my sins, nothing but the blood of Jesus? Oh precious is the flow . . . "

She wore jeans and a light blue turtleneck that accentuated her best features while hiding her worst. Her silver hair reflected the rays of the early spring sun. For a moment I could not breath.

She was preparing my birthday dinner—no Tilapia in sight—good wholesome beef chunk chili with whole tomatoes and cheddar cheese Mexican cornbread with jalapeno peppers.

Interrupted, Anna asked, "Jacob, why in the world would you choose chili for your birthday dinner?"

"Je vous désirez plus que la nourriture, ma femme chérie!"

"Jacob, I took German in college, not French."

"Ich wünsche Ihnen mehr als Nahrung, mein Liebling Frau!"

"Vielen Dank. Sie wollen mich zu Tilapia kochen? "

"Well obviously you won't cook me fried chicken and turnip greens, right? Or squirrel brains? I need some comfort food honey," I responded.

"Chili and cornbread, seem about right," she said.

Anna's chili was even better than Mammy Lee's and her cornbread, based on Mammy's recipe, benefited from Anna's improvisations and was the best I had ever had. On the side Anna had stacked Polish dill pickles in a white bowl. My cup runneth over!

"Honey would you run away with me and join the circus?"

"Absolutely. Meanwhile, will you set the table?"

# 19

I NIBBLED ON ANNA'S EAR.

"Leave me alone Jacob."

"Anna, I wonder what happened to Mammy Lee?"

We both poured ourselves another glass of wine—I preferred a chilled Italian Pinot Grigio and Anna usually chose a Chilean Malbec.

For generations, the Stevens boys had had their own mammy. Dad had Orleander. I had Lee.

White southerners created the Mammy myth to redeem the relationship between black women and white men severely eroded by the Civil War. 100 years after the War, southerners, especially males, held fast to the myth of the mammy to claim that the racial problem was solved.

Armed with collard greens, black-eyed peas, and a sturdy dusting cloth, my mammy, and women like her, affectionately called "girls," or "the help," single-handedly maintained this fragile world that was Jim Crow Arkansas. Mammy Lee was parent, servant, and benevolent despot all rolled into one. This 285-pound, six-foot tall, woman was omnipresent. Chewing tobacco, limping slightly, and occasionally rubbing a lucky Mercury-head dime tied around her ankle with kite string, Mammy propelled me forward through all adversity. She helped me interpret reality and assuaged youthful insecurities with cornbread and ceaseless love.

Mammy was there when I walked for the first time. She dressed me each morning—until I was age 5! She combed my hair before I went to school. Asked me how it went when I returned.

"How was school? Did you take any tests? Did you do well? Did you behave?"

She taught me to pray, to sing, and to whistle.

"Mr. Jake youse have to listen to God as well as speak to Him."

She taught me how to blow bubbles with Bazooka Bubble Gum.

"Hold your mouth just so, put your tongue into the gum, and then blow. Like this!"

A magnificent pink bubble enveloped her substantial lips and would have floated her to the moon if she were not so heavy.

Mammy was there when I lost my first tooth and told me about the tooth fairy. She refuted claims by my peers that there was no Santa Claus.

"Jake those children know they won't get anything for Christmas."

I believed her. She cooked for me. She decided, who my friends would be. She insisted that I lower the toilet seat after tinkling—something I never quite grasped, as Anna will attest—since after all there were four males and one female (Mammy did not count since she used the bathroom in her garage apartment).

We memorized books of the Bible in order. She taught me to sing "This Little Light of Mine" and "Deep and Wide."

"This little light of mine," we sang, "I'm going to let is shine."

"Put it under a bushel——NO!"

Mammy and her white boy were certainly not going to put their lights under any bushel baskets.

Mammy Lee showed me where to find the fattest and longest fishing worms.

"Put a wet blanket on the ground, Mr. Jake," Mammy advised. "And tomorrow morning you will have the best fishing worms in southeast Arkansas."

And Mammy was right. She was right about a lot of things.

We dug for pirate treasure. We buried time capsules in the Delta soil, anticipating the day that we together would retrieve them. That day never came and earthworms and shrews are playing with my cat-eye marbles and silver jacks.

She taught me to speak. I spoke, I still speak, with a slight Ebonics edge. She told me about the disciples, Moses, and Zachariah. She taught me my multiplication tables, how to yo yo, and how to hold my breath under water.

Other adults, including my parents, macromanaged my life, but it was Mammy Lee, who actually was in my daily life. Mammy Lee empowered my soul to be all that I would later be. Notwithstanding the injustice of the whole arrangement, I loved Mammy with as much love as I have ever loved a person in my life.

In short, because she was not my parent, she was more than a parent. It was as if she, and I, did not know where to draw the line. There were no boundaries on our love. I loved her far beyond what her role could have asked.

Such a love can change a life.

Mammy called me "Mr. Jake" and she said "yes sir" and "no sir" to me——even when I was in pre-school! We all knew, who was in charge of this world. But, somehow she managed to love me anyway.

I can still feel her as she held me and squeezed, as if a hug and a shake could cure anything! She smelled like garlic and everything about her was epic in volume, size, and proportion.

There was desperation about Lee. Her world was changing quickly, too quickly, and her discomfort grew. I loved Lee, I loved my homeland, this way of life, and in a way, and they—Mammy Lee and my south—were one and the same.

I talked to Mammy about Bo.

"Child, they is some bad people in the world. No doubt about it. But God is in control and He will judge the good and the bad," she said.

"Then Uncle Evan is going to Hell?" Uncle Evan's eternal destination has been an issue of speculation all my life.

"Maybe. Judging and so forth ain't our job. We is just to love one another and try to forgive," Mammy offered.

Mammy continued to discuss Bo.

"Bo in a better place, Mr. Jake, he is with his daddy in Heaven," Mammy explained. "He ain't got no pain, no sorrows."

I had never heard God called "daddy." Seemed sacrilegious to me. "Mammy, does God like to hunt squirrels?"

"No, no. I means God loves us like a daddy does his childrens. He not a mean old cuss that don't love his children. He not like Mr. Evan who judges people according to their color. He love everybody."

Mammy always was a gifted theologian. She could explain inscrutable theological concepts in the most elementary terms.

"We gonna see Bo someday, Mr. Jake," Mammy continued. "And he gonna meet us at the pearly gates!"

Mammy loved a white boy, who ranked her in every way, but who desperately needed her nurturing care and direction. She never disappointed me. She was never too busy to pull me in her lap and let me rest in her arms.

She chose to love me and wherever I go, whatever I will become, I carry with me the love I received from Mammy. She was the first person who really knew and accepted me just as I am, have been, and will be.

Mammy really listened to me and to have someone listen to you is a sort of religious experience. Real listening is a kind of prayer, for as she listened, she penetrated through human ego to my heart. My times with Mammy Lee, and even my memories of being with Mammy Lee, left me with a sense of awe that it felt like I had entered into a holy place and communed with the heart of being itself.

# 20

ANNA CONTINUED STIRRING the chili.

I loved to watch Anna cook. Not only was I rewarded with her excellent cuisine, but I also loved to be near her. She was always so busy! Her life pulled her in so many directions! But cooking required concentrated effort in one direction at one place. That left the rest of her open to me!

I would wash dishes, set the table—anything to spend time with her. We would drink wine together; review the day; talk about our children and grandchildren. We were always amazed at what a great job we did. Our mutual congratulatory nepotism, if slightly exaggerated, was harmless enough.

I could not get enough of Anna. In truth, I was spoiled. For over thirty years I had mostly worked out of our home—it was either the church office or my writing den for almost my entire career. Anna, too, besides spending several years teaching, worked at home too. I was grateful for this on my 59th birthday. . .

TJ, the only son of Mammy Lee, loved sound: the guttural rumble of an approaching diesel locomotive haltingly moving through nearby railroad yards, the whoosh of a speeding auto across the nearby aqueduct bypass. TJ sat in awe as the whirling roundhouse deftly tamed an angry juggernaut and changed its direction with the greatest of ease.

TJ and I both listened to the same trains. I heard them from Mamaw's house; TJ heard them from his mother's shack on Railroad Street.

TJ knew the sound of each locomotive. Each one had its signature noise. The Tennessee Queen pulled into the round house——which quite literally was 200 yards from his house——every night at 9PM. It was an old steam engine and would be replaced by a diesel locomotive before he was thirteen. He loved to hear the old Tennessee approach the round house, and like a tired horse, release hissing steam in both celebration of the end of a run and the anticipation of the beginning of another.

"Welcome home old girl!" TJ smiled.

A locomotive—not the Tennessee Queen—brought my grandfather home from Monroe or New Orleans or Memphis. He did not know my grandfather, nor did he yet know me. He merely felt the rumble of the train and heard the clap of the brakes. There was no metaphor attached, for none of his people worked on the railroad. So we shared the same sensory experience, but in a different universe.

Above all, we shared his mother, Mammy Lee. Mammy was my mom from Monday to Saturday noon, and then his mom for the next day and a half.

The world into which TJ was born was, on one level, dark and foreboding. He was born in an old shack next to the railroad tracks. It was a well-maintained house, but hardly more than a shanty. Or so it looked to me, a boy, who lived in a veritable mansion. TJ's house was only whitewashed, not painted. It was from an old Jerome, Arkansas, German prison camp barracks; my dad purchased it for Mammy Lee at a modest price, and it was moved by Marcos Bertucci, who, in spite of the fact that he was an ex-World War II Italian prisoner of war, considered a Jerome Prison camp and later Pedlam to be a better place to live than Milan, Italy.

There was no plumbing in the house, only an outside pump shared with TJ's neighbor. In spite of water being everywhere abundant, after being primed the old mechanical suction hand pump dispensed water with severe parsimony, as if it begrudged the partakers any notion of generosity and plenty. The front porch of TJ's house was slightly sagging on the south corner. On the porch was a barrel planter full of daffodil bulbs that burst out in gracious yellow beauty for one brief moment in early spring.

There was no light to draw anyone home. There were no streetlights in colored town. Electricity was available, and black residents paid taxes, but Pedlam city officials discouraged all interaction between the white and black communities that was not monitored by and beneficial to the white community. Commingling with blacks in the same soft, white street illumination was too much for white Pedlam to chance. Besides, light in colored town was superfluous. Blacks did not need to be out after dark and, if they were, it was the consensus of white Pedlam that they were up to no good.

Darkness suited TJ just fine. In the summer he would sit on his porch, holding an RC Cola or sweet tea, being careful to compensate for the sloping front porch, and enjoyed the pure, pristine southern night sky that was undiluted by precious white Pedlam light.

Every afternoon, TJ closely examined his pet, Zedediah, a Walker Collie mix, for fat blood-sucking ticks. He carefully extracted them from Zedediah's ear or leg and squashed them on the sidewalk. Over time he created a sort of macabre smiley face as if to warn marauding miniature trespassers that TJ's house meant death and destruction.

Black Pedlam found that race mixing inevitably led to white exploitation. In Pedlam, race mixing was both a social concern as much as a biological concern. The determination of boundaries between human groups was something to which white Pedlam gave its utmost attention.

We did not want to live next to people of another "race" or have our children go to school with them or attend church with them. Thus there was no meaningful interaction between whites and blacks in any Pedlam institution except in ways that were defined and strictly controlled by whites—and the whites liked it that way.

But, so did most blacks. Mammy Lee and TJ liked living in a place where there were few whites. They preferred it that way. Our white superiority was based not on natural, biological premises, but on property and terror. Black Pedlam correctly perceived that racism was more than individual bad choices by whites: it was a systemic phenomenon, an evil power. And blacks wanted no part of it.

To some people, marriage across the color line spelled the eventual end of white hegemony maintained by separatism. Yet others regarded it as a blatant sellout to systemic evil. Racial mixing stood as a powerful reminder of subjugation and domination. The memory of black-white mixing abuse (masters' demanding sexual favors from black slaves) was stronger than the promise of sustaining multiethnic relationships. The black church, the most sanguine of black institutions, therefore tacitly embraced segregation because historically such mixing brought exploitation to black families.

"TJ," Mammy explained, "Generally white folks needs to be kept at a distance. They can help you, but they can just as fast hurt you. Work with them if you must. Get in and then get out."

In short, black Pedlam knew that, when they mixed with whites, they inevitably got the short end of the stick. Moreover, all week the Pedlam blacks were abused by white privilege. There was no great desire to have whites in their churches on Sunday morning or in their homes the rest of the week. Hence the Pedlam community, white and black, held a substantial and mostly overt aversion toward race mixing.

Most of the black community opposed integration of any sort, including school integration. Black leaders observed that interaction with white Americans ultimately led to blacks' being ancillary, subordinate, and abused.

Yet the truth was that TJ never thought about such injustice at all. Colored town was full of extended family and friends. It was safe and inviting. All were equally subordinate to the whites and this created a sort of blessed, friendly egalitarianism.

While Mammy took care of me, TJ lived next door with his absent father's sister. On the weekend he came home to live with his mom. TJ did not take it well. He missed his mother a great deal, and he cried when she left on Monday morning. He would sit on his porch every Saturday afternoon when my dad brought her home. Sometimes I would go with Dad. I did not enjoy seeing TJ hug my Mammy with such proprietary enthusiasm.

TJ was my age, born a few months before me. My parents allowed Mammy to take a few weeks off, but by the time I was born, Mammy had returned. In fact, Mammy nursed TJ and me during the first few months of my life—although eventually TJ abdicated to me. I loved the feel of her breasts on my youthful cheeks and it was my place of refuge in moments of crisis.

All that I gained, TJ lost.

I wept when she left me on Saturday afternoon and TJ wept when my mother picked her up Monday morning. Yet, in one-way TJ held an advantage. Mammy's husband, TJ's father, had hoboed on a train when TJ was three and no one saw him again. On Saturday and Sunday night TJ slept with his mom. I knew this was true because Mammy talked about it.

"I'se gonna snuggle with you Mr. Jake like I snuggle with my TJ," she laughed.

But my "snuggle" was a controlled hug and nothing like the generous affection that TJ experienced. I once asked mom if Mammy could sleep with me.

"No, Jake. Nigras do sleep in white people's houses."

So I experienced reverse discrimination: the one I most loved could only be mine from 9-5 and never on weekends.

TJ and I were brothers, who never met, never were to meet.

# 21

Donny Baleigh Jones and Floyd William Stuart were sure that they were the most fortunate boys in Choctaw County. They were returning from the Venetian Café in Greenville, Mississippi, in Donny's 1948 black Ford truck. Their truck tires were humming on the pavement that was slowly recovering from a late April 85 degree-day. Donny had bought what he thought were mud tires, but in fact they were snow tires that Mr. Dubois had craftily sold Donny. They just looked cool to Donny, who had no idea what real mud tires looked like and did not care much anyway. The Ford Truck, with a floor starter, and real spare, was, without a doubt, one of the coolest vehicles in the Arkansas Delta.

18-year-old Donny bought 17-year-old Floyd his first Budweiser. Donny initiated his good friend Floyd into the adult world by treating Floyd to lasagna and to Budweiser.

"To our moms and to our country," Donny toasted.

"To the Falcons and to my good friend, Donny," Floyd reciprocated.

At the night's end neither boy was drunk—neither could afford to buy more than one beer—but both were inebriated by the prospect of what great things were coming. Donny Baleigh Jones and Floyd William Stuart were United States Marines, or would be. Both were due to report to the Marine Corps at Camp Pendleton by the end of the week. They would leave on a Continental Trailways bus in the morning and this was, in their estimation, a fitting closure to their adolescence and the beginning of their adulthood.

Both boys had grown up on Canebrake Bayou, Pedlam, Arkansas. Canebrake Bayou, previously called South Highway, was a community enclosed by colored town on the West and the Choctaw Country Club on the East. It was an amalgamation of some of these richest, and poorest, white citizens of Pedlam, Arkansas.

Neither boy had been on an interstate highway, but in 1965 there were not that many around anyway. Donny and Floyd were on the Pedlam Falcon football team. They were never starters, but managed to obtain the coveted Pedlam Falcon sport's jacket with an embroidered golden falcon and the letter "F." In Pedlam parlance, these possessions were better than gold.

Nor could they rate the cheerleaders, as far as girls go, but did manage to date clarinet and flute players in the band.

By all estimation they were good boys. They attended Pedlam First United Methodist Church and were active in the United Methodist Youth Group.

They loved God, Pedlam Falcons, and the United States of America, in that order.

The black Ford sped along State Highway 82 across the narrow Greenville Mississippi River Bridge. The old truck bounced over expansion joints that were really not needed in tropical southern Arkansas.

The WPA in the Great Depression built the Greenville Bridge and participants were expected to pay for it for the next generation. A modest toll was exacted for each passenger. Also, after a Boll Weevil infestation in 1948, the Mississippi State Police stopped and examined each entering vehicle. Apparently

Mississippi boll weevils were less virulent, because Arkansas authorities did not bother to examine cars from Mississippi. Pedlam youth, just for the fun of it, would often hide friends in the trunks of cars.

Mississippi State Highway 82 became Arkansas State 144 on the Arkansas side. The road and the state police were friendlier.

Eutaw was only a few miles from the Bridge and the boys were not speeding. Why should they? They wanted to enjoy this night for the rest of their lives! Grand Lake was on their right and on their left was the El Chico Restaurant that had the best Mexican food in three states.

But Donny and Floyd had no time for chicken enchiladas. For one thing, they were exhausted. They were farm boys and were used to getting up early in the morning. Neither enjoyed late nights and nine o'clock was a late night.

They were both excited. Tomorrow was to be their first intrastate bus ride. They planned to sit together in the front seat. Riding in the front seat made them feel as if they were in the best seat of a Ferris wheel, every turn extended them into open air. They had always wanted to get that seat on the school bus from Canebrake Bayou, but Dubby Boyles had made them sit in the middle of the bus, closest to the black kids as they could be. Bubby Boyles wasn't going to be on the bus tomorrow and moreover, they deserved to sit wherever they wanted—they were joining the Corps.

Jed King, who lived a few houses down from Donny, joined the US Marines in 1962. In early 1965 the North Vietnamese 324B Division crossed the Demilitarized Zone (DMZ) and attacked Jed's 3rd Marine Division. The battle was won, but shrapnel severed Jed's spinal cord and he would never walk again.

Marines were not drafting, at least not yet. That would come later. Two boys for the U. S. Army and one boy for the U. S. Marines. That was why Cooter Roberts reported to the Draft Board thinking he was going into the Army and ended up in the Marines. It was all the same to him.

But Donny and Floyd volunteered. They wanted to serve in the Corps. Floyd's daddy had to grant special permission, but both boys were accepted.

They joined up to honor Jed. They got the idea by watching a John Wayne movie The Sons of Katie Elder. In that movie, the brothers honored their deceased mother, and in Donny and Floyd's estimation, their country, by banding together and taking care of each other. Donny and Floyd were impressed by the filial fidelity exhibited among these sibling boys.

John Elder, played by John Wayne, speaking to the youngest brother Bud, "All we want to do is make you end up rich and respectable. You fight us every step of the way."

Bud Elder played by Michael Anderson, Jr., responded, "I don't want to be rich and respectable. I want to be just like the rest of you."

The Sons of Katie Elder, Donny, and Floyd found something bigger than themselves and intended to embrace it with gusto.

The Ford turned north at Eutaw and headed straight toward Pedlam. Floyd was fast asleep.

Donny and Floyd crossed the Choctaw County Line about halfway between Eutaw and Pedlam at the Twin City Diner. This gaudy truck stop was neither a diner nor between two cities. In fact, neither Pedlam nor Eutaw officially was a "city" since neither town offered more than 4000 residents. Nor was it a diner. The small café's modest menu, offered three choices—hamburger and fries, eggs and fries, or hot dogs and fries.

Donny needed to buy gasoline. He was reluctant to buy fuel at Twin Cities. The Esso station was the most expensive gas in Choctaw County—$.39/gallon. It preyed on unwary outsiders traveling between Little Rock, Arkansas, and Vicksburg, Mississippi. Choctaw County visitors were used to paying such exorbitant prices in Little Rock or Fort Smith and didn't seem to mind paying similar prices down here. Donny minded though. And he was sure that Floyd would not pitch in.

Donny pulled up behind a 1964 Ford Falcon with New York License plate MZX 248. The blue and white license plate was, in Donny's estimation, the ugliest thing he had ever seen. It made Donny proud to think that his license plate was red and white and had "Land of Opportunity" in blue on the bottom. He added a "Pedlam Falcon" vanity plate up front.

A gasoline attendant was servicing the New York car. On the driver's side was a young man, who was about Donny's age. He had entered Twin Cities Café to pay for his gas. Another kid about thirteen or fourteen years old, sat on the rider's side. Both were black.

Donny thought he knew the kid, but could not recall his name. He had never seen the other driver.

The driver lit a Pall Mall and held the door for Mattie Sue, one of the waitresses, at Twin Cities. With great skill, the young man held the door, lit his cigarette, and smiled at Mattie Sue as she entered.

Mattie Sue, wearing an industrial, standard waitress outfit that included frills on both sleeves and a white collar, was coming to work.

"Thank you," Mattie Sue said, making eye contact with the young man. "Haven't seen you around before have I?" she flirted.

"No, not from these parts."

"Where are you from?"

Still holding the door, the young man smiled, "New York City."

"Wow! I have always wanted to go there."

"Honey you can come home with me anytime!"

Mattie Sue smiled encouragingly.

"How about we get together after your shift and plan our trip?" the young man pursued.

"Sure. I am off at 11."

"Let me take my nephew home and I will come back and get you."

The young man leaned down and kissed Mattie Sue on the cheek and whispered something in her ear. She laughed.

Donny was initially impressed with such skill——to light a cigarette, hold a door, and to talk to Mattie Sue for so long was no small feat——but then Donny was outraged.

He had never witnessed such a time——a black man kissing a white woman in that way.

The kid, on the rider's side was horrified too, and then, fearful. His cousin from New York City might do such a harmless act in Brooklyn, but not in Choctaw County.

"Let's go! Quickly!" the young boy exclaimed.

His older cousin, however, was in no hurry and slowly pulled out of the Twin Cities Esso onto Highway 144 and headed north to Pedlam.

Donny, with disorienting rage, entered the station office that connected with the Twin Cities Café, and paid the attendant.

"Mattie Sue," Donny asked, "Are you all right?"

"What? Sure Donny, what's up?"

Donny did not answer. He was a Marine and he knew what he had to do.

With clenched fists, he walked back to his truck and grabbed his dad's Smith and Wesson 22 magnum single shot pistol from behind the seat. It was no big deal. Every pickup truck south of the Mason Dixon Line carried at least one weapon, usually two.

Without waking Floyd, Donny loaded the 22 and held it in his right hand on his lap.

Then he sped down Highway 144 toward the Falcon, which was carefully staying within the speed limit.

Within two miles, he pulled next to the Falcon and then forced it off the road. He authoritatively parked in front of it.

Donny calmly stepped out of his truck, like Jimmy Stewart approached Liberty Valence in *The Man Who Shot Liberty Valence*.

Under his breath Donny hummed James Taylor's title song:

> When Liberty Valance rode to town
> The women folk would hide, they'd hide.
> When Liberty Valance walked around
> The men would step aside
> Cause the point of a gun was the only law
> That Liberty understood.
> When it came to shootin' straight and fast,
> He was mighty good.

Rolling down his window, Elrod, in a New York accent exclaimed in consternation, "What the Hell!"

Donny made no reply and raised his pistol.

Elrod saw Donny's pistol. He quickly turned to warn his nephew.

The muzzle flash burned Elrod's ear and the whizzing 22 round entered the back of his head and deposited skull bone, brain matter, and blood onto TJ. The bullet continued through TJ's right hand that he put up to defend himself and into the car door frame.

Elrod's blood sprayed on Donny's right cheek too. He instinctively wiped it on his hand and then on Elrod's shirt.

While Donny coolly reloaded the magnum, TJ, crying, struggled to open the car door with his left hand. Even at this desperate moment TJ knew it was futile to beg for mercy.

"Bang!" The penetrating 22 bullet passed through TJ's cerebellum and, like the first shot, lodged in the rider's door.

The shot was not fatal. With his clouded eyes wide open, and gasping for breath, TJ suffocated on his own blood. Gory bubbles gurgled from his open mouth.

Brown eyes staring into space, Elrod and TJ quivered for a moment and then died.

It took Donny less than a minute to kill both boys. It felt good. The acrid gunfire smoke, and the sweet smell of fresh blood reminded Donny of deer hunting with his dad. He dipped his index finger into Elrod's blood and licked it. It tasted like warm, salty caramel.

The gunfire woke up Floyd, who exclaimed, "What the Hell!"

The irony of the repeated comment that Donny had heard twice within the last minute was not lost on him. He smiled.

The Ford Falcon engine purred in thoughtful repose on the side of Highway 144. To Donny it appeared that the boys might be sleeping. Or perhaps they were spotlighting deer. Or maybe they needed to relieve themselves.

Remembering this dad's admonition, 'Donny, make sure your weapon is unloaded and always wipe off your print marks before they rust the barrel,' Donny returned to his truck and carefully sprayed and then wiped off his dad's 22 magnum with WD 40 oil, which every Arkansan kept in his truck for just such a need. Quickly he wrapped the 22 in an old, soiled white T-shirt, and returned it to the back of his truck seat.

He liked the smell of WD 40 but it was not as pleasant as the smell of blood. He suddenly realized that this was his last night at home for a long time and it might be years before he could go hunting again. He was as pensive as a Quaker in morning meeting.

Floyd, too, perhaps, grasped the gravity of the occasion and said nothing else.

The truck was idling in unison with the Falcon and at first refused to break fellowship when Donny manually shifted the gear into first.

The old Ford groaned, and then lurched forward onto Highway 144.

Donny rolled down his window. He heard the hum of locusts and the chirp of crickets. A barn owl hooted. On the radio Johnny Cash sang, "I keep a close watch on this heart of mine. I keep my eyes wide open all the time." The evening was full of a pleasant EPN toxophene insecticide smell that had been sprayed on nearby cotton fields.

Donny turned right onto Highway 28 at the abandoned Stevenson farmhouse and drove with purpose and calmness to River Bend, Arkansas, to turn himself into Sheriff Cletus Compton.

## 22

THE CHOCTAW COUNTY COURTHOUSE in Riverbend, Arkansas, was a white, impressive dwelling. Built when the Mississippi River still lapped the edge of the levee, the courthouse presaged decades of prosperity and growth. It was made even more remarkable since no physical structure equaled, much less surpassed, the courthouse. It was the indisputable pinnacle in Choctaw County. Dedicated to the Masonic order, its virile copper dome replicated a phallic symbol.

An opera house performed Carmen and Rigoletto. It was also used as an unofficial city hall; at other times, it became a dance hall, and Riverbend residents enjoyed Memphis Blues and Dixieland Jazz. The opera house was also the location for boxing and wrestling exhibitions, including an exhibition by John L. Sullivan and Jack Dempsey. The town had several churches and two doctors by this time. Old Wormwood had his following too—14 saloons lined the levee offering imbibing spirits and fleshly diversions.

However, the Mississippi River changed course and abandoned Riverbend, the 1927 Flood devastated the community, and by the 1960s it was a shell of a town. The impressive Courthouse, with its 1927 Flood marks, was a crouching mastodon dispensing judicial justice and fiduciary benevolence to its adoring subjects.

Fifty-five year old, six foot two inch, stocky and determined both in body and demeanor, with grey free brown hair Sheriff Cletus Compton drew strength from his office. He dressed in a khaki uniform, with a dark brown hat banded with a black ribbon tied with two gold pistols dangling at the end. On his right index finger was a gaudy Masonic ring. When Cletus was excited the golden pistols danced on the flap of his hat. They were dancing now.

Donny had explained, in great detail, how he had shot the two boys. He did so with forced calmness. He did not feel any remorse, but he did worry about what Sheriff Compton would say. In that sense, Donny and Floyd, were very upset.

He placed the hand with the Masonic ring on Donny Baleigh Jones' shoulder.

"Donny and Floyd! For God's sake boys! Why did you do this the night before you left?"

The two boys and Sheriff Compton were standing in the Courthouse parking lot. The boys caught Cletus as he was leaving work. He only lived a few blocks away and was walking home for supper.

"Sheriff we was . . ."

Cletus interrupted the boys before they answered his question.

"Wait here, boys. I will be back in a few minutes."

Cletus had to stop his deputy, Dishough Morris, before he departed.

Dishough was an archetypal Choctaw good old boy—five foot eight, 180 pounds, and an impressive beer gut. He smoked Virginia Slims Menthols and dared anyone to tease him.

He had the night shift, but Cletus had sent him home—there was only one prisoner. Cletus sent him home too—he had knifed another black man at a bar in Reed, Arkansas, the night before, but clearly the man was contrite and his victim was going to live anyway.

The remorseful prisoner was following Dishough down the steps.

"Send the boy home, Dishough, and wait for me at the police car."

"Yes sir, Sheriff." Deputy Dishough was always formal with his boss when others could hear."

"Sheriff, is that the Jones' truck?"

"Yeah, Dishough. I will tell you about it in a minute."

Cletus paused for a moment and spit tobacco juice on the parking lot.

Cletus walked back to Donny and Floyd.

Donny and Floyd were noticeably upset. Donny was playing with his shirt buttons and Floyd stood with his hands in his pockets. Both looked down to the ground.

"Boys," Cletus continued, "You are both stupid crackers."

"Sheriff Compton, the nigger was kissing Mattie Sue!" Donny offered.

Floyd shook his head in agreement.

"Hell, boys, everybody kisses Mattie Sue. It ain't worth killng a couple of nigras. Couldn't you just have scared 'em or something? Did you have to blow their brains out?" Cletus replied with genuine consternation.

The two U. S. Marines appeared to be ready to cry.

"Well, the deed is done," Cletus said with profound finality, and some disgust. "Ain't nothing we can do about it now."

Those boys were wrong to shoot those two blacks, especially on the last night home. This could ruin their careers. It would ruin their families if folks found out. Those boys were stupid to do such a thing.

On the distant Mississippi River, a riverboat blew its foghorn. It was a hopeful sound, even though everyone knew it would never again be sounded next to the River Bend levee.

"Go on home boys," Cletus sighed. He was tempted to lecture them but it seemed futile.

"Don't tell anyone. I will tell your daddies and anyone else, who might need to know," Cletus said.

Cletus would do it. Once, when he was 14 he had taken his much much-loved black lab Lucky to the woods and shot her. Lucky was in misery and his dad could not afford a vet. So Cletus took care of business. The family supposed Lucky just wandered off. Cletus never told anyone the truth. The benign untruth was preferable to the hurting truth.

"For now don't tell anyone, do you 'her me, boys? No one!"

"Yes sir, Sheriff."

"Semper fi," Cletus said.

The boys returned to their truck and Donny drove home with profound relief. It was barely 10PM.

Cletus was born in River Bend, Arkansas. He had never lived anywhere else. In 1948 he was elected sheriff. By 1965 he was wildly popular.

His office had twenty-five plaster death face impressions of his apprehended executed criminals. All were males and all were blacks. All had been executed in the electric chair at Cummins Prison Farm less than 30 miles away.

Not that the sheriff was opposed to rehabilitation. Cletus

regularly rehabilitated his white criminals, but experience had taught him that black crime required more circumspect interventions.

For one thing, blacks, especially males, according to Cletus, were prone to violence, especially against their own kind. Therefore, he felt it was both fair, and judicious, to ignore all of the non-violent black crime—prostitution for instance—and most of the violent crime—like bar fighting—as long as only blacks were involved. Sheriff Compton, a conscientious steward of county resources, mostly let blacks do between themselves whatever they pleased.

Murder, of course, even among blacks was a different matter. All white juries were quick to convict defendants. Twenty-five of these convicted murderers decorated Cletus' office. It saved the county a ton of money and no one really minded or cared, for that matter. At least none of his white constituency, which was the only one that mattered since none of the blacks voted anyway.

When a white killed a black, if there was justification, or an accident, Cletus ignored the whole thing.

The year before16 year old Homer Horton boy, while deer hunting, had accidently shot and killed a black man, Bugger Malone, following the deer dogs on a horse. The horse was killed too. Cletus told Homer's dad, Winchester, to ante-up for the dead horse and everyone was satisfied.

In a rare instance when a renegade black killed a white, in malfeasance or otherwise, Cletus quietly let the Klan take care of it. If for some reason the Klan, did not come through, Cletus arrested the alleged perpetrator and he was meted justice in a courtroom. The outcome, whether in the hands of the Klan, or in the hands of an all white jury, was the same. In the 19 years that Cletus had served as sheriff, not one single black was ever acquitted if he was charged with harming a white. He had a 100% conviction rate.

Cletus was a good and just lawman. To him criminal justice was sacred. Criminal justice was the system upholding and sustaining the laws of the land.

Sheriff Compton, a lifelong member of River Bend Baptist Church, understood that crime began with sin. Sin required some sort of retributive justice. The penalty for crime must be proportionate to the harm actually caused.

Thus, Sheriff Compton saw the law as righteous retribution. He was a law and order sheriff, but also understood that judgment could be softened by mercy. However, a better ideal, in his mind, was to keep the crime from ever happening at all.

In effect, this is the way Sheriff Compton proposed to handle the problem of the two dead black boys that Donny had shot. It would be as if the crime never happened at all.

Cletus and Dishough found the Ford Falcon still running on Highway 144.

Dishough knew his automobiles. A small, lightweight 90 hp straight-6 with a single-barrel carburetor, powered the 1964 Falcon. Body styles included two- and four-door sedans. This one was a two-door, with a New York license plate. Dishough had never driven such a fine automobile and was thrilled at the possibility.

One of the boys was slumped over the steering wheel. Dishough pushed him against the other. The driver fell against

TJ, whom Dishough knew, and his head banged the window. They looked like they were two best friends sleeping off a bad night.

Blood and cephalic matter, though, were everywhere.

Without any thought of preserving evidence, with paper towels that Dishough thoughtfully had brought from the Courthouse, he wiped the inside of the window and the steering wheel. Next, he spread a couple of Piggly Wiggly grocery sacks on the front car seat.

Cletus walked over to the Ford Falcon.

"Dishough," Cletus said. "Follow me."

Dishough felt completely comfortable driving with two corpses.

"Boys you should have known better than to touch a white woman, even if she is Mattie Sue," Dishough offered.

Then, in thoughtful sympathy, he added, "But it don't mean you had to die this way. It is a shame."

Later, at the Courthouse Cletus said, "Now Dishough, you know to keep quiet about this."

It was not a question.

High in the pantheon of southern morality was loyalty. Dishough would remain taciturn and Cletus could count on this and in the common sharing of this unfortunate event camaraderie blazed brilliantly. Like solder under a welder's torch, nothing could break the bond between these two men once they shared a secret and a promise.

It was 11:30 PM and Cletus had to unlock the Courthouse to phone his brother-in law, Raleigh Parmentier, the County Coroner.

Raleigh, like almost every coroner in Arkansas, was elected, not appointed, and very few had a medical degree. Raleigh in fact worked at the Dermott glove factory before his brother-in-law helped him get elected ten years ago.

"Raleigh, this is Cletus. How are you? How is the family?"

"Fine, Cletus. I was heading for bed," Raleigh finished. He wondered why Cletus was phoning so late—Cletus went to bed right after the 10 O'clock news.

Raleigh continued, "Thanks for asking. How about Laura Lou? The kids?"

"She is fine and so are the kids."

With a perfunctory tone unusual for Sheriff Cletus Compton, he said, "Raleigh, I need to tell you something. It cannot wait until the morning. I have a couple of dead nigra boys here. Murder suicide."

"Murder suicide?"

Cletus paused for effect.

"Yeah, murder suicide."

Cletus resisted asking his brother-in-law if he was hard of hearing.

"One boy shot the other one and then shot himself. They both died instantly."

Raleigh, discerning Cletus' impatience, was quick to move the exchange along.

"Those people can never keep their pants zipped and their liquor in their cupboards in a full moon."

"Don't know about the women Raleigh, but I am pretty sure these boys were drinking,"

Cletus doubted that they were indeed drinking. He knew

one of the boys was only 13.

"One of the boys was TJ, a Pedlam boy," he finished.

Cletus wanting to end this conversation as soon as possible continued without waiting for Raleigh to reply.

"Both of the boys were shot, more or less in the back of the head."

This seemed unusual, even to Raleigh, and in spite of Cletus' annoyance and the latest of the hour, Raleigh had to push a little harder.

"I have been in a pissing match with Cletus since I was 12," Raleigh thought. "I am pretty sure I have got the old boy now!"

Cletus was forever catching more fish, killing the largest deer, and marrying the prettiest girl. Now, perhaps Raleigh could precipitate perplexity and regain some of the high ground he had lost.

"A murder suicide and both boys were shot in the back of the head? Cletus could you commit suicide by shooting yourself in the back of the head?"

Cletus would have none of it.

"Maybe."

Raleigh read a slight tone of irritation in his brother-in-law. He knew when to retreat. He had prodded his friend enough for the night.

"Ok I see. It is just a couple of niggers anyway. Do you need me to come over and sign the death certificate?"

Raleigh lived in Pedlam, nine miles away, and knew that Cletus would never stay at the Courthouse to wait for Raleigh to drive over.

"No I will take care of everything in the morning. Just wanted to tell you. Tell Cyndi-Beth hi and Goodnight."

Both Cletus and Raleigh were glad that was over!

"Will do, Cletus. Goodnight."

The next morning Sheriff Compton, on behalf of Raleigh Parmentier, filed a death certificate with Joanna Marie Davis, the county clerk. Later that day, at the same time that Donny and Floyd boarded the Continental Trailways bus to California, the bodies of Elrod and TJ were delivered to the Tiberius Wade Funeral Home. Sheriff Compton had not told Mammy Lee, who had no way to know that her son and nephew were dead. In fact, it was not until around 2:30 PM that Sheriff Compton visited my house.

I was home alone with Mammy Lee. Both my brothers were in school, but I was recovering from a strep infection. Lying on the living sofa, very near the front door, I was reading *Silas Marner* by George Eliot. Old Silas was about to find Eppie lost in the woods.

From my place, I could see and hear everything that Cletus said and did.

"Lee," Sheriff Compton said. "How are you?"

"Tolerable well, Mr. Cletus," Lee said with some anxiety. "And how is Mrs. Laura Lou?"

"She is fine."

It was not rare for the sheriff to visit colored town, but Lee was quite disturbed to see him at her employer's house.

"Lee, we need to talk. Are you alone?"

"Mr. Jake is sick and home from school. But he is busy reading his book."

"Lee," Cletus, anxious to get this over with, began, "I regret to tell you that your boy, and his cousin, Elrod, passed last night."

At first Mammy said nothing. She stared toward the garage and even I, a thirteen year old, knew that she was looking far beyond the garage to a place I had never been and might never go.

Mammy with no emotion, as if she knew that this would inevitably happen one day, asked, "Mr. Cletus how did it happen?"

With a sympathetic, compassionate face, Sheriff Compton, replied, "Lee, the boys killed each other. Perhaps they were in a fight. Perhaps they were on drugs. Perhaps they were drunk. One killed the other and then he killed himself. We are investigating, but we are not hopeful that we will ever know exactly why this happened. It was a murder suicide, Lee. A murder suicide."

Cletus must have been upset. No one had ever heard him say such a string of sentences; offer so much explanation, to a black person.

Mammy Lee, in a moment of unplanned peril, stated—did not ask—if she would have asked it would have been permissible—but she bluntly stated, "Mr. Cletus, my TJ was thirteen years old."

I saw something on the face of Sheriff Compton that I will never forget. It was the personae of pure, unadulterated malfeasance.

I had seen it before and would see it again, but every time I saw it, I was terrified. Mostly southern altruism and décor maintained sincere control. A smile, a nod, a politeness that transcended time and mitigated all impropriety. It disarmed the most reluctant detractor.

This was the face that charmed revisionist historians, and good-natured people everywhere, who saw us southerners as poor victims of northern aggression, of pasty-faced industrialists. They saw us as gentle loving people, who only needed to be understood to be liked.

But, there were moments, like now, when that facade descended, and we were what we really were. And Lee, inadvertently, at her own peril, had unveiled Cletus, and unleashed the wrath of southern racial fury, and we all knew that it was the wrong thing to do at this time and this place.

"Oh," she said apologetically. "I understand. Where are the bodies?"

To Sheriff Compton, by most accounts a kind and decent man, who faithfully upheld the law, the death of two black boys was unfortunate. But to destroy the lives of two white ones, because of the death of two black ones, was unthinkable. The trade of two black boys for two white boys was a reasonable, rational, and necessary trade. Even a preferable one.

Sheriff Cletus Compton drove away and no one ever talked about Elrod and TJ again.

I would never forget that moment. Mammy Lee was washing the bathroom before Sheriff Compton arrived. She smelled of borax bleach. I love that smell today. Like the strong odor of Magnolia blossoms, the smell of bleach reminds me of Mammy and draws me again back to a time when she was in my life.

Her sudden disappearance in the late summer of my 13th year was disconcerting, but not surprising. In some ways it was time. I no longer needed a mammy and, besides, by this time, Dad's business was failing and my parents could not afford a girl.

The first day I spent without Mammy I stood in my yard and watched Spunky Jones' low-flying bi-plane spray DDT on the field behind our house. Dad paid Spunky Jones $25 to kill mosquitoes before they multiplied and ruined all later summer barbeques. I walked out into the field, looked up into the sky. Spunky washed me clean with sticky DDT and methyl.

Later, I would ride my bicycle for three miles to look for Mammy only to find her house empty. The first thing I did when I obtained my driver's license was to drive to Mammy's house. It was still empty.

With no return address I mailed my dreams to the cosmos.

# 23

My birthday meal was excellent.

"Anna, I wish you would have known Brother Balfour."

The United Methodist system, like any meritorious structure, awarded its middle management, the clergy, according to seniority, performance, and other exigencies. Pedlam, five years before Brother Balfour's entrance, had wisely placed itself higher on the seniority list by building a beautiful parsonage. This happened because of competition from the Southern Baptists and because the United Methodists would never have the customer base (membership roll) to rival competing churches. Therefore, to compete, Pedlam First built the most awesome parsonage in Southern Arkansas. The Baptists had the most impressive choir, the Pentecostals had the biggest baptism font, the Presbyterians had the largest stain class window, the Episcopalians had the largest pulpit with a big eagle, but the Methodists—we had the most important ecclesiological structure in Pedlam — a grand parsonage!

In 1947, it was the most modern and impressive United Methodist parsonage in the entire Little Rock Conference. It had an automatic sprinkler system, in-ground pool, two-car garage, and an address on the most prestigious boulevard (Pedlam status addresses always resided on "boulevards," not "streets).

Yet the plan, so carefully conceived, backfired. It did draw many of the Arkansas United Methodist high seniority clergy, but also the odd clergyperson. The bishop used Pedlam as a promotion for pastors, who deserved good accommodations, but whose abilities did not warrant a serious, substantial church. Therefore, instead of offering a legitimate competition to the Baptists, et al., we became a stepping-stone to retirement.

Brother DeWayne Waudell, for instance, baptized my older brother in the last year of his completely forgettable tenure at First UMC.

"I baptize you in the name of the Father, Son, and the Holy Spirit, in the name of Jesus!" Brother Waudell quietly pronounced as he sprinkled holy water on my brother. Most Methodist infants were baptized in the name of the Father, Son, and Holy Spirit, but Brother Waudell grew up in an Oneness Pentecostal Church that believed the baptism did not take effect unless the person was baptized "in the name of Jesus." Brother Waudell was always a thoughtful ecumenicist.

He was slightly deaf, so he delivered his sermons very loudly, out of thoughtfulness to other hearing-impaired congregants. As it was, Wally Waldine, who lived across the street and had no problem hearing, was grateful. He decided to take church in his front yard, sitting in a lawn chair with a Good News Bible on his lap. The first Sunday of every month, though, the ushers Oren James and Parker Yancy brought the communion elements over to Wally. Oren placed the host on a shellacked picture of Roy Rogers and Trigger tastefully decorating a TV tray.

Brother Addison Henderson followed Brother Waudell and asked to be called "Pastor Addison," a Yankee-style appellation. Pastor Henderson baptized me. Later, my mother was sure that this was a prophetic moment.

Brother Raywin Ashton, who followed Brother Addison, labored in the vineyard, until his son Berthard impregnated Blanche Kemp, the sixteen-year-old daughter of the president of the Trustee Board. Brother Krandall Star from Montrose, Arkansas, came out of retirement to replace Brother Ashton. Other than the murder of Bo, his tenure was so ordinary that the church was sure the bishop had made a mistake.

About the time that John Glenn took his memorable flight in space, Brother Billy Bob Baker replaced Brother Star. He ran away with Candy Lynn, secretary of the Primitive Baptist Church, when Candy's husband attended the annual Cotton Grower's Convention in Stuttgart, Arkansas. Brother Billy Bob's replacement, Brother Charlie Don Ferguson, accepted a job in public relations with the Farm Bureau. Brother Cleanth Curtis served for only two years because he had a stroke and lost all movement on his left side. The young people thought it grand to have a pastor, who talked and walked like Frankenstein, but the adults were not amused and they petitioned the Bishop for relief.

Pastor Waylon Wynter came next. He stayed until 1968, when he felt called to join the Air Force as a chaplain. Wearing his impressive blue officer's uniform, we earnestly wished we could trade the regulation boring black academic robe that our pastors wore for Brother Wynter's dashing uniform.

Then Brother Hoyt Balfour arrived.

Brother Balfour came a week before Confederate Memorial Day. Memorial Day was a time of somber reflection upon the sacrifices of our glorious forefathers.

Schools were dismissed, and we lined the streets of Pedlam,

waving our Confederate stars and bars and the Union stars and stripes, to show that we were evolving, if unrepentant patriots. In a moving ceremony, Uncle Evan, wearing a Confederate major general's uniform, inspected his Klan Coven, all dressed in butternut uniforms, including period rifles and bowie knives, and standing at attention in front of Pedlam City Hall. Our parades, like everything else in Pedlam, were segregated. Whites lined up on Main Street; Blacks gathered on Railroad Street. All were expected to display both Confederate and Union flags and memorabilia. Some irascible Pedlam whites claimed Pedlam blacks preferred the Union Jack, but honestly it was difficult to tell. In retrospect, I wonder why any blacks would come to a parade full of the KKK, but, of course, in light of what happened to Bo and TJ, I knew the answer.

At the front of Uncle Evan's Coven was Pedlam High School's marching band, alternately playing, "Dixie" and "The Star-Spangled Banner." Bringing up the rear was the First Baptist Church choir with Confederate flags in their lapel, singing "The Bonnie Blue Flag."

The parade ended at First United Methodist's educational building, a miniature version of the Montgomery State House, where President Jefferson Davis was inaugurated in early 1861. To introduce our distinguished speaker, Uncle Evan ascended the church steps—the same stairs on which I tore a hole in my Sunday pants by sliding down a concrete rail—letting the tip of his Army surplus sword tap, tap, tap on each step. The most unforgettable Confederate Memorial Day of was in 1954, when 110-year-old Bodean Matthews, a former member of General Nathan Bedford Forrest's famed Escort Company, talked about the War for Southern Independence and his part in it. That evening a relatively unknown Tupelo, Mississippi boy, Elvis Presley sang in the old VFW Lodge.

A pastor distinguished only by his mediocrity, Hoyt Balfour was over six feet tall and had a dark, olive complexion that was accentuated by completely white—not grey—hair. He had a decided foreign and jaundiced look, as though he had not eaten enough turnip greens. Tiberius Winston, the Pedlam postmaster, once looked that way; Mrs. Winston fed Tiberius turnip greens and Earl Gray tea for two months before Tiberius got all his color back. Mrs. Iris Hudspeth, the church gossip, speculated that Brother Balfour was a Messianic Jew, who had survived the Holocaust. Others were sure he was an escaped Native American from the North Arkansas Cherokee Reservation. Brother Balfour spoke with a distinctly East Texas accent that made the Jewish conjecture bogus. The Cherokee theory lingered for years.

Brother Balfour wore black clergy vestments with velvet running down the middle on each side of the front buttons. Red, white, green, and purple silk stoles with hand-embroidered crosses graced Brother Balfour's robe. On Boy Scout's day, he wore a bright yellow linen stole with tasteful Cub Scout Wolf patches on each end. This was a gift from Bayleigh Thompson, the 285-pound den mother for Pedlam Cub Scout Troup 449. Bayleigh wore a matching yellow dress with a cute little Wolf patch on each shoulder.

In time, Pedlam summers cured Brother Balfour's vestments, as completely as hickory smoke cured our country hams. By June 30, Brother Balfour's robe smelled so bad that Jamella

Jackson's family, who for two generations had homesteaded the right front pew, resettled in the back left side of the sanctuary. When Brother Balfour walked down the aisle to greet departing congregants, his black vestments wafted stale tobacco smoke and unwashed body odor throughout the church. Swaying like ecstatic Pentecostals, faithful churchgoers alternately leaned this way and that to avoid this malodorous encounter. As an act of pity, Mom lied to Brother Balfour that it was my family's practice regularly to dry-clean the clergy vestments gratis on a biweekly basis.

Brother Balfour wore penny loafers with optimistic Crisco-shined Roosevelt-head dimes in the top slits. At the end of the service, when he strode down the aisle to greet departing parishioners, his dimes caught the cascading light from the late morning Pedlam sun and sparkled like newly acquired diamonds.

Juicy Fruit gum hid his unfiltered Pall Mall breath. He would drive to Halley, Arkansas, to obtain cigarettes so no unscrupulous store clerk would reveal his secret to Pedlamites. Of course, 90 percent of Pedlam adults smoked, but such blameworthy behavior among the clergy was not tolerated. The Episcopalian priest, with his bright pink shirts and clergy collar, smoked a black walnut pipe full of pungent, aromatic fruit-tinged tobacco, bathing his congregation with bayberry incense. The Presbyterian pastor smoked lightly filtered Marlboro cigarettes and drank California Chardonnay so unapologetically that everyone thought he was heading to Hell. The Baptists were too full of probity to violate the temple of the Holy Spirit with nicotine or liquor.

Brother Balfour was married to a former Orthodox Presbyterian, who faithfully attended Pedlam First UMC and never smiled; she sat in the third row from the front, right side, behind godly ninety-eight-year-old senile Mrs. Zenna Nolan wearing magnolia blooms in her hair, and right in front of Mr. Opie Wilson, an alcoholic, who smelled like Jim Bean. This seemed to be about the best place for a preacher's wife: behind the church's most celebrated scion and ahead of the church's most incorrigible reprobate. She could draw sustenance from one and beam benevolence to the other.

Brother Balfour's two boys were archetype preacher kids. Their shoes were always shined. They attended all church functions—including the women's auxiliary club. They rarely spoke, and when they did, they spoke with oxymoronic southern accents in grammatically correct sentences, avoiding all colloquialisms and hyperboles.

Brother Balfour dutifully warned us against "immoral thoughts." Most of us had not had an "immoral thought" since millionaire Fredda Oralene married a Missionary Baptist. In solemn grief, and with futility, for two years we left her pew spot vacant. Finally Miss Clementine Carter abandoned her spot and claimed Fredda's pew. Miss Clementine's old spot had a broken hymnal holder, and her Methodist Hymnal regularly fell on her foot. Meanwhile, Rufus Martin, whose stomach had terrible problems and growled with intense ferocity, claimed Miss Clementine's pew.

Having shared the same pew, even at different times, we hoped that confirmed bachelor Mr. Rufus and old maid Miss Clementine would get together. And they did briefly. One

Sunday Mr. Rufus donated daffodils for the front altar and later gave them to Miss Clementine. She was so wooed by Mr. Rufus's chivalric act that she moved back to her old pew to sit next to him, in spite of the broken hymnal holder and Mr. Rufus's gurgling gut. Sadly, the budding romance was terminated sooner than anyone expected because the rumbling was serious and not merely the outcome of too many pinto beans the night before: Mr. Rufus died of stomach cancer. Every spring for the rest of her life, Miss Clementine put a bouquet of daffodils on Mr. Rufus's grave.

Brother Balfour's liturgies never varied in scope and sequence—only in liturgical content.

At 10:40 AM, the organist began the prelude. At 10:45, Brother Balfour called the congregation to order with a Call to Worship.

> I will extol the Lord at all times; his praise
> will always be on my lips. My soul will boast
> in the Lord; let the afflicted hear and rejoice.
> Glorify the Lord with me; let us exalt his
> name together. Psalm 34:1-3

Brother Balfour then reverently announced, "Let us continue to worship the Lord by singing..."

He stepped aside and let the Pedlam First United Methodist Choir lead us in our opening, rousing hymn, proclaiming the lordship of our God, and admitting frankly that everything else in Creation was as filthy rags: "How Great Thou Art" or "A Mighty Fortress."

Then we begin the nadir point of the celebration—the Confession of Sins. Brother Balfour apologized for inviting us to confess our sins. "You should not think I am better than any of you because I am your pastor." He assured us that he was the most perfidious sinner in Pedlam. We believed him.

He led us in a somber, truthful unison prayer of confession.

> Most merciful God, we confess that we have
> sinned against You in thought, word, and deed…

We were delighted to reach the Assurance of Pardon. Brother Balfour often reminded us that he sometimes wished he were a Roman Catholic priest (we sometimes wished he was too) because the priest could pronounce the forgiveness of sins: now that was power! Brother Balfour was a sinner like the rest of us and could only invite us to accept God's forgiveness. Of course, he earnestly hoped that we would accept divine forgiveness and do so with a grateful heart:

> The Lord is compassionate and gracious, slow
> to anger and abounding in loving-kindness.

To prepare us for the apex of the service—the Offering—we sang a sanguine, subjective hymn like "What a Friend We Have in Jesus" or "What a Privilege to Carry Everything to God in Prayer."

It was offering time now. Brother Balfour thanked us for our generous donations.

"You are the most generous congregation in the world,"

he told us, "yet we cannot out give God."

For Brother Balfour's entire tenure we were reminded, weekly, that we could not out give God, something with which we manifestly agreed. Still, though, we could under give Him, and we did this regularly.

The most venerated male church officers (never a female: everyone knew you could not trust women with money) would come forward with the golden offering plates to collect the morning offering. I remember one usher, Woodrow Gleason, who was struggling with Parkinson's disease. He would stand in front of you with his golden plate and shake, until you ante-upped what you owed the Lord. It was quite effective. And as long as Woodrow collected money for the Lord, the Deity received a fair haul from the saints at Pedlam First United Methodist Church.

During the offering the choir would sing its anthem. Inevitably after the offering was collected, we had to endure three more verses of near cacophony. With the ushers Oren James and Parker Yancy standing purposefully, holding the First United Methodist Church's gifts, tithes, and offerings (and an occasional monopoly dollar deposited in jest by Larry Cantrell), saints (and Opie Wilson) waited until the doxology.

The doxology punctuated the end of the tithes-and-offerings interlude. We could hardly wait until the doxology, which was the oldest and most enthusiastic song of praise in the Protestant liturgy. We were grateful that we had escaped Woodrow Gleason's agonizing shakedown. Now as the choir finished its off-key anthems, we were almost half finished with morning worship.

> Praise God, from Whom all blessings flow;
> Praise Him, all creatures here below;
> Praise Him above, ye heavenly host;
> Praise Father, Son, and Holy Ghost.

To add a little drama, we all kept Mrs. Musick and her twelve-year-old wayward grandson Bartholomew in our prayers and in the corner of our eye. Bartholomew was a Lutheran from Jonesboro, so Mrs. Musick kidnapped her grandson every chance she could so that Bartholomew might hear the true gospel. Bartholomew carefully stalked his victims. We all looked to our arms when Bartholomew was in the house. No one was safe.

Often Bartholomew timed his sneak attack during the prayer of confession, while his victim was most contrite and vulnerable. Before the assurance of pardon was pronounced, poor Mrs. Musick was often hanged and quartered. At the end of the doxology, in celebration of the midpoint of our service, Bartholomew would inevitably commit some historic atrocity. Once he deposited his used Bazooka bubble gum on Mrs. Musick's open red-letter Bible. Another time he put a tack on Mr. Bilberry's seat, so that when he sat down after the doxology, he immediately sprang up in ecstatic religious fervor: "Oh shit!" Brother Balfour did his best to persuade Mrs. Musick that the Lutherans were just as good a bunch of Christians as we were and probably missed Bartholomew terribly. We doubted either to be true.

Morning petitioning, called the pastoral prayer, was upon

us. Brother Balfour liked the pastoral prayer time. He soared with the angels! Yes, Brother Balfour prayed with aplomb and gusto. Oh, the depth of the riches of the wisdom and knowledge of God!

We joined Brother Balfour with our wayward hearts and prayed protection for Buddy Lee, visiting his cousin in Natchez, Mississippi. Of course everyone in the congregation, except Brother Balfour and Buddy's wife Cheryl, knew that his "cousin" was really another woman with whom he was having an affair.

Next, Brother Balfour asked God to intervene on behalf of the United States of America, in danger of succumbing to the ravages of big government and menacing communist sympathizers. And while, He was at it, would God please ravage the godless Viet Cong and bring our boys back home soon? He also hoped that God would return to our public schools—even though each morning the Pedlam High School principal read a Bible passage over the loudspeaker, we stood and prayed the Lord's Prayer, and Mrs. Hawthorne even had her homeroom hold hands and sing "Kumbaya."

Brother Balfour finished by asking God to please help the doctors make Dannielynn, Freebird, Jabbo, and Lynyrd feel better. Brother Balfour was careful to list all the sick in his pastoral prayer so we would know he was on duty the rest of the week, taking care of his flock. Some of the more charismatic Methodists wanted Brother Balfour to ask God for a miracle, but most conceded that God did not do miracles in Pedlam First United Methodist Church. Brother Balfour finished with a rousing ending that felt as though he just could not relax his hold on God: "in the inestimable awesome, irrefutable, loving, magnificent, gracious, wonderful name of the one and the only begotten Son of God, our lovely and loving Savior, Jesus Christ. Amen."

Now it was time for the sermon. We all were grateful to see Brother Balfour unhook his Timex and place it on the pulpit. We were pleased. He was pleased. Our eyes met. Like a troop of cavalry on campaign, we had a singularity of purpose that drew us into glory!

The propitious moment had arrived! He knew, we knew, that he had about twelve minutes to ameliorate our obdurate souls.

To show our solidarity with Brother Balfour in this auspicious event, and hoping to hasten him along, we offered an occasional "Amen!" It was a soft "Amen," in the tone of voice one would use with a loved one. "Amen!"

Once Brother Balfour, in the Spirit, forgot himself, however, and on minute 22, to help Brother Balfour reach a conclusion, Kenny Hemingway yelled "Amen!" It worked. The organist immediately chimed in with a couple of verses of "Standing on the Promises." Brother Balfour, having regained his balance, simply went along with the charade and never said a thing.

Other than the prayer of confession, this was the only time we officially were allowed to speak. There might be other sounds, like coughing or crying, Bubba Baldwin's passing gas (he had a stay-out-of-jail pass for this nasty habit since we all knew he could not help it), or deaf Hugh Morris's "whispering" to his wife, Agnes——but these were unsanctioned by the

Holy Spirit and generally ignored.

"Brothers and Sisters, friends and guests, Falcon fans and others," he began. And then for 192 times in his years at Pedlam, Brother Balfour paused for effect, hoping we would laugh. We never did.

His sermon titles were catchy. "On the Road Again" was a discussion of Paul's Letter to the Romans. "In the Wilderness, but Not Lost" was about the journey across the wilderness to the Promised Land. He titled his annual stewardship message "The Sermon on the Amount." Once his secretary, Mimi Daniels, made a typing mistake, and the bulletin listed a sermon as "To Pee or Not to Pee" instead of "To Bee or Not to Bee." Brother Balfour was elaborating on Paul's chastising the Galatians for their overemphasis on works rather than grace. He meant to talk about how busy bees were, but that they could not make the honey without the worker bees—but it was too late. About half of the male congregants took his advice, and crowded into the fellowship hall's bathroom right before morning prayers.

Everything after the sermon was downhill sliding. From this point onward, we never sang, but one or two verses of any hymn. Our hearts were heading elsewhere, dreaming of barbecue ribs, or country club mashed potatoes, or the Sunday afternoon Arkansas Travelers baseball game. We were present in body, but not in mind and spirit.

Finally, the propitious moment arrived: the benediction. Brother Balfour gave the longest benedictions in recorded Pedlam First United Methodist Church history:

> Now God himself and our Father, and our Lord Jesus Christ, direct our way unto you......

Our hearts soared! Brother Balfour was not finished:

> Grace and peace be multiplied unto you through the knowledge of God....

He took a breath.

> Now the God of peace, that brought again from the dead our Lord Jesus, that great shepherd of the sheep, through the blood of the everlasting covenant, make you perfect in every good work
>
> In the name of the Father, the Son, and the Holy Spirit, go in peace.

That was one admonition we readily obeyed!

And now our cup runneth over! With an 11:45 benediction, wherever we were going, we were going to get there before anyone else. The Episcopalians gave us a run for the money, and the Presbyterians were not far behind. Nobody worried about the Baptists: they might not show up until 1:30 PM. Our hearts were warm, our bellies were empty, our womenfolk and children were smiling—we were the Pedlam First United Methodist Church! We had run the race and fought the good fight. We had received expiation for our sins, and we were set for the highlight of the Lord's Day, our heavenly reward: Ottie Lee's hickory-smoked pork ribs. And neither life, nor death, nor principalities, nor powers, nor what was, what is, nor what would be, would separate us from the delectable, savory, scrumptious Ottie Lee's pork ribs.

All day on Saturday, at an open-air four-pole court with a rusty tin roof, Ottie cooked the best hickory-smoked pork ribs in Choctaw County, arguably the best in the entire world. He smoked the ribs in a huge, homemade barbecue pit made from an old silver propane tank, with most of the silver paint burned off. The first few batches had a decidedly metal taste; politely no one mentioned that. After a few fires, there was nothing better to eat in the whole world. The secret was the moist, green river-bottom hickory that he used to smoke his ribs. Only in the last hour or so did he put his famous, secret barbecue sauce on the ribs. He only made a certain amount of this food of the gods, and I was fairly certain no Baptist or Pentecostal ever tasted one of Ottie's delectable barbecue ribs.

Brother Balfour favored the lectionary, but no matter what he preached, Ottie Lee's ribs reminded us of the goodness of God's person and of His creation.

Observing a caravan of pickup trucks arriving, Ottie Lee warned his wife, "Ouida Joe, get out here! The Methodists are here!"

Then, before the Baptists arrived, Ottie warned his patrons. "The Baptists are coming! Put away your beers!"

It was a standing joke and we all enjoyed it even though Ottie repeated it every week.

Otis Lee's ribs were irrefutable proof that we served a first-class God. For a moment, we wondered how anyone could attend any other church, in any other town, in any other place in the world. We truly were a blessed people, and we knew it!

# 24

AFTER OUR BIRTHDAY SUPPER, Anna and I sat at our kitchen table and watched rusty chested robins capture earthworms.

Twenty years ago our hedges were nicely manicured. The previous owner was careful to impose discipline and restraint on our hedges. However, neglect encouraged our feisty sentinels to expand beyond healthy horticultural self-discipline. In fact, riotous privet hedges very nearly blocked our view of the front yard. As it was, we could only see the right corner, near our springhouse.

Abundant, chilly May spring water bubbled to the surface forcing reluctant, gasping earthworms to hazard frosty mornings and hungry robins. Grateful rusty chested avengers hopped from point to point decapitating unwary burrowing waves of muscular contractions, which alternately shortened and lengthened in spasmodic movements.

Anna, sensing how much I enjoyed talking about the past, prompted me again.

"Tell me again about Theodis. You always enjoy talking about Theodis."

I did enjoy talking about Theodis Murphy. The problem was I could no longer differentiate between memory and nostalgia. Memory learned from the past; nostalgia tried to retrieve the past. Nostalgia was the horrible death that Bo endured. Memory was the life that he enjoyed. A life I enjoyed with him. I had to retrieve that. My reunion was a sideshow that was in danger of derailing the train, but even that was merely a diversion. The main show was the memory of Uncle Evan, Bo, TJ, Big Daddy, Mamaw, Big Momma, Mom, and Dad. They were characters in a play in which I had to write the final scene.

My life had progressed from ascendant promise, to supreme demand, to sovereign absence. If that was so, the promises of God that were mine in the spring of 1971 when I was born again had been forgotten or lost, and in this business, losing memory of something, was losing it altogether.

"Anna, my seventeenth year was the most cynical year of my life. I was as grumpy, and scurrilous as a bear. I was full of mocking disrespect for everything religious. In retrospect, I guess God was preparing me for conversion!"

"Jacob, you still have your moments. You inevitably say 'no' every time I ask you to do something. And, your obnoxious streak is a mile long," Anna scolded in her best 5th grade voice.

"Oh, shut up!" I joked. Except on my birthday I would never say shut up to this woman.

Spring in Southeast Arkansas was nothing like our spring. It was not tentative. There were no intermittent days of warm and then cold. It was altogether warm. It was as if the world had turned in a new direction and the frigidity of January was replaced by the resolute warmth of April.

"The spring of 1971 showed promise. Long stretches of early summer warmth were punctuated by slow, steady, soaking rain. The resulting Delta spring was luxuriant with potential."

In the Laurel Highlands planting was a risky business. Only lettuce could be planted in April. In Arkansas, by the middle of February we had planted our onions, by March our lettuce, by April everything else.

"Anna, do you remember my dad's garden?"

Anna, who appeared to be interested, quipped, "Yes."

"Vegetable gardens were competitive enterprises to Pedlam males. As insecure males stole furtive and at times envious glances at peer genitalia in the school gym showers, we also looked with vegan envy at competitors' virile tomatoes and seductive squash. April was D-Day in the garden timeline."

"April too, was the time for the high school spring orgy aka prom. In 1971, though, Brother Balfour announced April revival. A revival in the middle of the Ides of Hedonism! Even the Baptists, hoping to scoop up repentant sinners, waited until May. Tasteful red-robed choirs sang 'Just as I am' and preachers waving massive and appropriately tattered black Scofield King James Bibles preached fiery, and very long, sermons. The Assembly of God held fiery July revivals. Fatuous, uneducated preachers with J. C. Penny white shirts, stained with sweat and splatters of the potluck spaghetti sauce, herded hundreds of sinners to the rough unsanded and unvarnished altar, where they found their way to Jesus."

"Only Brother Balfour would send Jonah into Nineveh and have a revival in April. All the rest of the religious folk had abandoned April, as they had Halloween, to debauchery. Game over."

"The truth was that we had never had a 'revival' at the Methodist Church. We would never do anything as pedestrian as hold a revival."

"And 'we are not having a revival now,' Brother Balfour

announced. 'We are having a Lay Witness Mission.'"

"What is a Lay Witness Mission?" Anna asked.

"A Lay Witness Mission was exactly that, a glut of testimonies shared by lay people to unsaved lay infidels so that they might give their hearts to Jesus."

"Nonetheless, Anna, a Lay Witness Mission was not a 'revival per se.' Sly Balfour!" I said.

Whatever the lay witness was, on second thought, we were all glad it occurred in April, when spiritual events were as scarce in Pedlam as a football game. We felt smart about the whole thing: we had a leg up on our main competition, the Southern Baptists. Besides, we gained no small comfort from knowing that the Baptists and Pentecostals had to endure two weeks of sublime hermeneutics and innumerable sermons on John 3:16. We could apparently slide through the whole thing in one weekend, unscathed!

United Methodist laypeople, men, women, and children, from Oologah, Oklahoma, would share their testimonies with us Friday through Sunday morning. No preaching, no altar calls. Just testimonies.

Wilomena Lamoyne, from Pedlam First Baptist, was rumored to have given a testimony as long as Waylon Zebulon's filibuster in the Arkansas Legislature when Redell Trueman introduced legislation that alcoholic beverages could be sold in restaurants on Sunday. And her testimony, epic in duration, was also salacious in content. It turns out that Wilomena had danced with some Brinkley, Arkansas, boys without her husband's knowledge or permission. Wicked woman!

"United Methodist testimonies were generally more arcane, reticent, and short. After all, how much testimony would fit into a forty-five-minute worship service that occurred with regularity and boredom rivaling the choreography on the Lawrence Welk Show? We UMCs were careful to keep our metaphysics separate from our feelings. We never clapped during our songs and rarely quipped 'Amen' during our sermons."

"No argument here, Jacob. Those worship services remind me of our church services."

I generously ignored the dig.

"The team from Oologah arrived, and we fed them Mandell's cheeseburgers and hush puppies. We were pulling out all the stops to impress these saints. We were hoping that Pedlam's choice cuisine would mitigate any potential Oologah religious ardor."

"After Mandell's exquisite foray into the best that Pedlam had to offer, the evening began. What was extraordinary to me, as I remember on my 59th birthday, was the dullness of the event. Everything was predictable. The testimonies were rampant with banal archetypes and motifs."

"Jacob your profession has made you cynical!"

"Probably."

I continued. "Ima Jean Maxwell thought she was the happiest woman in the world, with two kids and a husband with a good job, and Oklahoma State University season tickets—but no, she was not really happy until she invited Jesus into her heart. Little Joe Tullis thought he loved Jesus since he grew up in the church and lived a godly life. He did not know Jesus. Little Joe ended his testimony with one of many clichés that only someone from Oologah would use: 'You know, standing in a garage does not make you a car.' Thankfully, Little Joe had his engine revved, and he was born again. Twyla Fay Mercer thought she was pregnant, but it turns out she was only full of gas. Still, this gentle nudge was enough for her to walk to the altar. Troy Allen Smith smoked Salem Lights and drank Wild Turkey Bourbon until the Holy Spirit baptized him, and now he spoke in tongues. He gave glory to God and was addicted to peppermints."

"These testimonies were inspiring, as testimonies go, but they did not 'warm my heart.' I remained a sinner after the Oologah folks left."

"Kenny Wayne, though, was saved and wore a Sooner baseball cap to remind himself of the weekend. Someone had told him, 'You aren't really saved until you tell others about the good news.' Kenny Wayne was saved and he was going to tell someone about it. He did have a lot of good news to tell: yet perhaps Mrs. Kenny Wayne should tell the good news because redeemed Kenny had broken up with his Tripp Junction girl-friend."

"Jacob, when are you going to talk about Theodis?"

"Hold your horses. I am there!"

"Kenny invited Theodis Murphy to the first available church service after the Lay Witness Mission: the Wednesday evening Bible Hour. In evangelistic zeal, Kenny Wayne hoped to save a descendant of Ham, yet he had no clue that our church did not save black people. Since Kenny was not sure exactly how to share Christ with Theodis, he invited Theodis to Wednesday service where Brother Balfour could take care of business."

"Theodis Murphy arrived then, in slacks and a sports coat. Not knowing that everyone else wore ratty jeans and modest blouses.

"Anna, Wednesday Bible Hour consisted of a series of hymns and readings from the Brown Cokesbury Methodist Hymnal and a homily by Brother Balfour. The whole thing was relatively harmless, and in perspective it was even shorter than the forty-five-minute Sunday morning service."

"Skeeter Jones, owner of the Majestic Theater, and chairman of the church worship committee, concerned about declining Wednesday night Bible Hour attendance, promised to give me a job if I would attend the services. I really wanted that job: all you had to do was pick up and tear tickets, and you got to see all the latest movies gratis."

"Yes and you also got to see some pretty risqué movies for free."

"Came with the job, Anna."

"Right. You still think you are Jon Voight in Midnight Cowboy, but at least you take off your boots."

I smiled.

"One distinguishing mark of Wednesday Bible Hour was that Brother Balfour included his approximation of an altar call. He did this with profound sincerity yet well-evidenced expectation that no one would respond. In sixteen years of ministry, no one had ever responded to Brother Balfour's invitation to know Jesus as Savior."

"Tonight, though, there was an urgent need to end quickly

so he was thinking of skipping the altar call altogether. The Price Is Right, a popular daytime game show and hosted by Bob Barker, was going to have a special evening show."

"The Price is Right was a pretty lame show, Jacob."

"Maybe to you folks in New Jersey, but not to Pedlam residents, who still bought washers and dryers at Oklahoma Tire and Supply Company."

"In any event, for some reason, Theodis Murphy wanted to give his heart to Jesus. This was a night of firsts: the first black person attended Wednesday Bible Hour and it appeared that he would be saved too."

"Brother Balfour, forgetting his previous invitation, asked, 'Theodis, what do you want?'"

" 'I want to invite Jesus into my heart,' Theodis replied."

" 'That is nice, Theodis.' Brother Balfour smiled. " 'Who would like to close in prayer?' "

But, then, it struck Brother Balfour—Theodis was giving his life to Christ! Brother Balfour's first convert!

" 'Brother Balfour, I want to dedicate my life to the Lord!' "

"Brother Balfour was not prepared for this and really had no conversion protocol from which to draw. Nonetheless, he was pleased. He gave Theodis a tract entitled 'Now That You Are Born Again' and then quickly grabbed his new brother's arm and moved him to his car. If Theodis hugged Brother Balfour, it would be tolerated. If Theodis hugged Roxanne, a Wednesday night regular, he would be castrated."

Anna, by this time was interested. "Pedlam First did have an interesting take on discipleship."

"Driving Theodis home, Brother Balfour, who had never been in colored town after 7PM, made every effort to avoid discussing what had just happened. 'Do you think the Falcons will take the state title this year?'"

"The rest of us made it home before The Price Is Right began. By then we had already forgotten Theodis, who surely was on his way to the Promised Land or colored town or somewhere, to enjoy being born again with his own people."

"I am sure God was very happy with your decision." Anna retorted.

"What did He have to do with anything we did that evening?" I asked.

"Ha! Ha!"

"Of course, as you know, Theodis returned to our church on Sunday morning."

"I guess he foolishly thought that since Jesus loved him all the time, and we appeared to love him on Wednesday night, that we would love him on Sunday morning too. He had read the pamphlet that Brother Balfour gave him. He thought he was our brother, and that was more important than anything else. Although he dared not go to the public library or sit on the first floor at the Majestic Theater, and could not even go to any of the public school washrooms except the one on the far side of the science labs, which was informally reserved for black students—still he thought he would be welcome at Pedlam First United Methodist Church,

Only one black had ever attended our church on Sunday morning. A Wharton graduate and the new vice president of the Pedlam Paper Mill, Marcus Danforth, transferred his membership from a Methodist Church in Chicago. Mrs. Ollie Smith fainted outright when Marcus sat in her deceased husband's pew. Marcus could not eat in our restaurants; his children could not swim in our pools. His children could attend our schools, they were always placed in remedial sections. Marcus, a lifelong Methodist, only visited our church once. Uncle Evan and his friends visited Marcus and burned a cross on his finely landscaped lawn."

"Go home!" Uncle Evan and his boys suggested.

"Marcus knew a sensible suggestion when he heard it so he transferred to a factory in Boise, Idaho."

"On this Sunday, like most Sundays, Oren Davis and Parker Smith were the designated ushers. A much-coveted post, ushering allowed the fortunate servant of God an extra cigarette and even another cup of coffee and a donut if the willing saints were able to get everyone seated before the Call to Worship. Ushers had very little to do between the Call to Worship and the offering.

Theodis smiled at Oren and Parker. Without looking up, Oren, thunderstruck, handed Theodis a bulletin. Unintentionally, he sat in Ribeye Rayford's empty seat."

"Ten minutes later, arriving late from a fishing trip to the Anthrax Hole, Ribeye tried to sit in his seat. Theodis reached for a pew hymnal that was dedicated to Ribeye's Uncle Harry Arnold. This was Ribeye's favorite hymnal, and no one used it, but Ribeye. Everyone in my church knew that."

"Ribeye growled (literally), but eventually sat next to the Widow Adams, whose false teeth inconveniently leaped from her mouth during the first hymn. Ribeye grimaced, but would be ready to catch Widow Adam's teeth when they launched themselves into space."

"The first hymn was everyone's favorite, 'Holy! Holy! Holy!'

> Holy, holy, holy! Lord God Almighty!
> Early in the morning our song shall rise to Thee.
> Holy, holy, holy! Merciful and mighty,
> God in three persons, blessed Trinity!

"Edna Marie Poole saw Theodis and stumbled backward. Earl Mays caught Edna Marie, but he sat on Emily Sue's glasses, which broke and protruded into Earl Mays's buttocks, which bled on Melinda Orwell's church pew cushion that the Women of Galilee had purchased from the proceeds of selling forty-eight blackberry pies."

> Holy, holy, holy! All the saints adore Thee,
> casting down their golden crowns around the glassy sea;

"Most Pedlam First Methodist congregants were experiencing confusion. Uncle Evan was full of unambiguous rage. He clearly saw the problem and did not underestimate his enemy. He knew perhaps more than anyone else the danger that a converted Theodis Murphy represented to our world. Tommy and Oren, with the very best Pedlam First UMC decorum and grace, politely asked Theodis to leave. Theodis Murphy left the church, but he never left me. Like an old Kodak film negative. I developed that scene for the next forty years, wondering, hoping, that I did not see what happened next. That there was actually a different outcome."

" 'Boy,' Oren said with surprising gentleness, 'you need to leave now and go to your own church.'"

# 25

ANNA AND I RETURNED TO OUR Anabaptist porch swing to observe whirling hummingbirds binge on our sugar water filled red plastic feeder. These beautiful but tiny creatures were no less aggressive in their defense of everything that they thought was their own. With aplomb rivaling their bigger aviary cousins, angry hummingbirds drove visitors away from their sugar water claim, which of course could feed every hummingbird within 50 miles. But, our spinning visitor did not know that and acted accordingly.

The kitchen telephone rang and Anna rose to answer.

"I will be back soon, Jacob."

The kitchen was only ten yards from our front porch, but careful Mennonite ingenuity required an inspired walk through wildly vibrant patches of red Achillea and chartreuse Alchemilla, which seized as much spring sun as they could. Our sinful predecessor apparently tried to put one up on his boring, Anabaptist God who preferred more subdued perennials and grasses.

With Anna's departure, I rehearsed again, in my mind, Theodis' departure from Pedlam First UMC.

There was no parting defiant act or obscene gesture. Theodis did not cry; he did not shout—I think we all hoped he would, as if such a response would justify our unchristian act.

In a moment of great love, enthusiasm, and hope, Theodis gave his heart to Jesus and assumed that, if Jesus loved him, we would love him too. This love propelled him to come to the first and perhaps only white Pedlam institution that had shown him approbation and love unencumbered by prejudice.

Theodis had a higher view of us than we had of ourselves: he thought that being born again meant really being born again, from above—that somehow we, along with him, had changed. Or rather, that we had already changed and would not make such ambitious claims on his soul in the name of our Lord unless we had changed to be like Jesus. Theodis had already ascended to the heavenly throne.

Theodis had met his Savior! While we labored in purgatory, Theodis was in the presence of the Savior.

At the same time, Theodis and Pedlam First both crashed into a huge tree on this April morning, and neither really died or lived, but remained in between. My church's vision of Heaven, Theodis discovered, was really only another type of Hell. Theodis lowered his head, said nothing, and walked away from our church and from Jesus. "Holy, holy, holy! Though the darkness hide Thee, though the eye of sinful man Thy glory may not see!"

> Brother Balfour saw everything and was obviously displeased. Not that he castigated us. We could handle that. We enjoyed pastors, who scolded us for our sins. We tolerated and even enjoyed paternalistic retribution. No, our pastor did the intolerable: Balfour wept! Right in the middle of morning worship, right where better men had stood, where much better pastors had labored, where our children had been baptized, Balfour wept! Right in the middle of morning worship, as if it were part of the liturgy, Balfour started crying! Not loud, uncon-

> trollable sobs, but quiet, deep crying, full of
> censure and deep anguish, like Jesus' weeping
> over Jerusalem, which did not recognize
> God's visit and "the things that make for
> peace!"

Old Man Henley, senile and almost deaf, remembering the last time he cried—when his wife died—started crying too. And then the children also were crying.

> Holy, holy, holy! Lord God Almighty!
> All Thy works shall praise Thy name,

With great empathy, Brother Balfour wept for all the injustice through generations that we had inflicted and would inflict on ourselves and on others. Brother Balfour wept. In Heaven's ears, the cries of Bo and Mammy Lee mingled in with Brother Balfour's sobs. Louise, and the hundreds of black students, who hid in back hallways in my desegregated school, afraid that like Enoch Marshall, they would be humiliated—as when Enoch had his bicycle stolen by some white boys and sold back to him for five dollars.

What infuriated us was that Hoyt Balfour, an outsider, had no business expressing such empathy, and certainly not publicly.

Brother Balfour wept with striking credibility because he had suffered, if possible, as much as Theodis. His weeping heaped piles of burning coals on our self-righteousness.

Our organist, sensing Brother Balfour's impropriety, judiciously played a verse of the last hymn over again, but softly.

On that April morning, my life went backward in time.

Back to the week before the Lay Witness Mission. Back to Uncle Evan's Bible Class. Back to Bo's smiling face and his clean windshield. Back to the moment I was born. I had become, using a term coined by Kurt Vonnegut, as it were, "unstuck in time."

On that fateful day, 50 years ago, on the Red Fork Road, we looked into the eyes of Bo and we knew prophetically, or rather we did not know, but should have, that he would return someday with a vengeance. As we peered into the dying eyes of Bo we were looking at our own destruction.

I was reborn. It was as if I relearned the truth, what I did not know then, but knew now: on that Sunday when Theodis Murphy visited my church, I had to die, really die. Not like preachers and revivalists understood. The way Flannery O'Connor and William Faulkner told it. With violence and meticulousness, I died.

I would have to die to everything, to everyone, and be reborn—or I would sink further into the Pedlam alternate universe, with its seductive familiarity—into the Delta swamp of iniquity, pretense, and injustice.

I had to be consumed as a fire consumed hardwood and forms charcoal. The charcoal will burn hotter and more dangerously than the wood itself. It was as if God had sent a fire that burned me unmercifully. Indeed, I had never known such pain as my conflicted soul endured during the fourth stanza of "Holy, Holy, Holy!" Yet at the end, then, I was something new. And something old.

Uncle Evan, Theodis, Ribeye were all real enough, but the tears of Brother Balfour were more real. They were the fire by night and the cloud by day that led me to the Promised Land. The weeping of Brother Balfour was the fire that burns, but does not consume on Mount Horeb. It was as if Balfour placed his staff into the Red Sea, and it parted. It was the power of Jesus Christ that called forth Lazarus from the grave. The same tears drove Peter, Paul, and the apostles over the known world and in one generation created the most comprehensive cultural revolution in world history.

It was as if the goddess Athena on the ship of Odysseus was guiding me home. My world as I knew it ended, and a new one began.

I was saved. I was a new man. A follower of Jesus.

Within half a year I went north. Always a wanderer. Always northward. I probed and searched and hoped I would find the fabled Northwest Passage. The legendary passage to the wealthy East Indies that would allow me to avoid the Strait of Magellan. Like Victor Frankenstein I looked for my monster in the frozen north. I would find the Northwest Passage and I would find my monster. The question was, would I hazard the passage and would I kill the monster.

## 26

"JACOB, THE PHONE IS FOR YOU."

"Happy birthday to you, happy birthday to you," Grace, who had inherited her dad's singing ability, sang. With that happy tune it was official: I was 59. The day was almost over. My 60th year had just begun.

Later I returned to the swing.

"Did she sing in tune this year?" Anna asked.

"Of course not, but, as you know, it was beautiful to me."

My four children were my cause célèbre. They give me life. Their life and affirmation, along with Anna's, propelled me into the future, sustained me in the present, and changed forever the past I once lived. They were more than enough compensation for all that I had lost.

My high school class devoured almost half of its brood. Like agile, robust wolf spider mothers we carried our egg sacs around with us. When our young spiderlings hatched they climbed onto our backs until partially grown. Then, we ravenously devoured our own children.

It was my 59th birthday, and in my mind, in my mind's eye, I walked past the empty chicken coop, across the treated-wood magic bridge—which I had painted white and shouldn't have because when you paint treated wood the paint doesn't stick, and it was unnecessary anyway—and I was again twirling the tire swing, but with no children shaking their feet at the fates.

Thinking about my 40th reunion felt like the first summer I was on the farm. I bought sheep and electric fencing to keep them in the pasture, fence that was more to keep the wild dogs out than it was to keep the sheep in. Being completely ignorant of these things, I bought an electric-fence tester. I must know if my fences worked. I touched one end of the tester to the fence, and I flinched. While now I knew for certain that the fence was "hot," I gathered that this must not be the proper use of the marvelous invention. Eventually I discovered that I was not to hold the other end of the wire tester, but that I was to stab it into the ground. Too long, I thought, I held the wire of my life in hand as it continued to shock me—yet not unto death. Misused electric-fence testers did not moderate mortality, but they made life uncomfortable.

Part of me wanted to be a part of the world I once knew: the Pedlam High School class of 1971. More than that, though, I wanted to have Anna and my children. I could not have both.

I enjoyed cultural affirmations that Grace, Nathan, and Emma would never experience. No one assumed I was going to steal his car. Security guards did not shadow me in a department store. White privilege gifted me with exotic treasures that my children would never have. My predominately white world assumed the universality of its own experiences, categorizing others as different and inferior while perceiving itself as normal. I liked it that way.

In John Barth's Floating Opera, the protagonist, Todd Andrews, was a lawyer, who has a detached, jaded view of the world. He won his cases by crafting intricate technical loopholes that reduce his cases to obvious absurdities. Comic relief was never far away. Life, Barth explained, was like a floating opera, full of joy. We were absorbed in the drama, thinking we know the tragic outcome, and then, in William Shakespeare fashion, a fool, a clown, walks on stage and urinates and the crowd roars with laughter. Barth reminded us that we mostly played the part of the clown, the fool,

The floating opera was presented on a barge of sorts, floating up and down a river. At certain points we saw the action, the drama, but too quickly the barge floated to a new location. For a moment we connected with the actors and actresses, we grasped all the subtleness of the opera. Then the opera passed us by, and we were left at the same place on the bank. We found ourselves in blissful ignorance, making up the rest of the story as we supposed, and at times fervently hoped, it would unfold. The floating opera drifted by again, and once more we were faced with all the angst or pleasure of insight and revelation.

On this day, my 59th birthday, I looked again at the floating opera and wondering if I understood after all what the opera narrative was. I was dazed by the choreography and entertained by the actors and actresses, but I was as unknowing and confused, and now discouraged, as I have been when the play first began. Or so it seemed until I remembered my children and my God.

I grew up in a place that made spurious claims on the souls of its passengers. The South I knew was gasping for breath as it struggled and nearly strangled among magnolia blossoms, mint juleps, and misplaced abnegation. It had lost its way, and apparently, so had I for a season at least.

I wanted to attend the reunion. I really did. When I thought about going, it felt like I was selling Joseph to Midianite traders (Genesis 37: 28). Like Uncle Lot I wanted to move my tents to Sodom and Gomorrah. Abraham and Anna could live in the howling wilderness. Give me the garlic of Egypt, the fleshpots of Nineveh.

"Anna, should I go to the reunion?"

She touched my hand. "If you like. I will go with you, but do what the God of Theodis, of Mammy Lee, of TJ tells you to do, Jacob."

When Anna and I decided to adopt our first child, Dad called me that vaporous evening of my discontent.

"Jake, please do not adopt. You will regret your decision. You will only raise someone else's problems."

Dad pleaded with me to change my mind and indeed wept in his plea.

"I must do this Dad. Anna and I have prayed about it and we feel it is the right decision for us."

When I said no to him for the first time, Dad did not know what to do. I had always done what he wished. He was completely disoriented, and so was I.

The Moabites and Ammonites waged war against me, and my soul cried out. Like King Jehoshaphat, I was facing enemies that would overwhelm me. Like the Greek mythical Tantalus, I stood in a pool of water beneath a fruit tree with low branches, with the fruit ever eluding my grasp, and the water always receding before I could take a drink.

Jenga, a game enjoyed by our family, was played with wooden blocks stacked in a tower formation. The object of the game was to take one and only one block from the tower and place it on the top. Points were awarded for how many times the players can do this. The game ended when the tower falls in any significant way. The loser was the person who makes the tower fall (whose turn it was when the tower falls); the winner was the person who has moved just before the loser.

All this time I thought that the tower fell when we adopted our children. It turned out that we had only removed some blocks to place them on the top. The game was not over: it just took the next player longer than expected to make the last move.

Anna, it turned out, had the needed block to put on top and then win the game. I thought that she toppled the tower when all she did was build a more beautiful thing. And we all won.

Dad called for Anna the last night he was alive. I was available, Mom was accessible, my brothers were nearby, but Dad wanted the Yankee. Anna rubbed his feet and prayed for him until sunrise, and, finally, in the early dawn, when the bass were churning the waters of King Tut, High Pocket Harris was stirring at Deer Camp, squirrels were playing in pecan trees at Four Mile Creek, Dad died.

## 27

On this late afternoon of my 59ᵀᴴ birthday, I looked again at the hills shading my farmhouse. The declining sun was already grasping the tops of hilltop poplars. Darting golden finches temporarily arrested the solar trek to the western horizon. However, the sun would not be delayed long in its inexorable journey to night.

On those hills, our whole family lay among four-leaf alfalfa clovers and broadleaf foxtails. We gifted each other with clover chains as we watched bald eagles soar slowly over pastures hunting tiny mice reclaiming cow manure undigested corn kernels. The majestic birds swooped down and grabbed wriggling mice that they took to their nest bound eaglets. Occasionally, marauding crows attacked these regal, diurnal predators. The swift eagles soared into the heavens, leaving tardy malevolent marauders cawing to empty skies.

The empty poplar-clothed hills, wearing the sun on their left shoulders, pleasured us with memories of our children.

Our children were all shades of white and black. They reminded us of late summer cotton fields, ripe with promise and hope. The fields were speckled with dazzling white puffs of black shell encased cotton. The spring deluge exacted its toll and the summer drought culled its due. Weevil, aphid, and worm, had done their worst. The wages of sin were death but God's grace prevailed. The rich Delta soil repaired broken cotton stems with fresh, green finery, sculptured from fertile Jurassic loam. In the end, the land and the cotton triumphed.

Excessive rain drowned and defoliated back corners of

ambiguous fields. Roadside dust coated shriveled plants and reminded farmer, and plant alike, that too much of anything, even life-giving water, would kill.

Anna and I loved our four children. They brought astonishment and grace into our lives. They made something new out of two very different people. We were parents, together, of a mysterious, God-created-family.

One white birth son came screaming into the world. He was anemic, and pale, like all white babies, we supposed, but we had never had one, so we could not know for sure. Our other three children were burnt brown chubby babies. Our birth son came from our loins, and shared some of our reticent pastiness. But, in truth, he was more like his siblings than his parents. Sibling promise pulled more vigorously than progenitor lifeblood.

Birth child, adopted siblings, all were the same to us. Not only in our eyes, because we loved our adopted and birth children with the same intensity and scope, but in God's eyes. In one lifetime, this litter of four, this brood of racial diversity, exploded the myth of homogeneity. The world would not be the same after these pillaging, cultural saboteurs built their snow forts on the hills and tree houses in the trees of the Laurel Highlands.

They were neither birthed by us, nor adopted by us. They were a new race, neither black nor white, but all at once and none at once. They were four new creations from the mind of God. With these four children, God inoculated the racist world with something new. Our tired world full of the plague of racism suddenly had its antidote. Our four children, unaligned with any social stigma, not corralled by any ethnic dogma, were a formidable foe to the loathsome parochialism that afflicted north and south alike. If they flourished, the world flourished too. If our multi-racial family failed because of evil praxis, on the other hand, then the world was doomed to divisive chicanery.

Anna and I knew, however, that good would prevail. These small ones we raised would transform the course of history. We had confidence in our God and confidence in ourselves. We deposited our ample idealism into the souls of two boys and two girls who stood with us on Mount Olympus and defied the gods of the age.

When I left Arkansas, I assumed that when I crossed the Mason-Dixon Line, I entered a foreign country. I fully expected that I would have to show my passport to security guards on the Mason Dixon line. I thought that strange-sounding northerners would check my visa and want to examine my birth certificate.

Surprising, no one seemed to care when I glided along Interstate 81 and crossed to Chambersburg, Pennsylvania.

I knew that Yankees pillaged the land, raped women, and forced little children to work in dreary factories, but I was sure I would not find racism in the Laurel Highlands. I knew that Yankees were responsible for treacherous social engineering, but I assumed it was because they liked black people and lived together in harmonious cultural diversity.

People might be lynched in Oxford, Mississippi, but surely not in Greensburg, Pennsylvania. As it turned out, here in the North my children were not physically accosted, yet they had to endure racial slurs in the grocery store and at church. Security guards carefully kept Nathan in their watchful eye in department stores while ignoring white infidel hoodlums. That was the extent of our harassment.

The truth is, I discovered, the same species thrived in Western Pennsylvania. Blacks were given the worst jobs in steel mills and were harassed in theaters. In the 1920's, in Johnstown, Pennsylvania, not too far from my house, the mayor made it illegal for blacks to live within the city limits. In the 1930s the Ku Klux Klan held weekend rallies on all the surrounding hills.

It was a warm autumn night in the Laurel Highlands, with mid-October weather that belonged more to Pulaski, Tennessee, or Yazoo, Mississippi. By this time we expected our first snow, yet there was only a clear night and the seductive warmth of a gentle breeze.

The unseasonable heat made us uncomfortable. It made us think that there were other specters lurking in the pasture on this night.

The beauty and warmth of this night belonged to my neighbors. To the Jewish family living nearby, to the black-white couple living a mile away, to the gay couple on the hill, and it was a night of terror.

Over the horizon a glow of light kissed the distant woodlands. I could hear a moving rendition of "America, the Beautiful." The consoling glow and inspiring melody were disarming. More comfortable with the drone of crickets and the incessant hum of distant automobile traffic, my Suffolk sheep obviously did not appreciate the harmonic offering. Perhaps they saw the fear in their shepherd's eyes.

The music came from a neighbor's farm, where over two hundred members of the Ku Klux Klan and their families were singing patriotic songs. The glow on the horizon originated from three burning crosses on a neighboring property on whose farm this KKK rally was held.

Oscar Dennings was a quiet neighbor, and "neighbor" was a euphemism because he lived over a mile away as the crow flies, four miles in car mileage. In the winter he was virtually unreachable by humans.

I rarely saw Oscar although last winter Oscar and his John Deere tractor pulled my snow-bound Subaru Outback home from Marty Stoltzfus's farm. Neighbors were neighbors, and we never allowed our social relationships to be compromised by our politics. Until now.

I was not aware of his social or political propensities—although I supposed he was a conservative NRA Democrat—everyone around me was—and I knew he preferred to grow field corn instead of sweet corn. It turned out that he was also the leader of the county Ku Klux Klan.

A few months earlier, I visited Oscar's unchurched dad a few hours before he died. In the shared hospital room, while his neighbor moaned in morphine delirium, accompanied by a cacophonic respirator, Oscar's dad removed his oxygen facial mask and told me that Jesus Christ was his Savior, and then promptly went to be with Him.

In my church, baptism was important, but not a prerequisite to accessing one's eternal reward in Heaven. While my

Calvinism warred with Wolfgang Goethe's Sturm und Drang (storm and drive/stress), perhaps, like Faust, with poor Gertrude as a witness for the defense, Oscar's dad had found peace.

A few weeks later a waitress, who worked at the Iron Pot Cafe, the unofficial headquarters of the local KKK, phoned that Oscar and his friends planned "to kill the pastor with the nigger children."

Mom phoned Uncle Evan and asked him to intercede on my behalf.

"Evan, Jake is not a bad boy; he just married that Yankee," Mom began. "Can you phone the boys up North and put in a few good words for him?"

"They are too easy on wops, Polacks, niggers, and Jews for our liking," Uncle Evan apologetically informed my mom.

Targets were few and far between. In fact, my children were the only conveniently available victims. In a pinch, I suppose, Oscar and his boys could find a Jewish couple or two, and I know there was a mixed-race couple in Somerset, but my family was the most available target.

I knew some inebriated good old redneck boy might do something stupid. So I first phoned the local police chief, who did nothing: he was planning to attend Oscar's festivities with his whole family. So I phoned the local Pennsylvania State Police Barracks, which had a black officer in charge. The State Police contacted the FBI.

For two days Crown Victoria Fords full of FBI agents patrolled my property.

"It was impressive," the agent admitted.

ONE NATION, UNDER GOD was displayed on an attractive sign in Oscar's front yard. Two tables were borrowed from the local Brethren Church and used to register participants. After paying their fees, families were herded to another desk, where they registered for one or two workshops. Up to two were free with registration. Other workshops were $45 each.

The topics were interesting: "How to Maintain an AK-47," "Enemies of Liberty: The Negro Hordes," "How to Lobby Your Local Congressman." There were even some that I would want to attend: "The Advantages of Using Hard Coal vs. Soft Coal to Heat Your House," and my personal favorite, "How to Castrate a bull." A guest KKK member from Alabama taught this last topic, and I made no comment when the FBI agent wondered why a speaker from Alabama was brought in to discuss this particular topic.

The FBI agent continued, "It felt like I was attending a Boy Scout Jamboree, or a vacation Bible school."

The highlight of the evening was a spectacular cross-burning event, with participants clasping hands and swaying with the music: "O beautiful for spacious skies . . ."

Over the horizon, I saw the glow of the cross burning and I heard the echo of the song. Both were inspiring but reminded me of John Milton's description of Hell in Paradise Lost. There was a brilliant image of both utter darkness and the burning fire of God's judgment juxtaposed in the same place, much as sin and love coexisted in the human heart.

"Better to reign in Hell than serve in Heaven," Satan cried to God. I saw the cosmological battle between good and evil on the horizon and felt it in the center of my heart.

Confident in the providence of God and the care of the FBI, my whole family played Candyland all night and waited for the dawn.

# 28

BIRTHDAYS WERE ALWAYS AWKWARD events to mom. Because she had never really had a birthday party herself, Mom was not sure exactly how to do the thing with her three boys.

Therefore, she was grateful to turn the whole affair over to Mamaw, who, it turned out, had a knack for birthday parties. Every birthday was a different motif. For my third birthday I was Blackbeard the pirate. In kindergarten I was John Wayne. My eighth birthday was my favorite—I was a Great White Shark. We were treated to fresh Maine lobsters.

"Jake eat them slowly," Mamaw commanded.

The last time I saw mom alive was in 1998.

In a pre-1998 election interview, Larry King was gently scolding Al Gore on Mom's opaque Panasonic thirty-two-inch television. Electrons danced across this colander of late twentieth-century fantasy. Cable television's munificence clashed with waltzing electronic intruders. Bounteous contradictions were everywhere evident.

It did not matter, though, because my mother only accessed one-third of her available channels. The effort to ingress more exotic offerings in the upper numbers was fatuous anyway. She only watched CNN, the Weather Channel, and the History Channel. Even the local news did not interest her now. This was all the entertainment she needed, and to her, news was entertainment. Pedlam police radio criminal justice crackled in the background.

Mom was dying of pancreatic cancer.

She was lying under a brightly colored afghan crocheted

by Big Momma.

The ratty afghan, full of unraveled spaces, was woefully inadequate for anything, but the most menial task. It should have covered a box of wedding pictures or an antiquated kitchen appliance, but its ambition was to cover my mother's unhealthy body. It offered minimum succor.

If the gappy afghan was inadequate in boundary and respite, Mom nonetheless needed the bright color to tease vigor from her embattled torso and pallid skin. Big Momma, with violent protest against everything bland that was in her wretched existence, knit bright chartreuse, gold, and pinks into her afghan. Her cacophonic choices doomed the afghan to family coffers or to the most desperate recipient, who had no ardor for natural, appealing, subtle hues or had no affordable choice anyway. My mother, though, long the sufferer of Big Momma's neglect, sought to draw from her mother's afghan what she could not have in life.

Mom's knee and her lower thigh peeked through frayed Afghan acrylic like a reptile hiding in the burnished flora of a viscous jungle thicket.

This was a prodigious offering for this parsimoniously modest woman who never willingly shared her soul or body with anyone. In fact, only her husband and her pre-pubescent little boys had ever seen her nude. She was not nude now, but I was shocked this evening to see so much skin. I was struck with a sort of nostalgia of innocent four and five-year-old bathroom post-shower memories of my mom whose ample breasts even then were flaccid and droopy. Her caesarean scars acquired from delivering my brother spread like lava paths across her white skin. The rare vulnerability and bounteousness of her nudity, even to a child, was unusual and appreciated. I still retained a wispy, pleasant hope I would peer into her soul one last time.

Always a robust woman, Mom was now a declining 109 pounds. Her wasted skin was hung from her ample frame. She once sported nearly 200 pounds with wit and vigor, and her ill-violated body now reeked of deficiency and limitation.
Mom ignored all this. The cancerous interlopers had conquered her corporeal existence, and they were now skirmishing with her spirit.

With her blonde frosted wig slightly askew on her forehead, Mom nodded in agreement with Larry King.

Mom was a seasoned multitask person, who preferred investing in several endeavors all at once rather than languishing in a contrived sequence of activities. She never prioritized: everything was equally important and must be accomplished altogether. Mom felt that she was wasting a moment if it was not graced with three or four projects. Today, for instance, she was watching television, listening to her police radio, chewing a pencil, and completing the New York Times crossword puzzle.

Not that Mom would concede defeat. It was not her style. However, she was no Achilles, exactly, but more a Hector. She went reluctantly into battle with very little bravado. She knew the outcome of the coming contest. "Now see him flying; to his fears resign'd."

Her contest started with an innocuous stomachache. Ordinary in extent but not in duration, it nonetheless was an aberration in my mother's medical portfolio. In her lifetime she had consumed truckloads of black-eyed peas, Cajun spicy gumbo, and rich turpitudes of fatty stew—all with no apparent retributive justice. Until now.

The stomachaches ended and the anemia began. In most medical communities, anemia was a sign that something was amiss in the gastrointestinal universe. In the southern Arkansas universe, where medicine was more empathic than empirical, too much fried chicken or too little turnip greens caused anemia. This diagnosis worked well enough, perhaps better than conventional interventions for colds, flu, and the occasional gallbladder attack. However, in the really big things, like pancreatic cancer, dietetic intercession was dilatory and inevitably, therefore, nugatory.

Mom, who walked three miles a day and thought she could defy the Baals, regularly ate chicken gizzards fried in lard, shrugged her shoulders and forgot about the whole thing. In fact, her commitment to homeopathic interventions satiated her most obdurate doubt, so that, even after inert remedies like Geritol and BC Powder failed, she still refused to visit her doctor. Then finally she did. Dr. P. J. Dudley, whose medicinal skills were slightly better than Greek humourism, with his stethoscope and pieces of a jelly donut protruding from his mouth, pronounced that my mother's disorder, more a loss of equilibrium than anything else, required nothing more than continent nocturnal rest and massive doses of Vitamin C.

Yet my mother, always ready to embrace even a shadow of a delusion, could not deny that she felt bad. To question a doctor-friend's diagnosis was worse than a serious illness: it was downright unfriendly, something my mother manifestly refused to be. Nevertheless, my mom, a wanton hussy, surreptitiously phoned Missy Rockett's physician, Dr. E. P. Donahue, in Bowie, Arkansas. To ask for a second opinion was not only rude; it was also inviting an epidemic of gossip, something that Mom ordinarily enjoyed, provided it was about someone else. It would be a nice narrative, however, if this was a false alarm and she could garnish some sympathy and attention along the way—without needing to pay the metaphysical gods for her largesse of composure in the face of imminent declination from prosperity and vigor. Moreover, Missy Rockett was from Maryland, a suspect border state. The State of Maryland, and Missy Rockett, might have a star in the Confederate flag, but everyone knew they were really not kosher southerners and therefore could not be trusted for anything more pertinent that second opinion physicians.

With confident sanguineness, venerable Dr. E. P. Donahue, throat reflector protruding from his head, oversized Masonic ring dominating his left middle finger, pronounced Mom to be in remarkably good health. Dr. Donahue, the second opinion, who had delivered Missy's two boys, was infallible. Once promulgated, the medical pope's edicts were sacred magisterium.

To obtain two unequivocal opinions from such august personages would satiate the most suspicious impulse. For a while, then, Mom was satisfied and tried her best to resume her old routines.

Yet Mom's malady was already fatal. Her ample stamina and delusional obstinacy propelled her forward for almost a year, but the carcinoma had already ambushed her. No one could tell, though, because she was otherwise in such great health. She was like a beautiful stallion whose robustness and wholesomeness camouflaged its malevolent metastasis in a concealed interior.

"My health," my mother ironically shrugged, "killed me."

Finally our family surgeon and good friend Dr. Johnny Joe Jones, one of Dr. Donahue's cardinals, "called the hogs" with Mom one last time before she went into the operating room. When he opened her up with his scalpel, Mom was mellifluent with metastatic carcinoma.

Dr. Johnny Joe was the best surgeon in Arkansas. There was one, Dr. Robert P. Howell, who was as good, but it was rumored that he was a Unitarian. Worse, he enjoyed Jack Daniels too much. That was OK if one sought his services on a Wednesday. He was sober on Wednesdays out of respect for his Assembly of God mother, who always went to church on Wednesdays. And it was Thursday. Besides no one could trust even a sober Unitarian anyway.

Trained in Houston, the medical school Mecca of the South—everyone wanted a doctor trained in Houston: "He must be good if he is from Houston"—Dr. Johnny Joe was a brilliant, skilled surgeon. He had assisted in the first heart transplant attempt (the patient died) in Arkansas. He was a Presbyterian. Everyone knew that the best doctors were Presbyterians, who went to medical school in Houston. In spite of one nasty habit—Dr. Johnny Joe chewed Red Chief Tobacco during surgery—he was much sought after.

"Wipe my mouth, Nurse," Dr. Johnny Joe told his assisting nurse.

Dr. Johnny Joe loved the Razorbacks. He never missed a game. Once, while removing Mrs. Nickle's appendix, the Razorback perennial nemesis the Texas Longhorns intercepted a pass and scored a touchdown. Reacting to this tragedy, Dr. Johnny Joe's scalpel accidentally filleted Mrs. Nickle's appendix and spleen.

No, my mother was fortunate to have him. He was accepting no new patients, but since he was a second cousin of Mom's old neighbor spiny Josephine Mae Stuart, he agreed to take my mom's case.

Five minutes after Johnny Joe's scalpel followed the approximate path of Mom's caesarean scar, he determined that the villainous cancer had begun only God knew where, but now the tumors were in the pancreas and had progressed and spread too far too quickly. Johnny Joe could do nothing but remove a particularly nefarious and ripe-with-cancer gallbladder. This small token of good was appreciated—Johnny Joe put it in a mason jar to show to the family—but it would only slightly delay my mother's death sentence. Deep inside my mother's liver, with his rubber-clad left hand, Johnny Joe rolled marble-size tumors between his thumb and index finger and prophesied, "she ain't gonna make it to dove season."

With buck season in full swing, Johnny Joe was still able to kill a four-pointer later that afternoon.

Mom went home to die. Mom did not know that her gallbladder had been removed until she received her hospital bill—we never told her. She thought it would be impolite to say anything. Johnny Joe could have taken out her heart, and she would still have been grateful.

Southern medicine was like that. Doctors politely did as they pleased with virtually no fear of litigations reprisal.

We Northerners want to know what our physicians do. We make them give us forms to sign, and we ask for long lectures. With no tinge of conscience, we often get second opinions. We look at their diplomas on their walls, and we want to know if they were board certified.

"Johnny Joe is a good boy," Mom said. "Josephine says he visits his mother every Saturday night."

For the first time my mother was hedged in. She could not beat this thing. Her chances of survival were zero, as adjudged by Dr. T. J. Jackson, the oncologist, a friend of Dr. Johnny Joe, who also was trained in Houston, but was a Texas Longhorn fan—a grievous shortcoming overcome only by his obvious doctoring skills.

But she never wanted to hear the truth. Neither Dr. Johnny Joe nor Dr. Jackson told Mom that she had a less than a year to live. She did not want to know, and they were too polite to tell her.

My Yankee blood boiled. I smelled malpractice here. Mom only smelled okra gumbo stewing in the kitchen.

It turns out, however, the okra gumbo probably did her more good anyway. Martha Lynn, her childhood Baptist friend, who secretly gambled with her on the grounded riverboats at Greenville, Mississippi, told her, "Honey, I am so sorry to hear you are going to die. And probably before the July Bonanza Night!"

"I'm sorry to hear that I'm going to miss the July Bonanza Night too," Mom calmly responded.

As if she were sipping a new brand of orange pekoe tea, Mom tried a little chemotherapy. No one dared die of cancer in 1999 without having a little chemotherapy. "Hospice care is for colored folks," my Mom said, "who do not have insurance." She meant to have all the medical care that Blue Cross and Blue Shield owed her. Unfortunately, it only succeeded in destroying what hair she had left and caused her to discard her last pack of Winston Lights.

"Mr. Vice President," Larry King asked as he leaned across his desk, "do you have anything else to add?"

Although we did not know it, these were the last few weeks of her life. Mom knew it. She had literally moved into her living room. She did not want to die in the backwaters of a bedroom. She did not want to die on the bed where she and my father had made love and dreamed dreams that neither lived to see.

Mom did not want to die on the periphery of life. She wanted to be in the middle of the action. Her living room controlled all access to her house. She was the gatekeeper and planned to man her station until she literally dropped dead. A captain at her helm. With her CB radio scanning for police gossip, with practically every light burning, with her television running day and night, Mom wanted to feel the ebullience of life until the bitter end.

If she could not defeat the fates, she wished to experience them with all the gusto she had remaining. She intended to watch Larry King Live until she took her last breath.

It was the final Christmas of her life. The family took turns caring for mom. In the final days, it was our turn and Anna traveled to Arkansas while I finished Advent with my congregation and would join Anna the day after Christmas.

Mom never said that she was "dying" or even "passing away." She was always "going to join Dad" or Big Momma. And so she did.

In a moment of great cosmic irony, as the sun set, much as it did today, Mom collapsed and died in the arms of Anna.

# 29

ANNA AND I WERE ALREADY MOVING toward the family room where I would read and Anna would knit until it was time to go to bed.

Darkness claimed garden boxes and the porch swing in the front yard and the sunset was blazing beautifully through a variety of evergreen trees in my backyard. The early evening breeze disturbed shimmering silver tinsel grasping the ends of prodigious branches. These trees were born again Christmas trees planted by the previous owner.

The Mennonite farmer planted sequentially 15 former Christmas trees. The oldest tree, almost 40 years old, was 100 yards from my back door. The youngest, only 25 years old, was 100 feet from my back door.

The faithful frugal saint required double duty from his trees, ancient evergreen warriors. As soon as he could spare the time after Thanksgiving, he exhumed small, thriving Scotch pine or Douglas fir trees from a woodlot at the end of our property. He did these things in secret since he did not wish his church elders to think he was precipitous in his celebration of the Savior's birth.

He secured the roots snug in a burlap bag full of Highlands's rocky soil and placed the tree in front of his living room bay window. No lights, however, or any other frivolity would be placed on this portentous visitor. It was only full of potential, not fact, like his plain wife, in simple garb, hid her pregnancy until neither saint nor gossiper would deny that new life was imminent.

Live Christmas trees, even Mennonite ones, must be, by necessity, diminutive. Because they were burdensome in weight, these wintry, celebratory guests could not be any taller than their sturdy bases could support or human benefactors could carry. Some ambitious trees scratched the short, parsimonious ceiling of the family room, which preserved all available warmth in the Arctic December winters. That was rare. It was a hardy, or well-populated family, indeed, that could deposit such a tall Yuletide visitor in front of a family room window. Live Christmas tree devotees learned quickly to compensate size with girth, lest the vigorous visitor harm those, who brought it home to its dwelling.

Hopeful that the sweltering heat from his anthracite coal stove would not extinguish the life from these erstwhile youthful evergreens, now Christmas trees, the hardy saint finally placed the sparse, religious decorations on his trees. Through the last few weeks before Christmas this vigorous guest delighted and enamored family and friends with its aboriginal charm.

However, it was apparent that this Anabaptist, paradigm of religious felicity, had nonetheless sinned. The backsliding farmer had placed silver tinsel on his tree. No upstanding, faithful, pious Christian would place something as facile and worldly as silver tinsel on a Christmas tree. Succumbing to errant pride, the crafty reprobate surreptitiously placed sparkling tinsel on God's beautiful creation, and in his desire to make merry my sly, previous owner, had presumed to add to what God had made so perfectly beautiful already, or so his bishop would say. Like a wily lover slipping into his courtesan's boudoir, the full bearded Mennonite, sitting in front of his Christmas tree, knowing full well he was violating the ordinances of God, that he was moving too close to Sodom and Gomorrah, sipped elderberry brandy, smoked his pipe, and observed the burnished tinsel shimmering in the declining bright enflamed sunset.

After Christmas, no doubt the careful farmer did his best to remove incriminating evidence before the former Christmas tree adorned his backyard and became a haven for bird and rodent. Decades later, silver tinsel waved at Western Pennsylvania sunsets, sometimes 50 or 60 feet in the air. I observed the tinsel now.

"Be sure that our sins will find us out," I thought.

The pious saint, in spite of his best effort, could not remove all his sin. He tried. It could not be. Wind and rain removed more, over the years, and brought some sanctified cheer to the man. But nothing could remove all the tinsel. These former Christmas trees, harbingers of hope and cheer, retained some of their bright oily, silver gifts and cast them into the heavens. Enterprising wrens and blackbirds snatched shiny tinsel to brighten thatch nest. No doubt the trees were grateful for the attention. These rebirth re-enactments seem to favor the vigorous monuments to Christmas extravagance. I know I was grateful. They graced my grandchildren with shadows in the most tepid summer afternoon and protected the north side of my farmhouse from the fiercest winter storm. In short, they were guardians of my land, guardians of my soul and I was grateful for my mischievous Mennonite predecessor, who risked all for the joy of tinsel filled Christmas.

This evening I observed these adorned trees swaying in the

early evening breeze and thanked God for these living commemorations, which would surely outlive me and even my children.

They spoke of times past. They lived as confidently as my memories lived. I saw the tinsel; I felt the temperate breeze impeded by the pine needles. I smelled the pleasure of decades of Christmases, even in May. I closed my eyes and I heard the joy again of my children as they opened their gifts. Again I saw my wife Anna sitting next to me these 34 Christmases past. I saw her now, even though it was May and Christmas was so far away. What was sin to an old sly Mennonite farmer was a sign of grace to this grateful Presbyterian.

It was true that the Pedlam Class of 1971 was rewriting history, but I wanted no part of it. I had already crossed the Rubicon, turned my eyes to Rome, and I knew it was only a matter of time before the Empire would fall.

On my 59th birthday my children would not use a bathroom behind my house. They would not call me "Mr. Jake." They bore my name and were my future. God Himself had rewritten my history. And there was no going back.

Over four decades ago I harassed black students, who came to my school. On my birthday I could not wait to hold my grandchildren, who were, like Solomon's loved one, darker than the black tents of Kedar.

In Plato's "Allegory of the Cave," Socrates described a scenario in which what people took to be real would actually be an illusion. He described a cave inhabited by prisoners, who had been chained since childhood: their legs and necks were held in place so that they were compelled to gaze farther into the cave and at a wall in front of them. That was their world.

Behind the prisoners and at the cave's mouth was an enormous fire, and between the fire and the prisoners walked strangers. On the wall the prisoners saw moving shadows of things and people, but could not touch them. There was no real sound—only off-the-wall echo of the noise produced from the walkway.

For 17 years before I met Christ I thought the shadows to be real things and the echoes to be real sounds created by the shadows, not just reflections of reality, since they were all I had ever seen or heard. While I was growing up in Pedlam, we occasionally, not often, would guess what the shadows were.

You might suppose that when I was freed, permitted to stand up and go as I pleased, and saw the things that had cast the shadows, I would no longer believe in the shadows. Strangely, though, I wanted to believe that the shadows on the wall were more real than what I had seen. I looked at the fire, and I did not like it. I yearned to move back into the darkness and look again at shadows. To join my old Pedlam friends. I had seen the light. I could no longer pretend that shadows were real. But, I did not like my new freedom. So I whored with wanton mistresses. I wrote comments on the Facebook pages of my Pedlam friends, hoping they would tag "like." I wrote blogs, posted comments, pleaded with my old Pedlam family to grant me some approbation.

Eventually, though, like Odysseus I buried my good friend Elpenor and resisted the song of the Sirens. In my 17 years I had sailed between the whirlpool and the cliff, between Scylla and Charybdis. Theodis Murphy and Brother Balfour rescued me from Ogygia Island. I built a ship and sailed for Ithaca, and I would find my Penelope at last. As my 60th year began, I aimed a deadly arrow at Antinous, who was about to take up a two-handled gold cup to drink his wine and already had it in his hands. He had no thought of death: who among all the revelers would think that one man, however brave, would stand alone among so many and kill them? I did. I beat the odds.

God called me to an alternative life. Only God Himself could do that. Building a life with Anna was a start.

The juxtaposition of hope and history was a knotty problem for me. It posed a central question: "If bad things happen to us, how can a good God be in control?" My cry was the cry of Joseph when he was speaking to his naughty brothers: "You intended to harm me, but God intended it for good."

Uncle Evan had a delusional "history" that was much like a Nazi propaganda film, but it was not a "history." It was a past made up of venal images, obscured remembrances, and visceral prejudices that stewed in his poor, conflicted mind.

My history was immutable and it was big enough to love Uncle Evan and my four children and a Yankee wife too. And in my soul these six people warred in eternal variance.

Again, in a real sense, racism existing for generations in my family history, in my community history, ended in my story. The destructive historical cycle ended. My ancestors were slave-owners. Their great, great, great grandchildren were black. The cycle was complete. The curse was ended.

Brother Balfour introduced me to a God, who meant business. A God, who changed history. Not some disambiguation grounded in warm fuzzy feelings. Not the God of Uncle Evan, but the God of Abraham, Isaac, and now Jacob. I was named again, claimed again, by my God. A God, who loved the world so much that He sent his only begotten Son to die for my sins.

I began the journey to Ithaca, on that April morning in 1971 when Hoyt Balfour cried and when Theodis Murphy was escorted from Pedlam First United Methodist Church. I was finally coming home.

I will never be home, really, though, until, like Dante, I reach that celestial kingdom, that place where I see a "living light encircling me, leaving me so enveloped by its veil of radiance that I could see no thing."

Hoyt Balfour did not last the year. The bishop moved him to an obscure church in North Arkansas, as close as possible to Massachusetts.

I did not go to my fortieth high school reunion. I did not trifle with this thing. I discovered that my world was not after all a human artifact: God created it and He could change all things.

The God I met, on the day when Theodis came to church, was the God, who made all things new. Once the cat was out of the bag in my life, so to speak, I knew that my world as I knew it was finished. To me, that was a central part of my transformation that Brother Balfour initiated on that April Sunday morning in 1971.

That was when I realized that the way I treated people of color was a moral issue. Whatever categories I chose to define my relationships affected my soul. Racism, with all its kaleidoscopic manifestations, was systemically demonic and individually destructive. I knew that now.

Most of all, on this 59th birthday, I was hopeful.

The beginning of my conversion was the point when I accepted the limits of logic and the paradoxes of life.

It was from this place, on the eve of my 40th reunion, that I recognized with eternal effect that the Spirit of God knew better than I did what it meant for me to be me. God alone defined, who I was. I experienced again grace. Never would God reject me. No matter how the controlling ego may struggle to bury or redefine this fact, once I knew this, there were irreversible yet always good consequences.

While I was thankful for my Pedlam community, especially my community of faith, the church, it was that very same community that both betrayed, and then brought me into close proximity with the One, who saved my soul.

I was drawn into spiritual communion by the living presence of Christ—not because I had been socialized or accepted by anyone, nor because I had experienced anything. My life, my wholeness, my salvation—it all was acquired outside myself.

A strong sense of other was part of what defined and transformed me. In my life the concept of other was the process by which Pedlam excluded others, whom they wanted to subordinate and control. Part of my journey to health and to wholeness, part of what Christ did for me when I was reborn, was that I learned to construct roles for life giving and myself that were healthy. In the way that air departs from a jar when water was poured in, so rejection, unforgivingness, and hopelessness flowed out when Christ's love poured in.

One outcome of my new life in Christ was the renewed social relations that were even more real than those I once had. One thing was clear by this morning on my 59th birthday: the intimacy in the Spirit of Christ not only was more significant than any human relationships, but it was better than that. God redefined relationships with past, present, and future family, friends, and acquaintances.

In that sense I reclaimed the Lord's Supper on my 59th birthday. No longer did I need to take communion with good people; I only wished to be with redeemed people. We altogether needed the grace of God.

In Katherine Anne Porter's "The Jilting of Granny Weatherall," a dying elderly woman was flowing in and out of consciousness. She remembered her "jilting" when her former fiancé stood her up at the altar. At first Granny was bitter, but over the years she forgave the guilty jilter. "Yes, she had changed her mind after sixty years. . . . I forgot him. I had a husband just the same and my children and my house like any other woman. A good house too, and a good husband that I loved and fine children out of him. Better than I had hoped for even." Yes Granny, and I, found a way to forgive. To do this in remembrance of Him.

A poor French cook in the film *Babette's Feast* living on a desolate peninsula was asked to prepare a cheerless, somber meal in memory of the community's deceased pastor. Babette would not fix a dreary meal—she fixed a gourmet feast instead. Never before had the people tasted anything like it. Their entire lives were changed by the repast. They would remember it for the rest of their lives! The Lord's Supper was to me, again, Babette's feast.

My life I discovered, with my wife Anna, our four children, and yes, even Bo, TJ, Mammy, and even Uncle Evan, was a supper without comparison!

On the night that our Lord was betrayed He took bread, and after giving thanks, broke it and said, "Take. Eat. This is my body that is broken for you."

I reclaimed the Lord's Supper. I could not resist the richness and generosity of the Lord's fare!

God was there when Bo was begging for mercy; when Uncle Evan was teaching Bible class; when Donny shot TJ. God's justice and love would not—could not be appeased by unjust sufferings. On this my 59th birthday I enjoyed again the sovereignty and providential rule of a gracious God. More than that, I grasped the love and grace of God so eloquently expressed in the person of Jesus Christ my Savior. That made all the difference.

I was home. I was at peace. I had been jilted, and I did some jilting, but in the final analysis God was good and alive. I would see Bo, TJ, Mammy, Mom, Dad, Mamaw, Daddy Ray, Big Daddy, Big Momma, and, yes, even Evan Nash, again someday. We would remember together the Delta sunrises and reminisce about hunting and fishing trips that were ours once, but would be ours again.

On this day I had Anna and whatever time God had given us to be together on this earth. And it was more than enough.

In the Laurel Highlands, darkness was serious business. No major metropolitan area compromised our dusky night. We saw transcontinental streaking airplanes dodge falling stars in our expansive sky. Passengers dozed in their reclining seats while Anna and I sat in our family room on the edge of the world.

Anna put away her knitting. "Time for bed, Jacob."

I smiled.

Other books published by Harvard Square Editions

*Gates of Eden*, Charles Degelman
*Sazzae*, JL Morin
*Close*, Erika Raskin
*Living Treasures*, Yang Huang
*Dark Lady of Hollywood*, Diane Haithman
*A Weapon to End War*, Jonathan Ross
*Savior*, Anthony Caplan
*All at Once*, Alisa Clements

Send James P. Stobaugh your comments at
www.forsuchatimeasthis.com

CPSIA information can be obtained at www.ICGtesting.com
Printed in the USA
BVOW04s1105270414

351740BV00002B/16/P